HEART FAILURE

This Large Print Book carries the
Seal of Approval of N.A.V.H.

HEART FAILURE

RICHARD L. MABRY, M.D.

THORNDIKE PRESS
A part of Gale, Cengage Learning

GALE
CENGAGE Learning·

Farmington Hills, Mich • San Francisco • New York • Waterville, Maine
Meriden, Conn • Mason, Ohio • Chicago

Copyright © 2013 by Richard Mabry.
Scripture quotations are taken from the New King James Version of the Bible and the New American Standard Bible®, © The Lockman Foundation 1960, 1962, 1963, 1968, 1971, 1972, 1973, 1975, 1977, 1995. Used by permission.
Thorndike Press, a part of Gale, Cengage Learning.

LIBRARY OF CONGRESS CATALOGING-IN-PUBLICATION DATA

Mabry, Richard L.
    Heart failure / by Richard L. Mabry, MD. — Large print edition.
        pages ; cm. — (Thorndike Press large print Christian mystery)
    ISBN 978-1-4104-6565-8 (hardcover) — ISBN 1-4104-6565-9 (hardcover)
    1. Large type books. I. Title.
PS3613.A2H43 2014
813'.6—dc23   2013044060

Published in 2014 by arrangement with Thomas Nelson, Inc.

Printed in Mexico
1 2 3 4 5 6 7 18 17 16 15 14

This novel is dedicated to the pastors, staff, and my fellow members at Stonebriar Community Church.

ONE

Adam Davidson and Dr. Carrie Markham strolled out the doors of the Starplex Cinema into the warm darkness of the springtime evening. As they made their way through the few cars left on the parking lot, Adam's right hand found Carrie's left. She took it and squeezed, and his heart seemed to skip a beat. His fingers explored until they felt the outline of the diamond ring he'd placed there only a week ago.

She leaned in to briefly rest her head on his shoulder. "I never thought I could be this happy."

"Me either." And if he had his way, this was how it would be for the rest of their lives. Two people in love, enjoying their small-town lives, their only worry what movie to see on their regular Saturday night date.

A loud noise in the distance made them both stop. Then Adam saw a shower of color on the horizon, about where the ballpark would be. "Fireworks show. The Titans must have won." *Get a grip, Adam. Stop jumping at every noise. You're safe.*

When Adam first met Carrie eight months ago, she was fragile and hurting, as skittish as a baby deer, still bearing the scars from the death of her husband almost two years earlier. Her only interest seemed to be her medical practice. But, little by little, he'd seen her start to smile, to laugh, and eventually to love.

Carrie had restored the smile to Adam's life as well. He still had his own problems, even though he hadn't revealed them to her. He hoped he would never have to. But having her in his life made him certain that the life he now lived, so long as he lived it with her, would be all he ever wanted.

These things were supposed to take time, but in just a few short months each of them had decided that the other was the person needed to fill the hole in their lives. The culmination had come with Adam's proposal and Carrie's acceptance last week. They hadn't set a wedding date yet, but for now Adam was content to watch Carrie plan and bask in the glow of their shared happiness.

The couple reached Adam's car and

climbed in, but hadn't yet fastened their seat belts when Carrie said, "I think a chocolate — No, make that a hot fudge sundae." She leaned back in the passenger seat of Adam's little Subaru. "That would . . ."

As she was talking Adam saw a dark SUV approach from his right, moving at a snail's pace. When the vehicle was directly in front of Adam's Forester, its side window came down to reveal the glint of light on metal as the driver's hand extended outward.

Adam's next action was reflexive. If he was wrong, he could apologize. But if he was right — He was already moving when he heard the shots.

The impact of Adam's arm across her shoulder pushed her down until her head was below the level of the car's dashboard. Then Carrie heard it — a flat crack, followed by two more in rapid succession. Muffled thuds sounded above her, and she pictured bullets boring into the headrests at the place where her head and Adam's had been seconds ago. Carrie cringed against an expected shower of glass, but only a few tiny pieces sprinkled down on her.

The faint ringing in her ears after the shots didn't mask the screech of tires and roar of an engine. When the noise subsided, all that remained was the rapid thud of her heartbeat echoing in her ears.

Carrie huddled with her head down, her breath cut off as much by fear as by the pressure of Adam's body atop hers, a human shield. She felt his soft breath in her ear as he whispered, "Are you all right?"

"I . . . I think so. How about you?"

"I'm okay." The pressure holding her down lessened. "Stay down until I tell you it's safe." Carrie turned her head to catch a glimpse of Adam peering cautiously over the dashboard.

Her heart threatened to jump out of her chest while her mind wrestled with what just happened. After a seeming eternity, Adam bent down and said in a hushed tone, "I think they've gone. You can sit up."

Carrie raised her head barely enough to peer through the damaged windshield. When nothing moved in her field of vision, she eased upward to perch on the edge of her seat. A few cars were still on the lot of the theater after the last Saturday night show, probably the vehicles of employees closing down for the night. There hadn't been many people in the movie theater.

"Are you sure you're not hurt?" Adam's voice, full of concern, brought Carrie back to the moment. He brushed a bit of glass from her seat with a handkerchief, then tossed it onto the floor of the car.

Carrie unfolded from her crouched position and eased farther onto the seat. "Scared, is all," she said. "You okay?"

"Not a scratch."

He reached across to hug her, and she turned to find shelter in his arms. They stayed that way for a long moment, and the trembling inside her slowly eased. "What . . . what was that about?"

"Nothing for you to worry about." Adam's voice and manner were calm, and Carrie felt comforted by his very presence. Then, as suddenly as the turn of a page, he released her and swung around to face forward in the driver's seat. His next words were terse, clipped. "We have to get out of here." He reached for the ignition, key in hand.

"Wait a minute!" Carrie pulled her cell phone from her purse and held it out to him. "We can't leave. We need to call 911."

Adam took her arm, a bit more firmly than necessary, and pushed the phone away. He shook his head. "No!"

She flinched at the negative response and the tone in which Adam delivered it. "Why?

Someone shot at us. We should call the police."

Adam's voice was quiet, his words terse. "Look, I don't have time to explain. Let's go."

What's the matter with him? She took a deep breath and let it out slowly. Twice she started to speak. Twice she stopped.

Adam turned the key and reached for the gearshift lever.

Carrie saw his jaw clench. She was terrified, but Adam wasn't so much scared as — she searched for the right word — he was *cold* and determined. The sudden change frightened her. "If this was a drive-by, we need to report it. Maybe the police can catch them before they kill someone."

"Just let me handle this," Adam said. "Right now, let's get out of here. I want you someplace safe."

Although Adam's voice was low, there was an intensity to his words that Carrie had never heard before. "You have to trust me," he said. "There are things you don't know, things that make it dangerous for me to deal with the police right now." He pointed to her seat belt. "Buckle up and let's leave. I'll explain soon."

Carrie wanted to argue, but she could see it was no use. She put away her phone and fastened her seat belt.

The lights on the theater marquee went out. In the distance a siren sounded, faint at first but growing louder. "We're out of here," Adam said. He put the car in gear and eased out of the parking lot, peering through the starred windshield to navigate the dark streets.

Carrie studied Adam as he drove. Most men would be shaking after such a close encounter with death. But he wasn't. Why would that be? Was he used to being shot at? She shook her head. That was plain silly.

She thought she knew him — after all, they were engaged. Carrie glanced at him again. Maybe she didn't know Adam as well as she'd thought. That scared her even more than what they'd just experienced.

They rode in silence for a few moments, and during that time Carrie recreated the shooting in her mind. Then something clicked — something she hadn't realized until then. She turned to Adam. "You pushed me down before the shots were fired. You didn't react to the shots. You knew they were coming."

Adam glanced at her but didn't respond.

Carrie thought about it once more. "I'm sure of it. You shoved me below the dashboard, then I heard three shots. How did you know what was about to happen?"

He continued to peer into the night. "I was backed into the parking space so I had a good view of the cars moving down the aisle in front of us. A black SUV pulled even with us, and the barrel of a pistol came out the driver's side window. That was when I pushed you down."

"Lucky you saw it."

Adam shook his head. "Luck had nothing to do with it. I'm always watching."

His response made her shiver. She hugged herself and sat silent for the balance of the trip.

When they slowed for the turn into Carrie's driveway, Adam said, "Is there room in your garage for my car?"

"I suppose so. Why?"

"I don't want to leave it at the curb or in the driveway where someone can see it. Open the garage and let me pull in. We'll talk once we're safely in your house."

Carrie found the garage remote on her key ring and raised the door. When they were inside the house, with the garage door closed, she took a seat on the living room sofa. Adam went through the small house, drawing drapes, closing blinds, and making sure all the doors and windows were locked.

Finally he returned to where Carrie

waited. He started to sit beside her on the sofa, apparently thought better of it, and sank into a chair. "I've wrestled with this all the way home. I thought I was finally safe, but maybe I'm not. I know what I'm going to tell you may change things between us, but you deserve an explanation."

That was the understatement of the year. Thirty minutes ago she and Adam were a newly engaged couple, winding down an enjoyable evening. By now they should be feeding each other ice cream like two lovebirds, talking seriously and making plans about their future together. But instead . . . "Yes," she said, "you owe me an explanation, a big one. So explain."

"Let me say this first. What I'm about to tell you started long before I met you. My life has changed in the past eight months. I'm different, and it's because of you. I'm . . ." Adam leaned toward her. He clenched and unclenched his fists. "To begin with, Adam Davidson isn't my real name."

Two

"To begin with, Adam Davidson isn't my real name." It seemed to Adam as though all the air went out of the room as soon as those words were out of his mouth.

Carrie took a deep breath. "What do you mean?"

Adam swallowed . . . hard. Then, like a diver finally deciding to plunge off the high board, he said, "My real name is Keith Branson. I'm on the run. If the wrong people find me, I'm a dead man." He swallowed again. "I hope and pray I'm wrong, but what happened tonight may mean they've found me."

He watched emotions trace across Carrie's face like words running across an electronic billboard: puzzlement, disbelief, fear, anger. The ache in his heart grew with every passing second.

He'd thought maybe he'd finally found safety. He'd hoped he'd never have to share

16

this information with her. But his hopes were dashed when the bullets flew through the windshield. Maybe he'd never be safe. And now he'd brought Carrie into it. He had to tell her, no matter the cost to their relationship. He loved her too much to let her keep believing the lie.

"What have you done? Are you running from the police?" She almost shouted the next words. "What's going on?"

"Long story," Adam said. "First, I'm not running from the police. But I'm not who you think I am either. I'm not a paralegal, although I'm working as one. I'm a lawyer, and I'm running away from some very bad men — men who want to kill me."

"If you're hiding from criminals, wouldn't the police protect you?"

"Maybe, maybe not. But that would mean letting them know my real identity. And no matter how the police may try to keep it confidential, somehow that information is going to leak out. It has before. If it reaches the wrong ears . . . I'm dead." He shook his head. "Of course, it may already be too late."

The color drained from Carrie's face. She snatched a ragged breath. In a low voice she said, "Let me get this straight. You're telling me you're living here under a false identity.

17

But it's not because you've done anything wrong."

"Right, I —"

Carrie continued as though Adam hadn't spoken. "When you didn't want to call the police after someone shot at us, I thought maybe you had a bunch of unpaid tickets, unpaid alimony, something like that." Her voice rose with every word. "But now you tell me you're hiding from someone who might kill you?"

"Yes," he said. "Now can I explain?"

"Go ahead. I want to know everything, Adam. Or should I call you Keith?" She clenched her fists. "Or is there another name for me to learn?"

He took a deep breath through his nose, let it out through his mouth. Repeated the process. *Be calm. You fouled up, but maybe you can salvage things.* "Please, call me Adam. I came here for a fresh start, and that's when I became Adam. That's when I met you. That's when I fell in love with you."

"If you're in love with me, why didn't you tell me the truth?" Carrie lowered her voice to a quiet tone that pierced Adam's heart more than any shout could. "Why did you — no, why did *we* almost have to die before you told me about your past? Why did it take a shooting to make you tell me that

18

everything I know about you is a lie?"

"When I first met you, I told you the same story I'd told before, in so many other places. It had become a habit, a way of life for me. Then when we got to know each other, after we fell in love, I didn't want to spoil things by telling you the truth." His mouth was dry, his throat threatened to close off his words, but he didn't want to interrupt his story by asking for water. "I was wrong to keep all this from you. I admit it. I've been agonizing since you accepted my proposal, wondering when and how I'd break the news to you."

For a moment Adam couldn't read her expression. Then her words removed any doubt. She was hurt — hurt deeply. "And you think now is the time?"

"What happened tonight may mean that the people who've been hunting me for so long have found me." He looked down. "I'm sorry I waited, but I have to tell you the truth now. I love you too much to keep it a secret any longer."

"You say you love me, yet you hid your past from me. It took a *shooting* to change your mind. That doesn't sound like love to me."

Adam felt like one of the early Christians, the ones whose limbs were tied to horses that literally pulled them apart. "I admit it. I've put off doing this. I was afraid, because telling you who I am . . ." He took a deep breath, then another. There was a catch in his voice when he spoke again. "I love you, Carrie. More than I've loved anyone in my life."

Carrie hugged herself like a woman trapped in a deep freeze. "So what happened tonight? Was someone trying to kill you?"

"I can't be totally sure. Maybe someone's found me, maybe it was a random drive-by shooting. But I know one thing for sure. If my true identity gets out, even in the most innocent fashion, Charlie DeLuca will find me and try to kill me . . . and you too, once he discovers that I love you."

Carrie's expression shifted from puzzled to terrified. "So just being with you puts my life in danger?" She almost whispered the next words. "How could you do this to me? Were you using me? Did being part of a couple let you blend in to the population?"

"No! Absolutely not."

Carrie turned away from him and stared at the opposite wall. "What are you going to do next?"

"Tomorrow morning I'll call the police and tell them I found my car parked at the curb with three bullet holes in the windshield. I'll do my best to make them believe this was a case of malicious mischief. I can't have them digging too deeply into my identity. Because if they do, I might as well pack up and get out of town."

Her back still to Adam, Carrie said, "What if the police want to talk to me about the shooting?"

"They won't. Not if I tell it the way I've described." Adam rose and began pacing. "Believe me, more than anything I want to keep you out of this."

Carrie spun to face Adam. When she spoke, her tone was cold. "I think you'd better go."

Adam stood, then stopped. "Carrie, I'm really sorry. I hope you can forgive me." He looked directly into Carrie's eyes. "I meant the things I said when I proposed. I still mean them. I love you."

For Adam time froze as Carrie stared, first at him, then at the ring on her finger, then back at him. Finally she put both hands in front of her, and Adam's heart dropped when he saw the twisting motion she made.

"Carrie, please don't —"

She took two steps toward him and held out her hand, the engagement ring in her open palm. "I don't know what to think right now. But it doesn't seem right for me to keep wearing this. I don't know whether I love you, or fear you, or feel sorry for you, or . . . I don't know." She shook her head. Tears streaked her cheeks.

Adam took the ring and noticed that her hand, like his, was trembling. He couldn't let it end this way. He had to make it right. "Carrie, please, we need to talk again. Will you call me?"

"I don't know." Carrie shook her head. "I honestly don't know."

Carrie listened to the hum of the motor as the garage door closed. She wasn't sure whether it was closing a chapter in her life or opening the door to an entirely different one. She was tempted to go to the window and peep through the blinds to watch Adam drive away. Maybe she should do that, a visual punctuation mark to the end of their relationship. But she wasn't sure she wanted it to end. She wasn't sure about anything anymore.

She took out her cell phone and punched in a number she knew like her own. It was late, but she needed to talk with someone. No, not just someone — to Julie.

The phone rang four times before a sleepy female voice said, "Yates residence."

"Julie, it's Carrie. I'm so sorry for calling
—"

The voice dropped to a whisper. "No
problem. Let me take this into the living
room. I don't want to wake Barry."

Carrie had been pacing when she placed
the call. Now she slumped into an easy chair
and dangled her legs over the arm, unconsciously assuming the posture she'd taken
so many years ago when she was a high
school student chatting on the phone for
hours on end with her best friend.

"Okay, now I can talk," Julie said. "What's
up?"

"I'm sorry for calling so late, but I had to
talk with someone. I was almost killed tonight."

"Are you okay?"

"I'm fine, just shaken."

"What happened?"

"Someone shot at the car where Adam
and I were sitting. They missed, but my
world's been turned upside down."

"I don't doubt it," Julie said. "I mean, having someone take a shot at you —"

"There's more. It's Adam. He's not the
person I thought he was."

Who did I think he was? Carrie thought
back to her first meeting with Adam, and it
made her heart ache. A little more than

eight months earlier, she was talking with friends in the foyer after church when a man she knew slightly approached. "Excuse me, Carrie. This is Adam. He's new in town, and I'm trying to introduce him around."

The man called Adam was prototypically "tall, dark, and handsome": a bit over six feet tall, olive complexion, brown hair with a slight wave, guileless gray eyes. He told her his name was Adam Davidson. He was a paralegal, recently out of a messy divorce, looking to start over in a new location. They exchanged handshakes and phone numbers, and Carrie forgot about it until he called the next day . . . and the next. Finally she agreed to show him around town. Then they had lunch at a restaurant she liked. Lunches led to dinners, and soon Carrie realized she was no longer a tour guide. She and Adam were dating — and getting more serious with each date.

During that time he was never anything but attentive, charming, and apparently taken with her. And she'd felt the same way. He listened to her talk about her late husband. She cried on his shoulder. And she experienced something she never thought she'd have again — love.

Carrie forced herself back to the present. "I don't know if I should tell you . . ." She snatched a deep breath, afraid for Adam, yet feeling the desperate need for her friend's assurances.

"What is it? This sounds ominous."

"You have to promise not to tell a soul, not even Barry."

"Okay . . ."

Carrie tightened her grip on the phone. "I've already told you that someone took a shot at Adam's car after we left the last show at the movies. Well, Adam refused to call the police to report it. When I pressed him, he told me his real name wasn't Adam Davidson. He's on the run — not from the law but from what he calls bad men. And it's critical that his true identity be kept a secret."

"He called them bad men. So does that make him a *good* man?" Julie asked.

"I don't know. What really hurts is that he's been lying to me! I feel as though I've been part of a play, and I'm only now getting to know the actor playing opposite me," Carrie said. "I'm confused."

"So . . ." Julie hesitated, and Carrie could tell she was treading lightly. "So is the engagement still on?"

"I gave him back the ring. Now I don't know what I'm going to do."

"You have to answer one question: do you

love him?"

Carrie shook her head, even though there was no one to see it. "I love Adam . . . or thought I did. But now I don't know who Adam is." She glanced at the clock. "It's late. I need to let you go. I wish we could get together to talk about this. You always help."

"Barry's going to be in Dallas soon, maybe next week. Why don't I plan to go with him? We can meet somewhere halfway between Dallas and Jameson. I'll give you a call and set it up."

"Thanks, Julie."

"And in the meantime," her friend said, "pray about it."

"I'm not sure I can," Carrie said. "I —"

"I know. Some well-meaning people told you that if you prayed hard enough, John wouldn't die. But he did. That doesn't mean you have to stop praying. God doesn't always answer prayers the way we want, but He sees the big picture. And He loves you."

Carrie didn't respond.

"I'll call you soon," was all Julie said.

Later, as Carrie lay in bed, she stared upward into the dark and wondered if Julie was right. Maybe prayer would help. Even if God didn't answer, it might help get this burden off her shoulders. Of course, since

John's death, her belief in the power of prayer had gone downhill. But it was worth a try. She began, "God, I don't know what to do. Please give me wisdom to deal with this." But soon she found herself on a familiar track, wondering why her prayers for her husband hadn't been answered. Grief mixed with anger boiled up yet again, stirring a pain that was always there, just under the surface. Finally she rolled over, buried her head in the pillow, and sobbed herself to sleep.

The first thing Sunday morning, Adam dug out his phone directory and looked up the non-emergency number for the Jameson Police Department. "This is Adam Davidson. I left my car parked at the curb in front of my apartment last night, and when I came out this morning, I discovered three bullet holes in the windshield."

After Adam gave the necessary information, the man on the other end of the line asked him to stay where he was and meet the patrolman who'd be there soon.

"How soon?"

"Maybe an hour. Maybe a bit longer."

Adam didn't argue. He knew that complaints like this didn't carry a sense of urgency like those where the caller was in immediate danger. Besides, he could use the time to make another phone call.

He didn't have to look up this number. Several times Adam had started to program it into his cell phone's speed dial, but for the sake of security, he decided to store it only in his memory. The call was answered on the second ring.

"Branson."

The voice brought an image to Adam's mind and a smile to his lips — an image of a man who looked like a slightly stockier, slightly older version of himself. "Dave, it's me."

"Keith?"

"You mean Adam."

"Sorry, old habits die hard." A door closed softly in the background. "Okay, what's up?"

"Someone shot at me last night. Might be a random drive-by, but I can't risk thinking that way. I have to assume I was the target."

Adam envisioned his older brother rubbing his chin, a sure sign he was thinking. "So I guess you're about to leave again. Adam, are you sure you want to live the rest of your life this way? Always on the run, always looking over your shoulder. Changing names and locations so often that you sometimes wake up wondering who you are, where you are."

"No, I'm not going to run anymore," Adam said. "You forget, I'm in love. I just asked Carrie to marry me, and if she'll still have me, I'm prepared to stay and fight."

"You're sure?"

Was he sure? He'd spent most of the night thinking about that question. "Yes. I'm convinced God brought Carrie into my life to complete it." He sipped from the mug at his elbow and grimaced when he found the coffee had gone cold.

"Does she know who you are? And does she understand the situation?"

"Not the whole story, but enough. Last night I told her that Adam Davidson isn't my real name and that I'm on the run from some dangerous people."

"And what did she say?"

"About what you'd expect. She's angry, hurt, confused. Besides all that, she realizes she's in danger by being close to me." The simple act of saying the words made Adam's throat tighten, a lump that all the coffee in the world couldn't wash away.

The silence on the other end of the line dragged on so long Adam thought they'd been disconnected. Then Dave said, "Where do you go from here?"

"I'm not sure yet. A lot depends on Carrie, I guess. If I stay, I put both of us in danger. If I go, I lose her." David felt tears forming. *Stop that. Real men don't cry. Or maybe they do if they've really fouled up and possibly lost the woman they love.*

"Are you praying about it?" David asked.

"Of course. I've prayed every day since I left Chicago. Sometimes it's the only thing that's kept me going."

Before Dave could respond, Adam heard the doorbell. "Gotta go. Police are here to take a report on the shooting."

Even after leaving his original identity, Adam had always been truthful with law officers. Not only was it part of his nature, it was an obligation. As a lawyer he'd been an officer of the court — still was, although his license was in his original name — sworn to uphold the law, cooperate with authorities, never withhold pertinent information. Now what he was about to tell the policeman at the door would be an outright lie. *And so it begins.*

Adam wondered where it would end.

THREE

Carrie awoke on Sunday morning to a gray world. Sheets of rain beat against her windowpane, matching her mood. Maybe this was a good day to stay in bed. She burrowed deeper into the covers and thought about the changes in her life.

The shooting in the movie parking lot had shaken her. Then Adam's revelation turned her world upside down. She didn't really want to go to church. She wanted to hide her head, block out the world. But church was a habit she'd acquired years ago, and Carrie knew that ultimately she'd leave the safety of her bed and get dressed. Duty or desire, it made no difference. Church was on her agenda today.

She visited the coffee pot, then set about getting ready to face the world. As she did, she took stock of herself in the mirror. Her blond hair was cut in a no-nonsense short style that framed a face others told her was

31

attractive. Her green eyes saw things clearly without the need for glasses, although obviously they had been unable to penetrate Adam's disguise. She was an attractive professional, still in the prime of life. But after John's death she'd put up an invisible fence that might as well have had warning signs on it. *I've been hurt. I'm healing, but I'm still vulnerable. Stay away.*

When she met him, she'd opened the gate and let Adam in. In hindsight that was probably a huge mistake, one with which she'd have to deal. And now her world had changed again. Her ringless finger felt peculiar. Even more peculiar was a morning without the usual call from Adam, a day without a lunch or dinner date. She'd adjusted before. She'd do it again. Carrie wiped away the tears that formed in the corners of her eyes. Maybe church would help, maybe not.

She slipped into a simple green dress, gulped the last of her coffee, and grabbed an umbrella. *Ready or not, world, here I come. But be aware. The gate is closed again.*

The organ was sounding the final notes of the prelude when Carrie slipped into the half-filled sanctuary. She stowed her umbrella under her seat and tried to put her mind in neutral. Maybe the service would calm her heart. Maybe it would help her find the answers to the questions nipping at the edges of her thoughts like a pack of wild dogs. She hoped so.

Carrie found it hard to focus on the service. She went through the motions, but her concentration kept slipping. She sang the hymns without letting the lyrics sink in. She stood for the reading of the Scripture, but the words washed over her like waves on a beach. There was no comfort there. And through it all, her emotions were all over the place.

She alternated between anger at Adam for the lies he'd told and disgust at herself for believing them. Carrie revisited her sorrow for John's death and the part she might have played in it. She was wracked with pain thinking of her short time with John, snatched from her after only five years of marriage. Her heart ached as she realized the perfect life she'd envisioned with Adam was now disappearing as well, replaced by a situation that was dangerous at best and fatal at worst.

Carrie considered slipping out during the offertory, but then the pastor stepped to the pulpit and it was too late for her to move without attracting attention. The preacher seemed to stare straight into her soul, and his first words tied her stomach in knots. "Let not your heart be troubled."

The Scripture should have made Carrie relax, but instead it gave her the sensation of being trapped in an elevator in free fall. In an instant she was transported back to a scene from almost two years ago, a scene she'd never forget but wished she could. Her mind's eye saw the same pastor, the same pulpit. But this time there was a bronze casket at the front of the church, banked on either side by floral tributes that assaulted her nostrils with a sickly sweet scent.

Instead of her current seat in one of the back rows, Carrie was in the front row, with John's sister and her husband on one side, John's mother and father on the other. Carrie's parents hadn't bothered to come. Even the death of their son-in-law couldn't bridge the rift between them and Carrie, the chasm that developed when she embraced Christianity in her first year of medical school.

That day the pastor had read that same Scripture: "Let not your heart be troubled." She supposed the message he brought was one of comfort and hope, but other than the opening verses from the Bible, Carrie couldn't recall a single word he spoke. There'd been music and words of tribute from a couple of friends. But all Carrie could think about during the entire service was, *We should have had decades together, but all we had was five years. It was such a freak thing — a punctured coronary artery during a routine procedure. I'm a doctor — why couldn't I save him?* She squeezed her eyes shut to hold back tears. What did she do wrong? Why did God let it happen? Why?

The swelling notes of the organ brought Carrie back to the present. She'd apparently stood at the proper time. She'd managed to bow her head with the rest of the congregation for the closing prayer. As she joined the crowd filing out, she thought about the morning's Scripture passage. "Let not your heart be troubled." The words brought a wry, mirthless smile to her lips. *Sorry, God. I can't help it. My heart's been troubled too long.*

Carrie was halfway home, driving on automatic pilot, when the ring of her cell phone interrupted her thoughts. She pulled into the parking area of a nearly deserted strip shopping center and dug the phone from her purse. The Emergency Room was calling.

"Dr. Markham," she answered.

"This is Doris in the ER. We have an

elderly man here with severe dyspnea. He says he's seen Dr. Avery in your group, but not for at least a year. You're on call, but do you want us to try Dr. Avery?"

"No, I'll see him. Get an EKG and chest film. Oh, and draw some blood chemistries and a CBC. I'll be there in ten minutes." Carrie laid her cell phone on the seat behind her and aimed her Prius toward the hospital. She kept her eyes focused on the road, but her mind wasn't on the hospital or the patient waiting there for her. It was on Adam — her relationship with him, the secret he'd told her, their future together . . . if they had one.

She wondered if there was any way out of this living nightmare. She'd have to talk with Adam again. There were too many questions still unanswered. But she dreaded their next conversation. What could she say? She still didn't know what she should do. She'd thought she loved Adam, but who, really, was Adam Davidson?

Carrie was still debating her next move when she pulled into the hospital parking lot. *Enough of that.* She plunged through the double doors of the Emergency Room, ready to immerse herself in the practice of medicine. Her personal life could go on hold for a bit.

The patient's name was Gus Elsik. He lay propped on the gurney in a full sitting position, struggling to breathe despite the oxygen mask on his face. The sheet had slipped to expose one swollen ankle. Carrie noted the distended neck veins. The diagnosis was already pretty clear to her, but she'd go through the necessary steps to be certain.

The patient was obviously in no condition to talk, so Carrie addressed her questions to the woman in a blouse and jeans who stood beside the gurney, fresh lines of worry adding to the ones that creased her face already.

"I'm Dr. Markham. What happened?"

"My father's having trouble breathing."

"Is this a new thing?"

The woman shook her head. "No, I took him to the clinic last year when he was having the same kind of trouble, just not as severe. He saw Dr. Avery, who said it was some kind of problem with his heart. The doctor gave him some pills, but after he started feeling better, Daddy stopped taking them."

"And when did he start getting short of breath?"

"It's been going on for a couple of weeks. Maybe more. When it got to where he couldn't walk from his room — he stays with us — when he couldn't walk from his bedroom to the dining room without resting to catch his breath, I insisted that we come here."

Gus's other symptoms confirmed Carrie's diagnosis: swelling of the feet and ankles, moist cough, waking up at night short of breath, having to sit upright to breathe. "What you have," she said to Gus, "is congestive heart failure. I'm going to admit you to the hospital, do some tests, and start treatment. I'll contact Dr. Avery. He'll see you tomorrow and follow up."

Gus's daughter asked, "Is it serious?"

"It's serious, but I've seen worse. We should be able to get this under control with some medications to get rid of the excess fluid and improve the heart function."

"What . . . did . . . you . . . call . . . it?" Gus asked, a gasp for air separating each word.

"Congestive heart failure. But don't let the words scare you. We're going to keep your heart going for a good while yet." She encouraged him with a smile and a pat on his shoulder.

As she sat at the nurse's station to write orders, Carrie thought about heart failure. There was the kind Gus developed, the kind that medications could help. Then there was what she was feeling right now: the heart pain, the anguish, the emotional turmoil that no amount of medicine would improve. That was the worst kind of heart failure.

A Scripture verse popped unbidden into her head. She didn't recall the source — somewhere in the Old Testament — and she wasn't sure of the exact quotation, but the gist was that God promised to give a new heart. *You didn't give my husband a new one, God, so that's one strike. I don't know about Adam's heart. And I'm still waiting for my new heart.*

As soon as the clock in his kitchen showed eight a.m. on Monday, Adam dialed the law office where he worked. He hoped Brittany, the receptionist, wasn't running late. He had a lot to do, but the first thing was to square his absence with his employers.

He was about to hang up when there was a click on the line and he heard, "Hartley and Evans, may I help you?"

"Brittany, this is Adam."

"Where are you? Are you okay?"

"That's why I'm calling," Adam said. "Somebody decided to shoot up my car during the night. I've got to arrange to repair the damage, get a rental car, all that stuff. Would you tell . . . ?" Who? Bruce Hartley was the senior lawyer in the two-person firm. But it wasn't always possible to predict how Bruce would react. The other partner, Janice Evans, was the better choice. "Would you tell Janice what's happened? I'll get there as soon as I can."

Adam's next call was to his insurance agent. He expected to leave a message, then waste most of the morning waiting for a call back. Instead, the agent was at his desk and proved both sympathetic and extremely helpful. When he found out Adam's car was drivable, he told him where to take it to have the damage repaired. He even arranged for a rental car to be delivered there.

By mid-morning, Adam pulled into the lot that served the two-story building owned and occupied by Hartley and Evans, Attorneys at Law. He parked his black Toyota Corolla rental in his assigned slot, tugged his briefcase from the passenger seat, and headed for the front door.

The briefcase was a constant reminder of Adam's journey. Along the way he'd parted with his expensive Halliburton case, a gift from his ex-wife. He couldn't recall into which river he'd tossed the brushed aluminum status symbol, a gesture to further separate himself from a life he could no longer live. Then, after Bruce Hartley suggested that the grocery bag in which he carried his lunch and a few files wasn't appropriate for a member of their staff, Adam found a scuffed leather briefcase in a pawnshop in town. It was this case that he now parked next to his desk before he slipped into his chair.

Bruce Hartley paused opposite Adam's open doorway. Adam had heard Brittany describe Hartley as "sixty-one, going on forty." The lawyer had a receding hairline that he tried to disguise with an expensive haircut, and a bulging waistline that custom-tailored suits did little to hide. Hartley was just out of marriage number two or three — Adam couldn't recall which — and rumor had it he was already looking for the next Mrs. Hartley, although why anyone would put up with the man's unpredictable moods was hard to imagine.

Hartley looked pointedly at his watch, then hurried on down the hall. Adam didn't know whether Janice Evans had passed on his reason for being late, but evidently Hartley didn't consider his employee's tardiness worthy of comment.

Adam was going through the phone message slips on his desk when Evans stopped by. Janice Evans was a decade younger than Hartley, and to Adam's way of thinking, the more level-headed, intelligent, and talented

41

of the two lawyers.

She wore a tasteful wedding and engagement ring set on the appropriate finger. Tiny pearl earrings were Evans's only other jewelry. Her perfectly styled ash-blond hair fell short of her shoulders. She wore designer glasses over gray eyes that seemed to see everything. He was no expert on women's clothes, but Adam was willing to bet that Evans's pants suit had a well-known label and cost several times more than his off-the-rack suit.

"Sorry to hear about your car," she said. "Get things wrapped up?"

Adam smiled up at her. "Yep. It's in the shop getting a new windshield and having the headrests redone."

"What did the police say?"

"Not much, actually. My own theory is that it was some high school kids with a gun, deciding to use my car for target practice." *How many more times am I going to have to tell this?*

"Well, be careful." Evans nodded once and retreated to her office.

A few minutes later Brittany eased up to Adam's desk and handed him several file folders.

"Anything urgent?" Adam asked as she shuffled through the stack.

"No. Usual stuff. But we missed you. The coffee you make is so much better than what I brew."

"Glad you like my touch," Adam said. "And unless someone shoots out my windshield again, I'll be in tomorrow to brew it for you." *That is, unless I'm dead.*

FOUR

Carrie stood behind her desk and rammed her arms into the sleeves of a fresh white coat. Why did the laundry think so much starch was needed for a professional look? Sometimes she thought the deliveryman should just stand her coats in a corner of her office instead of hanging them in her closet.

Carrie was trying to open the side pocket to admit her stethoscope when her nurse, Lila, stuck her head in the office door.

"And a very happy Monday to us all." Lila was a middle-aged divorcee, a bottle blonde, who still acted as if she were in her twenties. Today she looked as though she'd bitten the lime, only to reach for the tequila and find someone had hidden it.

"Party a bit too much over the weekend?" Carrie asked.

"Nope, didn't party enough. I had at least another day's worth of fun planned, but I turned around and it was time to start another week." Lila eased into a chair, crossed her legs, and looked up at Carrie, who now struggled to button her white coat. "How about you?"

There were two ways to get news spread throughout the twelve-doctor, multi-specialty clinic where Carrie worked: put a notice on the bulletin board or tell Lila. Carrie chose not to go either route. "Pretty routine." She checked her pockets, lifted her gaze to Lila, and smiled. "Let's get on with it."

Lila stood and gave a mock cheer. "Once more the Rushton Clinic moves into high gear."

The clinic's official name was Jameson Medical Associates, but everyone called it the Rushton Clinic after Dr. Phil Rushton, the managing partner. He'd put together the group of physicians, helped work out a system for dividing profits and sharing expenses, made the administrative decisions most doctors were happy to avoid, and still found time to be the foremost cardiac surgeon in the region.

Carrie was one of two internal medicine specialists in the group. Her training was as good or better than that of the other internist, Thad Avery, and their practice sizes were about equal. She had no quarrel with the arrangement except for occasions when Phil Rushton's actions made her grit her teeth. She was ready to see her first patient when a secretary hurried up. "The Emergency Room called. Mr. Berringer was brought in earlier by ambulance. Heart problems. The ER doc wants to know if you'd like to see him."

Lila, now quite professional, said, "I'll let patients know you've had an emergency. They can wait or we'll reschedule. Go ahead."

Carrie walked through the breezeway that connected the clinic with the hospital, then made her way to the ER. The charge nurse handed her a chart and pointed to a curtained cubicle.

Carrie flipped through the pages, noting the history of weakness, blurred vision, and a sense of palpitations, culminating in a fainting spell. The ER doctor had already ordered blood work, and the report was on the chart. Carrie scanned the figures, stopping when her eyes lit on the potassium level: 2.6 mEq/ml — definitely a contributory factor, and something that should be corrected as quickly as possible.

She pulled aside the curtains and took in the scene. "Mr. Berringer, what's going on?"

The older man, pale and sweating, turned his head slightly toward her. The oxygen mask on his face added a hollow timbre to his voice. "I wish I knew, Doctor." He opened his lips to say more, but instead closed his eyes, apparently spent by the effort.

Carrie turned to Berringer's wife, who stood beside the gurney, alternately blotting beads of perspiration from her husband's forehead and stroking his hand. "Mrs. Berringer, is your husband taking any medications other than the ones you told the emergency room doctor about?"

"Dr. Markham, they're all medicines you prescribed. Don't you have the list there?"

Carrie smiled at her and said gently, "Let's pretend I don't."

The woman frowned. "You know about the heart pills and the cholesterol medicine. And, of course, there are those little tiny pink pills, but I don't think they count. They're just water pills of some kind."

Carrie tried not to grind her teeth. "Do those little pink pills have a long name that's shortened to some letters?"

"Oh, yes." The woman's face brightened. "I remember. HCZT or HTCZ or something like that."

Hydrochlorothiazide, or HCTZ, was a

47

diuretic given to patients with high blood pressure, but it also could deplete potassium levels in the body. And when this occurred in patients who'd taken an overdose of digitalis, the combination had the potential to be lethal.

Soon Carrie was able to put together the story. Henry Berringer refused to be "one of those people who use little pillboxes" to tell him if he'd taken his medicine on that particular day, choosing instead to rely on his memory. Apparently, for the past several days he'd taken his pills two or three times a day. The resulting digitalis overdose at first manifested itself as nausea and lack of appetite. He complained of seeing a yellow halo around lights, something he blamed on his early cataracts. But when he fainted in the living room, his wife called 911. His pulse was fifty and irregular when the paramedics arrived.

"You've taken too much of some of your medicine," Carrie said to Mr. Berringer. "We need to make sure that doesn't happen again. In the meantime we're going to do some things to reverse the effects of that overdose."

Mrs. Berringer looked so relieved that Carrie thought she might burst into tears. "Thank you, Doctor," she mouthed as Carried slipped through the curtains with a promise to be back as soon as she could.

Carrie spent the next several hours shuttling between the clinic and the ER. Finally, thanks to atropine, Digibind, and intravenous potassium, Mr. Berringer's heart rate and rhythm were approaching normal levels. Carrie thought it would be best to watch him for a bit longer, and since he had a disturbance of cardiac rhythm and might have sustained heart muscle damage, there was no problem getting approval for his admission to the hospital's medicine floor. If serial EKGs and cardiac enzymes showed no further problems, she'd let him go home — but with a lecture about his need to become "one of those people who uses pillboxes." That was far better than becoming "one of those people who didn't take their medicine properly and died as a result."

Carrie was walking through the ER on her way back to her office when paramedic Rob Cole stopped her. "Dr. Markham, what's the latest on the man we brought in with the digitalis toxicity?"

"He's out of the woods," Carrie responded. "Good pickup on the diagnosis, by the way. He'd also taken too much HCTZ, so his potassium was in the cellar."

"Ouch. I noticed the atropine we gave him in the ambulance wasn't enough to get him straightened out. Glad he's doing better now."

"Thank you for asking."

Carrie turned away and had taken a step when Rob said, "Dr. Markham?"

She stopped and looked back at him. "Yes?"

He frowned and looked away. "Never mind. I'll ask another time."

As she traversed the enclosed breezeway that connected Centennial Hospital with the building that housed the Rushton Clinic, Carrie wondered what else Rob wanted to say. It seemed to her that, more and more, Rob went out of his way to run into her, sometimes in the ER when he and his partner dropped off a patient, occasionally in the cafeteria, once or twice in the halls.

It was flattering that he seemed to want to be around her. Rob was a little younger than Carrie, possessed of good looks that had all the nurses talking — wavy black hair, deep brown eyes, sparkling white teeth. There was no question he was what some of the staff would call "a hunk."

Get a grip, she told herself. *Stop wondering if Rob is coming on to you. This isn't junior high.* She looked at her bare finger and wondered if she'd acted hastily in giving back Adam's ring. Until thirty-six hours ago, Carrie was sure she was in love with Adam Davidson. But what about this new Adam? And what about their future? With the old Adam, it seemed certain and secure. Now it was uncertain and dangerous.

It was obvious that Mrs. Berringer loved her husband. She was right beside him in the ER, putting into practice her vow to love him in sickness and in health. Carrie had been ready to make that vow and more to Adam, but now was she really prepared to be with him "for better or for worse"? Especially if "worse" meant running from someone trying to take his life . . . and hers along with it? That was the question she had to answer. She was hurt at his deception, but it ate at her that if she really loved him, she wouldn't be running away when Adam needed her.

Carrie leaned against the wooden handrail that ran the length of the breezeway, pulled out her cell phone, then paused with her finger over the keys. She closed her eyes for a moment and tried to prepare for the call she was about to make. She at least needed to listen to his whole story. She'd set up another meeting with him. After that? She'd wait and see.

As hesitant as a child climbing onto a jungle gym for the first time, she pushed the speed-dial button.

When Adam felt the buzz of his cell phone in his pocket, he experienced the epitome of "mixed emotions." The display showed that the call came from Carrie — and she'd be calling for one of two reasons: to give him a chance to explain, or tell him to get out of her life and stay out.

"I'm glad you called," he said, hoping that her next words wouldn't make him a liar.

"Adam, I don't have long to talk. We need to finish our last conversation. But I want to meet somewhere safe. I don't want to be a target again."

Adam ran through the choices. He figured his apartment was out. If the gunman had found his car, he'd no doubt located where Adam lived as well. And there was no way he would lead a potential killer to Carrie's home. "How about the law firm where I work? Everyone is out of there by five — five thirty at the latest unless something unusual is going on."

"Is it safe?"

"I'm not sure any place is safe anymore, but this seems the best option. I'll leave the building with everyone else and drive around a bit to lose anyone who might be following me. Then I'll park a block away and come in the back door."

"So what do I do?"

Adam thought for a bit. "Hopefully the shooter doesn't know your car. The lot's well lit. Park right by the entrance and call me on my cell as soon as you get there. Hurry inside, and I'll double lock the doors behind you."

Carrie hesitated. If she said no to that idea, he wasn't sure what he'd do next. But finally he heard the rush of a long exhalation. "Fine. I'll be there as soon after six as I can make it."

"Thanks," Adam said. "I appreciate —" He stopped talking when he heard a click. Carrie had already ended the call. He stared at the dead phone, his heart sinking. He prayed their relationship wasn't broken beyond repair.

Outside the clinic exam room, Carrie scanned the information on her next patient. George Harris, age sixty-two, complaining of swollen feet and ankles. A number of diagnostic possibilities ran through her head, disorders like "congestive heart failure" and "deep vein thrombosis." That was what she liked about her internal medicine practice. Every day there were new challenges. Well, time to tackle this one.

She tapped on the door and stepped inside. The older man perched on the edge of the exam table had silver hair combed straight back. Blue eyes twinkled behind steel-rimmed glasses. He was already wearing an exam gown — Lila had seen to that — but he wore it with the same dignity as though it were a white tie and tails.

"Mr. Harris, I'm Dr. Markham. How can we help you today?"

"Frankly, I think I'm fine. But my daughter seems to have a different idea."

There was a distinct British accent there. Carrie checked the address on the man's papers and confirmed that he was local. Then the younger woman sitting in the corner spoke up and solved the mystery. "My father-in-law recently came to the United States to live with us. He says nothing is wrong, but we don't believe it's normal that his feet and ankles are so swollen."

Carrie eased onto the rolling stool, positioned it midway between patient and daughter, and looked first to one and then the other. "Suppose we get a little more history. Mr. Harris, when did you first notice this?"

As the story unfolded, Carrie mentally laid aside several possible diagnoses until only one stood as the prime suspect. Mr. Harris worked in Great Britain for years in an electronics manufacturing plant. His job had been to solder and weld various components, and although provisions were made to avoid inhalation of the fumes from his work, he and many of his fellow workers had hated the respirators, disliked the noise of the exhaust fans, so they plied their trade without them at every opportunity. And as a result, he now presented to Carrie with the consequences of decades of inhaling cadmium-laced fumes: facial puffiness, swollen ankles and feet, protruding belly. Why? Because his kidneys were failing, causing the loss of a protein called albumin from the body, with resultant accumulation of tissue fluid in these areas.

"We're going to start by checking some lab work," Carrie said when she'd finished her exam. "Lila will help you with that. I'd like to see you back again tomorrow, when we can go over the results and talk about treatment."

Carrie had just finished dictating her note when Lila appeared in the doorway of the cubicle. "Urinalysis and metabolic profile are cooking, but you don't seem to have any doubt about the diagnosis."

"No, I'm sure we're dealing with nephrotic syndrome. That poor family is about to have its life turned upside down." Special diet, medications to control blood pressure, regular trips to the dialysis lab. Carrie closed her eyes and balled her fists. *God, why do You let these things happen?*

Then again, why was God letting Adam break her heart? And why did God let good men like John die because a seemingly simple medical procedure went horribly wrong? As she headed for the next exam room, it was all Carrie could do to focus on the patient inside. She worked to put aside her situation with Adam. She struggled to stop thinking about the way her husband's life had ended . . . and the role she played in that terrible event. Carrie thought she might pause and pray for help and guidance but quickly dismissed the idea. That avenue had been closed for quite a while.

As Carrie pulled into the law office parking lot, her heart thudded against her chest wall. It wasn't only the potential danger that pushed her adrenaline level sky-high. It was the very real possibility that tonight Adam might tell her something that would fracture their relationship forever. She loved him —

that was clear to her. But how much could that love withstand?

She was about to find out.

The law offices occupied a small, two-story building. Adam had told her that the bottom floor contained offices, the upper story a conference room and law library. She punched his speed-dial number on her phone.

"Carrie?"

"I'm here."

"I'm unlocking the door now," Adam said.

She hurried the few steps from her car to the front entrance where Adam waited. They stepped into a reception area where a low-wattage light burned. The burgundy carpet was soft under her feet. Tasteful drapes of burgundy and tan framed the windows. Several upholstered chairs were situated along the walls. A cherry wood desk and chair faced outward from one corner, and behind it two lateral file cabinets of the same material flanked a door that probably led into a business office.

Adam pointed. "My office is back there."

Carrie walked down a hall lit dimly by security lights. In Adam's office, he flipped the light switch and gestured her to one of the two chairs across from his desk. He took the other and turned it sideways to face her.

Adam seemed to have aged overnight. His face was haggard and his eyes were red-rimmed, accented by dark circles beneath them. Carrie almost felt sorry for him — almost. She recalled the love she'd felt for him — still felt. She wondered what her emotions would be after she learned more of his story.

Carrie nodded at Adam, as though to say, "It's your turn."

"Okay. Let's hear the rest of it."

Adam leaned toward her and she saw him struggle to keep his voice calm. Though they were alone in the building, he spoke in a quiet voice. "Thank you," he said. "For meeting me . . . for giving me another chance."

Carrie shook her head. "I should at least hear the whole story. I owe you that much."

He moved as if to reach for her hand, then pulled back and let his own hands rest on the arms of his chair. "As I told you, I started life as Keith Branson. I went to law school at John Marshall in Chicago. While I was in school, I met a woman who worked in her father's law office. She seemed perfect, and I fell hard for her. After a relatively short engagement, Bella and I were married. When I graduated, her father, Charlie DeLuca, took me into his practice."

Carrie nodded but said nothing. She didn't want to stop the flow of his narrative.

Adam went on to tell about an idyllic first year of marriage. But soon he discovered his father-in-law's practice had a shady side. Charlie not only defended some of the biggest criminals in Chicago, he played a key role in laundering huge sums of money, was a cut-out in several narcotics rings, and acted as an advisor, if not a partner, for a group that controlled most of the prostitution in that part of the state.

Beads of sweat dotted Adam's brow. "I finally told Bella what I'd found out about her father's law practice — that it was part of a criminal enterprise — and that I wanted no part in it. She laughed and said, in effect, 'The money's good. Keep your mouth shut.' "

"But you didn't," Carrie said.

"I couldn't. I tried, but it was harder with each day that passed. Sometimes the arguments lasted well into the night. Then Bella told me she was pregnant."

Despite herself, Carrie caught her breath. Did Adam have a child?

"I was overjoyed," Adam continued. "But Bella didn't share my feelings. She wasn't ready for motherhood. She told me she was going to visit a friend. She came back in a

59

week and told me she'd lost the baby. It wasn't long before I found out that actually she'd had an abortion. That was the last straw for me."

"What did you do?"

Adam squeezed his eyes shut for a moment, as if he could drive away the images that plagued him. "I put together a detailed file to be used against my father-in-law and his associates. When I had everything ready, I contacted the District Attorney and said I was prepared to testify before a Grand Jury and at any resulting trial. In return, I wanted protection."

"Obviously, they said yes."

Adam nodded. "I told my wife and father-in-law that I needed some time away, packed a suitcase, and left. The next time I saw them was at his trial."

The DA assured Adam that the U.S. Marshalls Service would keep him safe until after the trial. He was ferried back to Chicago from Milwaukee to testify before the Grand Jury. After that, the marshalls moved him from city to city, always under a new name, until finally he came back to Chicago to testify at his father-in-law's trial. The process had been a slow one — two years, in fact. And as each day passed, Adam wondered if he'd made the right choice.

"What about your wife?" Carrie asked.

"Once she learned what I had done, she filed for no-fault divorce — in Illinois it's called 'irreconcilable differences.' My absence sped up the process. Before I returned for her father's trial, the divorce was final."

"And your father-in-law?"

"The jury convicted him of a whole laundry list of crimes. He ended up with a total sentence of thirty years. He should have gotten even more."

"So you're safe now. Why not resume your true identity? Why not go back to Chicago?"

Adam laughed without mirth. "My life wouldn't be worth ten cents. Charlie De-Luca was part of a big organization, not to mention his family members and people who owed him favors. As soon as his sentence was handed down, I'm certain the word went out to kill me."

Carrie thought about this. "What brought you here to Jameson eight months ago, then?"

"After the trial one of the places the Witness Security Program — it's usually shortened to WITSEC — had me working in was an office supply store in a small town in Iowa. One day a guy showed up with my picture, asking if anyone at work knew me. Apparently no one cared for the guy's attitude, so they told him they had no idea what he was talking about. But the more I thought about it, the more convinced I was that my new identity wasn't all that secret. After all, WITSEC has a lot of moving parts, and all Charlie DeLuca's family, or hired gun, or whoever had to do was spread around enough money and they'd find me. It was time to find somewhere else, but this time, on my own."

"So the program didn't move you here?"

"No, I moved myself. No one knows where I am now . . . or, at least, I thought that was true. But if that shooting Saturday night wasn't random, someone's found me, and until I know for sure, I don't want to talk with the police."

"Why?"

"When I was working in Charlie DeLuca's office, I learned he had contacts with cops on the take in police departments from California to New York. There's no reason to think that doesn't include Texas."

Carrie was shaking her head before he stopped talking. "Why didn't you choose a large town, like Dallas? Surely it would be easier to get lost there."

"It is, but it's also more likely that organized crime has a bigger presence in a large city than in someplace like Jameson. I'm close enough to Dallas to enjoy the benefits, but a smaller place like Jameson seemed a lot safer."

"So you haven't told anyone where you are?"

"Just one man. He's a marshall, but this move is totally off the books. Besides, I'd trust Dave with my life."

Carrie frowned. "Why?"

"He's my older brother. He's David Branson, Jr."

Carrie thought about the story she'd heard. It revealed an Adam who had the moral fiber to do the right thing, even if it meant losing his identity, his family . . . and perhaps his life. True, he should have told her the story before asking her to marry him, but she could see by the pain in his eyes as he told the story how much it cost him to reveal it now. This wasn't the Adam she thought she knew, but what she'd heard did nothing to erase her love for him.

Carrie was ready to say something to Adam when the crash of breaking glass made them both bolt from their chairs and hurry toward the front of the building. A large hole ringed with shards was all that remained of the plate glass window in the reception area. Smaller pieces of glass littered the carpet like diamonds. The drapes, one area of carpet, and two of the uphol-stered chairs in the room were on fire, send-ing tongues of flame licking outward, threat-ening a larger blaze. Wisps of acrid black smoke stung Carrie's eyes and seared her lungs.

"Are you okay?" Adam yelled.

Carrie stifled her coughing long enough to say, "Just fighting the smoke. Is there a fire extinguisher here?"

"It's in the hall," Adam said. "I'll get it. Call the fire department."

As Carrie dialed 911, her first thought was for their safety. But her second was that despite Adam's insistence on not being involved with the police, now he'd have to be. She wondered how he'd handle their questions — and where it might go from there.

FIVE

Adam had the fire extinguished by the time the fire department arrived, but the firemen spent another fifteen or twenty minutes making sure there were no areas that might burst into flames later.

The police arrived at almost the same time as the firemen. Facing them wasn't exactly what Adam wanted, but there was nothing to be done about it. He'd simply have to put the most innocent face he could on the incident.

The patrolman taking Adam's statement asked him, "Any idea why someone might have done this?"

Adam knew how this worked. He expected the question, and had his answer ready. "There are two lawyers who work here. The most likely explanation is that someone didn't like the way one of the attorneys handled his case."

"Any recent cases handled by the firm that

could have triggered this?"

"I don't know of any, but you should ask the lawyers. One of them should be here soon."

The patrolman looked at his notes. "When this call came in and you gave your name, the computer kicked out a recent report you made about vandalism to your car. Think someone's out to get you?"

Adam struggled to maintain a calm demeanor. "I doubt it. That was a simple case of vandalism. I don't think there's a connection here."

The questioning went on in that vein for what seemed like an hour, although when he glanced at his watch Adam found it had taken only twelve minutes. When it seemed the questions were coming to an end, the patrolman turned to Carrie and asked, "Anything to add, ma'am?"

Adam tried to send her a silent message. *Please don't say anything about what I've told you. Please.*

Carrie's face was smudged with soot, her blond hair was a mess, her green eyes were red-rimmed. She was the perfect picture of "let's get this over with so I can go home." She gave the patrolman a shy smile. "No, I have no idea who could have done this. Adam and I had some things to discuss, and we needed a quiet place to do it." She grimaced as she looked around. "Unfortunately, this wasn't it."

Adam breathed a sigh of relief when Janice Evans walked in. Now maybe the police and firemen would direct their questions to her. Before he could introduce Evans to Carrie, the attorney strode over and held out her hand. "Janice Evans. You must be Dr. Markham. Adam has mentioned you."

"I wish we could have met under better circumstances," Carrie said.

"It happens," Evans replied. "Sorry you were involved."

The policeman's first question to Evans was, "Any dissatisfied clients who might have done this?"

Her response was a calm shrug. "Sooner or later, someone decides his lawyer didn't do right by him. Some of them send nasty letters. A few file complaints with the bar association. But I must say I've never had one go quite this far." She grimaced as she turned to look at the damage. "After you're through talking with me, I'll call a client who's a general contractor. Maybe I can convince him to board up the window tonight." She nodded toward Carrie. "Adam, why don't you take Dr. Markham home? Come back here afterward so we can talk about keeping the practice running tomorrow."

"I have my car, thanks." Carrie nodded once to Evans, once to Adam, before she hurried toward the door.

"I'll see you out," Adam said, hurrying after her.

Carrie beeped her car unlocked and was inside it before Adam reached her. He stood there, wondering what Carrie's response would be to her second brush with danger in such a short period of time. Surely it couldn't be good.

Carrie lowered the car window. "Yes?"

He wasn't sure what to make of her tone, but the look on her face conveyed a desire to leave more strongly than any words could. He wanted to hold her, beg her to stay, assure her that his goal was to keep her safe, but she started the engine and looked ready to drive away.

"Carrie, I'm so sorry. I hate to leave things like this. We still have a lot to talk about."

"When? How? Each time we get together someone tries to kill you — and me in the bargain."

"Would you like me to follow you home to be sure you get inside safely?"

"I don't think that would make me any safer." Was that a faint smile, or a grimace?

"Look, Adam. I want to hear more of your story, and we'll figure out a way to do it. But right now I'm going to head home, where I'll lock all the doors, take a long shower, and try to sleep."

"When can I see you again? Will you call me?"

"Eventually, but give me awhile to think about all this." Carrie rolled up her window and put the car in reverse.

Adam watched her taillights fade into the distance, and his heart went with her.

Okay, God. Please don't take her from me. Help me out here. What do I do next?

"After you finish with this next patient, Dr. Rushton wants to see you in his office."

"Thanks, Lila. Tell him it won't be too long."

Carrie paused outside the exam room. Why did Phil Rushton want to see her? It couldn't be that he wanted her to do a pre-op evaluation on his patient. He routinely asked the other internist in the clinic, Thad Avery, to do that. Was there some problem? Phil was a confirmed nitpicker. And although things had been quiet between them since John's death, there had been a few differences of opinion between her and Phil in the past — situations where tempers almost reached the boiling point.

Phil Rushton was an excellent surgeon. But Carrie didn't particularly admire him as a person. He had divested himself of his wife and two children as quickly as possible after completing his residency training. Now, other than surgery, he had little else to occupy his time. True, he didn't always lord his status over his colleagues, but he wasn't above using his position as chief operating officer of the clinic to snoop and pry. She wondered what he had in mind this time. Whatever it was, she had an uneasy feeling that it wouldn't be good.

Carrie finished with her patient and made her way down the hall toward Phil's office. The door of an exam room opened, and Carrie stopped to let one of the nurses, holding a handful of papers, exit with a middle-aged man.

The nurse and patient came toward Carrie. When they were abreast of her, the man stopped and looked Carrie full in the face, his eyes narrowed in a frown that made her take a step back. She swallowed twice. "Hello, Mr. McDonald." He didn't reply, just stood silent, fixing her with that look before he turned to follow the nurse. *If looks could kill . . .*

It had been over a year since Calvin Mc-

Donald's wife died. Was he still angry about her death? Or angry with Carrie about the part she played? Carrie hurried on, trying to put the encounter out of her mind, as she had others that preceded it.

Phil occupied a corner office in the clinic, bigger in size and more expensively furnished than anyone else's. It even had its own door leading directly outside, so he could come and go without anyone — patients or colleagues — being the wiser.

Carrie tapped on the closed door and received a curt, "Come." She'd always hated that response, since it came out sounding like, "I'm terribly busy, but if you must, I grant you permission to enter."

She opened the door, took a step into the room, and raised her eyebrows in silent question. Phil looked up from his desk. "Come in. Close the door. Have a seat." He turned his attention back to the papers in his hand.

Phil Rushton was anything but a commanding picture. He was short, chunky, almost bald, and spoke in a high voice that reminded her of the lab experiment in high school where the students all inhaled helium. But he made up for what he lacked in appearance by a manner that said to all concerned, "I'm not just anybody — I'm *somebody* — and don't you forget it."

Carrie hitched one of the patient chairs closer to the desk, smoothed her skirt across the back of her thighs, and sat. Phil's attention was back on the paper in front of him, scribbling notes in the margin.

As she waited, Carrie looked around her. The walls of Phil's office were covered with diplomas and certificates that testified to the status he'd achieved: BS with honors from Northwestern University, MD degree and selection to Alpha Omega Alpha at the University of Chicago's Pritzker School of Medicine, chief resident in cardiothoracic surgery at Rush University Medical Center. He'd gone on to receive award after award while in practice. She'd heard the term before, even used it — this was his "I love me" wall.

After a moment she said, "You wanted to see me?"

Phil sighed gently, capped his gold-plated fountain pen, then dropped it on the desk. "Yes, Carrie. I sent for you." Phil leaned back and steepled his hands, displaying the long, manicured fingers that could do magic on the human heart in surgery. "I heard that you were one of the victims of a firebomb attack last night. What was that about?"

"Where did you hear that?" she blurted.

"At the hospital when I was on rounds," Phil replied in a cool voice. "I repeat — what was that about?"

Carrie bit back a retort. The question was valid, she guessed, although the manner in which it was asked was a bit demeaning. So typical of Phil. She took a deep breath. "My friend Adam and I went to his office so we could have some privacy while we talked. That's why I was there." Her words came faster than she intended. "One of the lawyers said she thought it was most likely a disgruntled client of the law firm, trying to exact some sort of revenge. The police seemed to agree." Just talking about it sent a chill down her spine, but she hurried on. "And, although you didn't ask, I wasn't harmed. Only shaken."

Phil leaned forward and fixed her with an earnest expression. "That was going to be my next question, Carrie. I'm glad you weren't hurt." He picked up his pen and began twirling it. "And you weren't involved in this? It had nothing to do with you or, for example, an unhappy patient?"

Carrie hadn't given serious consideration to the possibility. Surely the attack was meant for Adam, not her. But she wondered for a moment if Phil's eyes, eyes the color of winter rain, were seeing something that she missed. Then she thought of another pair of eyes, eyes that fixed her with a malevolent glare. Could a patient, Mr. McDonald or some other, go to this length to harm her? She'd have to think about that a bit. She hoped this was just Phil being Phil, making the moment melodramatic.

Carrie struggled to keep her tone even. "So far as I can see, the episode didn't have anything to do with me, except to scare me half to death. Now, are you through? I have patients to see."

Phil's voice softened slightly, but his eyes still seemed to probe her. "Carrie, I have to ask uncomfortable questions. It's part of my job as the clinic's managing partner."

No, it wasn't. Not this way, anyway. Could Phil be fishing for what her employment contract called "questionable behavior," trying to get rid of her? She wouldn't put it past him. *Stop it. You're being paranoid.*

Carrie stood up. "Sorry, but it still makes me uncomfortable to talk about the incident. Is that all?"

Phil rose and offered his hand across the desk. His smile was faint. She couldn't tell if it was sincere. "Carrie, we all know the stress you've been under since John's death. If there's anything I can do to help you . . ."

Phil let the sentence die.

74

"Nothing, but thank you." She drew in a deep breath. "Now, if you'll excuse me, I have patients to see."

Phil nodded, eased into his chair, and picked up his pen once more, effectively dismissing her.

As Carrie closed the door she decided that even if Phil weren't the senior member of the group, he'd still be in charge. The other doctors in the group would see to that. Sure, the clinic was in business to heal the sick, but to keep it going took money. And Phil Rushton generated a lot of money for the group. She hoped she'd never reach the point where she practiced medicine solely for the monetary rewards.

Going into medicine was a response to a call Carrie felt just as strongly as a call to ministry. Actually, it *was* her ministry, a ministry of healing. But Adam was trying to heal, in a manner of speaking, and so far she had done nothing to help him.

Sure, she was hurt because he'd lied to her, but she could see why he did it. She'd been about to let him back into her life, about to forgive him, when that firebomb came through the window. And what did she do? She ran away again. What did that make her?

Her next patient was an elderly gentleman. His appearance brought several descriptions to her mind: thin as a rail, pale as a ghost. The smile he gave her was the very definition of "putting on a brave front." His wife sat beside him, their hands touching.

Carrie smiled back at them. "Mr. Atkinson," she said, "I have your test results, and there's good news. The treatment seems to be working. Your blood count is much better. I think the leukemia is headed for remission."

Atkinson's face relaxed. Tears streaked his wife's cheeks. They both spoke at once. "Thank God." "Oh, Doctor, that's wonderful."

First Atkinson, then his wife moved forward to wrap Carrie in warm hugs. She luxuriated in the moment. Phil could have his certificates and awards, the satisfaction of pulling in the largest share of clinic income. But this was her reward. This was what she'd been called to do. This was why she practiced medicine.

Adam suffered through a restless night. He'd told Janice Evans he'd be there in the morning. After all, she had no idea the firebomb was meant for him. But weren't two attempts on his life enough to send him on his way, leaving Jameson and his would-be murderer behind? Not if the woman he loved was here, and that was exactly the case. He couldn't leave Carrie — not if there was any way to salvage their relationship.

He kept one eye on the rearview mirror as he drove to work. One of the schemes he'd turned over in his mind during the restless night was getting a gun. Dave had urged him to acquire one when he went into the Witness Security Program — even offered to help — but Adam refused. He couldn't bring himself to do it then, and he couldn't do it now. Maybe there was another way.

Twice he started to call Carrie, twice he pulled his hand away from his cell phone as though it were a fiery coal. No, she said she'd call. All he could do was wait.

The law office smelled of smoke. A large piece of plywood covered the front window. The burned chairs were gone, an empty spot where their replacements would sit. Workmen were on their knees, removing the damaged section of carpet. Despite all that, Hartley and Evans, attorneys at law, were open for business. No matter what else might happen, the legal machine continued to grind.

Adam slogged through the day, one ear tuned to his cell phone, waiting for a ring announcing a call from Carrie. But there was nothing.

"Would you take these papers over to the District Clerk's office? They need to be there by the end of business today." Bruce Hartley tossed a manila envelope onto Adam's desk. "Better hurry. They're about to close."

Adam looked at his watch. "I'm on my way. Then I'll head home. See you tomorrow." He shoved the envelope into his battered briefcase.

He was almost to the door when Bruce said, "By the way, was your girlfriend with you last night when someone lobbed that Molotov cocktail through the window?"

Adam paused with his hand on the knob. "Yes." He'd learned long ago never to give more information than was required.

"No danger of her suing us, is there?"

"Nope. But thanks for your concern."

Adam went out the door, leaving Bruce to decipher whether the last remark represented sarcasm or a sincere thanks. *If I were back practicing law, I'd run rings around him in court.*

During his short walk to the courthouse, Adam kept his head on a swivel. Every stranger was a potential threat. Each open window in the downtown area hid a sniper.

Soon he was back at the building that housed the law offices of Hartley and Evans. Adam paused in the parking lot and scanned the rows of cars still there. Where was his car? Had it been stolen? Then it dawned on him. It was in the shop, getting a new windshield and having the damaged front seats repaired. He located his black Toyota Corolla rental and used the remote to unlock the doors.

He hadn't heard from Carrie yet. Should he call her? No, he was determined to give her some time to process everything. In the meantime, he'd run some errands. If he hadn't heard from her later this evening, maybe he'd call.

Adam was almost to the cleaners when he noticed that the blue SUV behind him looked familiar. Had it been sitting near his car in the parking lot when he left?

When Adam first entered the Witness Security Program, Dave had given him some rudimentary lessons on how to handle a tail. He put them into practice now, changing lanes, turning without signaling, jumping green lights and running through the last second of yellow lights. Finally, just before he was ready to take a short segment the wrong way on a one-way street, Adam looked in the rearview mirror and saw that he was clear.

He spotted a parking garage and wheeled sharply into it. The time dragged, but Adam forced himself to sit for ten minutes before he started the car and nosed back into traffic. It took him another five minutes of deke and dodge before he was certain he'd lost his tail . . . if there had been one in the first place.

Adam's brain hadn't been idle while he sat in hiding. He headed for the facility from which his rental car had come. Once there, his car safely lost in a sea of other returns, he entered an office staffed by a single clerk with a phone to his ear and two lines blinking. The clerk hung up and looked at Adam expectantly.

Adam put his rental paperwork on the counter. "I know you're really slammed, but this car's running pretty rough. I'm afraid the last renter put some cheap gas into it before turning it in."

The clerk frowned at the telephone with its blinking buttons. "I'm sorry. Why don't we put you in another vehicle?"

Adam had given this some thought. Jameson was a typical midsized north Texas town. The vast majority of vehicles on the street were either pickups or SUVs. "Sure." Adam paused as though considering a fresh idea. "How about a pickup?"

Adam had barely finished speaking when the clerk pulled a set of keys from a drawer and pushed them toward him. "No problem. Got a Ford F-150, and I'll let you have it for the same price as the car you're driving. Slot 18A. Enjoy."

By now, new calls had added more blinking buttons to the phone. When the young man picked up the handset and took the next call, Adam eased the rental papers he'd been ready to give the clerk back into his pocket. Apparently the person on the other end of the phone had a significant bone to pick with the car rental company and had the clerk's full attention. During the heated exchange that followed, Adam hurried out the door.

Great. Now the rental company's paperwork showed his previous car, while he was driving the most common vehicle in the city.

A shiny black pickup waited for Adam in 18A. Perfect. He tossed his briefcase inside, adjusted the mirror and seat, and headed out of the lot. He still had to run those errands. After that, if Carrie agreed to see him, he needed a safe place for them to meet.

He didn't want to bring Carrie to his apartment for a variety of reasons, not the least of which was that the shooter probably knew where he lived. After the incident with the firebomb, it was obvious that the law office wasn't safe. And under no circumstances did Adam want to lead his stalker to Carrie's house. He needed a safe base of operation, not only a place to meet Carrie, but somewhere he could relax without fearing he'd be murdered in his sleep.

He'd check into a motel, and he had the perfect location in mind. He'd need to pick up clothes and toiletries from his apartment. Maybe if he parked a block away, went through alleys and used the back entrance, he could avoid detection. Not now, though. He'd postpone that until after dark.

Adam needed cash, so his first stop was an ATM, where he withdrew the daily maximum from his account. No problem there. Adam had one more stop to make. Then he'd be ready to go to ground.

After his next errand he climbed into his new pickup and took a roundabout route to one of the motels that ringed the outer part of the city. The one he chose wasn't part of a chain, but a small, family-owned motel that featured a row of cabins set back from the highway. He checked in and paid cash for three days.

When he filled out his registration, Adam put down a fictitious address and transposed two digits of his license plate. He entered *Ford* for his last name. Adam thought a moment before adding the first name *Edward,* figuring the clerk was too young to remember the Yankee pitcher Whitey Ford.

Once in his room, Adam used the prepaid cell phone he'd just purchased to call Carrie. She answered on the first ring. "Carrie, it's me, Adam." He took a deep breath. "I know I said I'd wait for you to call, but I can't wait any longer. Can you meet me at the Rancho Motel after dark?"

"Adam, I don't —"

"I'm in a motel for a reason," he hurried on. "I'm staying away from my apartment for now. There are parking areas in both front and back of a row of cabins. Park in the back, close to the breezeway where the ice machine is. Then walk straight through and turn left. I'm in cabin six."

The silence stretched on. Adam was about to say something more when Carrie said, "Okay."

"One more thing," Adam said. "Be careful as you drive here. Try to make sure you aren't followed."

Adam's call had caught Carrie in her car,

sitting in the doctor's parking lot after hospital rounds. She'd ended the call, and within seconds her phone rang again.

"Carrie, it's Julie. Can you talk now?"

"Sure. I'm glad you called. Are we still going to meet for lunch?"

"That's why I'm calling. Barry and I are going to be in Dallas tomorrow. Will that work?"

"Of course. I need some face time with you." Talking with her best friend had always helped Carrie put things in perspective. "Tell you what. I can arrange to get away a little after eleven, and my first afternoon patient isn't until two."

They settled on a restaurant halfway between Dallas and Jameson. Carrie wondered if she should warn Julie to be certain she wasn't followed, then dismissed the idea as paranoid.

As Carrie drove out of the parking lot, something she'd heard in med school crossed her mind. *Just because you're paranoid doesn't mean they aren't out to get you.* Maybe it wasn't paranoid to be careful — not if someone was trying to kill Adam . . . and her.

Six

Adam jumped up from his chair when he heard the tap on the door of Rancho Motel's cabin six. "Adam?" a small voice called.

He opened the door and waved Carrie inside. They exchanged an awkward hug, but when Adam made a motion to kiss her, Carrie pulled back, disguising the movement by tucking a strand of hair behind her ear. His heart sank.

Carrie settled into the room's only chair. "Do you think this is a safe place to meet?"

Adam eased onto the bed and sat with his back against the headboard. He'd asked himself the same question. "It's the safest place I could think of."

"Why didn't your caller ID show up on my phone when you called?" Carrie asked. "What I got was 'private call.' "

"I went to Best Buy and bought a prepaid cell phone. People, especially those on the wrong side of the law, call them 'throwaways.' I'll give you the number before you leave. From now on, use that when you call me."

"Why?"

"I understand that it's possible to locate a cell phone, even when it's not being used, by triangulating the cell towers it accesses. I don't know how sophisticated this guy who's after me really is or how much technology he has available, but I decided there was no reason to give him a way to pinpoint my location."

Carrie said, "Well, I can see that you're taking this seriously. But what's your next move? That is, if you don't mind telling me."

For maybe the hundredth time Adam regretted thinking he could get by without sharing his past with Carrie. But he couldn't change that. He leaned back against the headboard and closed his eyes. "I'm not sure what to do. Ordinarily I'd pack up and run again. But that would mean leaving you, and I can't do that."

"But if you stay, you're not safe. Right?" she said.

"You saw what's happened already. Does that seem safe to you?"

"What I can't understand is, if DeLuca went to prison, why is this still happening?"

"A connected mob guy can put out a hit

whether or not he's behind bars," Adam said. "You can bet that's exactly the message that went out before the prison door closed on Charlie DeLuca."

"So that's why you were in the Witness Protection Program," Carrie said.

"Witness Security Program," Adam corrected. "But, yes. No one knows where I am except my brother."

"Why Jameson? Why here?"

Adam forced a smile. "My grandmother grew up here. She went north and married my grandfather, but as a child I heard lots of stories about Texas, and specifically about Jameson, which was just a wide place in the road when she left. I looked it up on the Internet and found it had changed. Like the story of the three bears — not too large, not too small, but just right."

"So you essentially slipped away from federal protection? Would they take you back?"

"I left the program because there were too many ways DeLuca's people could find me. I don't see why it would be any safer for me to go back now."

"How did you get a job here?" Carrie asked.

"All it took was a couple of forged references and an obvious good grasp of the practice of law. It's not hard to be a paralegal when you're already an attorney." A faint smile crossed Adam's face. "Besides, Bruce Hartley got me cheap, and that's just his style."

"What about me — or maybe I should say, what about us? Was that all part of your cover?"

Adam was shaking his head while she was still talking. "Absolutely not. My first week here, when I slipped into the Jameson Community Church and saw you in the congregation, I knew I had to meet you."

"So when we were introduced that Sunday morning after church, it wasn't an accident?"

"No. Until I saw you, I never put much stock in that 'love at first sight' stuff. You changed my mind, right then and there. And the more I got to know you, the more certain I was that love was real." He took a deep breath, swallowed twice, and said, "Carrie, I loved you then. I still love you."

Carrie turned her head and wiped at her eyes. A long moment passed before she finally spoke, and when she did her voice was fragile, as though it was ready to crack. "When John died, I thought I'd never love anyone again. Life had lost its color. But I met you, and it didn't take long for me to think you'd come into my life to fill the hole that was there. I started to live again."

"I wasn't trying to —"

Carrie shook her head. "You did exactly what was needed. You let me talk about John. You dried my tears and let me lean on your shoulder. You gave me your love. And the gray turned to a rainbow again."

Adam's heart swelled.

"You introduced yourself as Adam. Then I found out you're really Keith. You may even have other names. But that doesn't matter. I've decided that what matters is I'm not ready to lose you. I love you, and I want us to be together."

Hope rose in Adam's chest. "Does that mean our engagement is on?" he asked. "Are you ready to wear the ring again?"

Carrie rose and moved to the window. She stared into the night for a long time before speaking. "Let's leave it at 'I love you' for now. We can talk about our future when all this is settled."

"So where do we go from here?" Adam asked. "You know the choices I have. What do you want me to do?"

Carrie turned from the window and looked into Adam's eyes. "I don't know what to tell you. All I know is that we're in this together."

Adam crossed the room and put his arms around her. They hugged and kissed, this time with the passion that had marked their relationship earlier.

When Carrie finally pulled away she looked at her watch. "I need to go. Give me your new cell phone number. I'll call you tomorrow."

Carrie entered the number into her phone, then moved toward the door, where she turned to face him. "Should I keep calling you Adam?"

He nodded. "You have to, in order to keep my identity a secret. Is that going to be a problem?"

"No. You're still the man I fell in love with. That's all that matters." She kissed him once more. "Good night. Be careful."

All through a night marked by tossing, turning, and brief periods of fitful sleep, Carrie pondered her situation and weighed the choices facing her and Adam. Her dreams were filled with flashbacks of John's death interspersed with vivid scenes of a gunman bursting into the church and shooting Adam dead during their wedding. She woke in a mass of tangled, sweat-soaked bedclothes.

Over a quick breakfast of coffee and toast, she considered her options and found none of them good. Driving on automatic pilot to the clinic, her mind was a muddle. Now it was time to go to work, to put everything else aside. Her patients deserved her full attention, and that was what they'd get.

She stood outside the exam room where her first patient waited when a familiar voice made her turn. Phil Rushton said, "Carrie, glad I ran into you. Do you have plans for lunch?"

Carrie made a conscious effort not to show her surprise. What was going on? Phil Rushton didn't ask colleagues to lunch. It was generally held that he didn't ever stop for lunch. He went straight from the operating room to his clinic so he could see his post-ops, evaluate possible preoperative patients sent to him by his colleagues, and do the hundred and one things involved in a busy and successful specialty surgical practice.

There was definitely something going on here — but she wasn't sure what it was. One explanation was that Phil was interested in her as something other than a colleague. But that didn't ring true with her. Phil rarely did anything that didn't benefit him, directly or indirectly. Once more Carrie wondered if he was angling to get her out of the clinic. She'd noticed some time ago that he favored the clinic's other internist, Thad Avery. Maybe Phil or Thad wanted to replace her on the clinic staff with a friend of theirs. Whatever the reason, she'd better tread carefully.

"I'm sorry, but I have a luncheon date."

"With that boyfriend of yours?"

"Actually, no." *As though it's any business of yours.* "I'm meeting a woman who's been my best friend for years."

"Can you cancel it?" Phil said. Was that a smile on his face? Unbelievable. "There's a little hole-in-the-wall café down the street. The food is great, but it seems no one's discovered it yet, so it's quiet. Just the place for us to talk privately."

Talk privately, as in break bad news? Carrie liked this less and less. "Phil, I —"

"Dr. Markham!"

Carrie's nurse, Lila, came speed walking down the hall toward her. Something was definitely wrong. Lila didn't hurry for anything except the direst of emergencies. "What?" Carrie said.

"The EMTs just brought Mrs. Lambert into the ER. Chest pain, syncope, shock — probably a coronary. The ER doc's with her now, but they need you there stat!"

"I'm on my way." Carrie turned to Phil with an "I'm sorry" look, then hurried away, glad for the interruption, but worried about her elderly patient who appeared to be having her third coronary event in the past two years.

As she walked briskly through the enclosed breezeway that connected the clinic with the hospital, Carrie thought about what lay ahead of her. She wondered if this was the heart attack that might be the final one for Mrs. Lambert. Well, not if Carrie could do something to prevent it.

There had been a time when Carrie prayed for her patients. Then John died. She hadn't offered up many prayers since then, but this seemed to be the time for one.

God, I know the ultimate result isn't in my hands, but in Yours. Please use me to restore Mrs. Lambert to health. The doors to the hospital were straight ahead of her. Time to see if she, or God, or the two of them together could keep her patient alive.

Carrie pushed through the double swinging doors into the confusion of the Emergency Room. Her eyes swept left and right as she hurried to her patient's side. If one ignored the sounds that formed a constant background — beeps and voices and the clatter of balky gurney wheels — and focused instead on all the moving parts, they'd see staff going about their business in an efficient manner, with no outward hint of the inward adrenaline rush some of them undoubtedly felt.

"Dr. Markham, your patient is over there." An ER nurse, whose name danced outside of Carrie's memory, indicated a cubicle surrounded by drawn curtains that moved like sails in the wind from the activity going on behind them.

"Thanks, Jane," Carrie said, thankful that the right name had come to her just in time.

She drew aside the curtains and saw what she'd expected. An ER doctor alternately focused on the green lines of a heart monitor and the lab slips in his hand. An elderly lady, thin and pale, lay motionless on the wheeled stretcher. Oxygen flowed into a clear plastic mask that covered her lower face. IVs dripped into both arms. Her vital signs, constantly displayed on yet another monitor, showed a blood pressure that was low but adequate.

"I'm here," Carrie said to the other doctor. "Fill me in."

He did so in a few sentences, using the medical-speak only a professional would understand. "If you don't need me, I've got an ER full of patients. But call if I can help." He slid through the curtains and was gone.

As Carrie moved to her side, the woman

on the stretcher opened her eyes, blinked, and squinted in recognition. "Dr. Markham. Am I dying?" Her voice was weak, and the effort of speaking seemed to exhaust her.

Carrie patted her hand. "Mrs. Lambert, you've had another heart attack — a pretty big one, according to what I see. We need to do a cardiac angiogram to see how to handle this."

Mrs. Lambert breathed out through pursed lips, then took in a deep breath. "So, another stent?"

"I'm —"

"It depends on what the angiogram shows. You may need an operation to supply more blood to your heart."

Carrie whirled to identify the speaker. Actually, his voice was easily identifiable to her — she'd heard it only minutes ago — but she couldn't believe Phil Rushton would try to claim the case without speaking to her first. "Phil, what —"

At that moment a man and woman in hospital scrubs pushed into the already crowded space and positioned themselves at the head and foot of the gurney. The woman spoke to Mrs. Lambert. "We're going to take you for an X-ray study of your heart." They busied themselves with changing from the wall oxygen supply to a tank under the gurney. The male member of the team unplugged the monitors, and in a moment they wheeled Mrs. Lambert away.

Carrie glared at Phil. "Can you tell me what's going on? And why you're taking over my patient without consulting me?"

Phil made a palms-out gesture. "Carrie, this is Mrs. Lambert's third infarction. I have no doubt that both her EKG and enzymes will confirm that it's a major one. Her daughter called the clinic right after you left and asked if I'd take charge of her case if she needed surgery. She gave me most of the history I need. We'll see what the angiogram shows, but I'm willing to bet that this time stents won't do it. Your patient will need bypass surgery. Now, unless you want to try to talk her and her daughter into going somewhere else, I think you'll agree I'm a good choice to do the operation. And the sooner we get to it, the better."

He was right, of course. Mrs. Lambert was a prime candidate for what medical professionals called a "cabbage." Not the leafy vegetable. She needed a coronary artery bypass graft, a procedure that bore the acronym CABG. Carrie had to admit the probable need for such surgery crossed her mind as she hurried to the ER. Mrs. Lambert shouldn't suffer because Carrie had her feelings ruffled. She shrugged. "Let's head for the angiography suite. I want to see what the angio shows."

"Are you sure you want to go back there?" Phil said. "After what happened to John —"

"I'll be fine," Carrie snapped. "I've been going to the angio suite since two weeks after John died. I'll be the first to admit it wasn't easy at first, but I did it." She turned on her heel and said over her shoulder, "I promise I won't break down, if that's what's bothering you. Now, are you coming?"

As Carrie hurried down the corridor, she wondered about the man matching her stride for stride. Professionally he was as competent as they came. She'd trust her life to Phil. Actually she'd trusted her husband's life to him. She might have assigned some blame to Phil in John's death, but now that some time had passed she realized he'd done all he could. The question that continued to plague her was whether she had done all she could as well.

Seven

Phil was right, of course. The angiogram showed almost total blockage of Mrs. Lambert's left anterior descending and left circumflex coronary arteries. In layman's terms, blood flow to the major portion of the heart muscle was cut off. "I'll talk with Mrs. Lambert and her daughter," Phil said.

Carrie knew she'd been dismissed, but she couldn't simply disappear. She'd cared for Mrs. Lambert through two other heart attacks and thought she'd formed a bond with the woman. Even if the daughter asked Phil Rushton to take over the case, Carrie felt an obligation to be there. "I want to go with you when you talk with them. She's my patient too." *At least for now.*

She stood by as Phil explained the procedure to Mrs. Lambert and obtained her permission for the surgery. No problem, the woman said. She knew how close to death she'd come — how close she still was. If

98

surgery was what was needed, she was ready.

Carrie's heart melted when Mrs. Lambert looked at her and said, "Dr. Markham, would you pray for me?" Carrie nodded her assent, afraid to speak. *I'll try, but my prayers haven't been too successful lately.* She squeezed Mrs. Lambert's hand and followed Phil out of the room.

They found the daughter, Mrs. Stinson, in the waiting room. Despite her earlier frustration about the call to Phil Rushton, Carrie sympathized with this harried, middle-aged woman who wore worry lines on her face like a combat badge. Mildred Lambert had lived with her daughter and son-in-law since her husband died over a year ago.

Carrie and Phil took two vacant chairs that flanked Mrs. Stinson. There was no one else within earshot, so this was as good a place as any to have the talk. "Your mother has had another heart attack," Carrie began. "And this was a big one — almost fatal. So Dr. Rushton needs to perform surgery."

Phil explained that Mrs. Lambert needed more blood flow to the heart, so he'd take a vein from her leg and hook it up to take the place of the clogged arteries. "We call it a bypass graft."

"Is it risky?" Mrs. Stinson's voice was

weak, and now tears flowed freely.

"Of course," Phil said, and went on to explain the potential risks. "But it's necessary surgery. Without it, your mother would almost certainly die."

Mrs. Stinson turned for the first time to Carrie, an unspoken question in her eyes.

Carrie nodded. "I agree."

A secretary came over to the group and handed Phil a clipboard. He glanced at it. "We have the op permit signed. Now I have to get ready." He rose and hurried away.

"Is Mother strong enough . . . ?" Mrs. Stinson let the words trail off.

"We believe so. The anesthesiologist is excellent. Dr. Rushton is the best heart surgeon around. The whole team is extremely competent. Your mother is in good hands." Carrie found herself reaching for Mrs. Stinson's hand. "I have to get back to the clinic. Dr. Rushton will see you as soon as the surgery is over, and I'll be back this evening. Is there anything I can do for you now?"

Mrs. Stinson blinked away tears. "Just keep us in your prayers."

Carrie nodded and left the room. She looked at her watch and decided that if she hurried, she could finish seeing her patients and still be on time for lunch with Julie. In the hallway, she heard someone calling her name. Carrie turned to see Rob Cole trotting toward her. "Dr. Markham, I'm glad I caught you."

"Rob, I really have to get back to the clinic. What's so important?"

"I wondered about Mrs. Lambert."

"Did you and your partner have that call?"

"Right. Her EKG showed a massive MI. Did she make it?"

"So far. And you were right — she had a myocardial infarction. Dr. Rushton is doing a CABG right now."

"Well, she's in good hands," Rob said. He ducked his head, and Carrie thought he looked about fourteen years old when he did. "Um, I know that you're a doctor and I'm only an EMT, but I was wondering if you'd like to have a cup of coffee together sometime."

Carrie put her hand on his arm. "Rob, I'm flattered, but I'm involved with someone else. Thank you, though."

Rob was a good-looking young man who'd just asked her out. And Phil, despite his usual demeanor, had sent some signals of interest as well. Some women probably would be thrilled to have that much attention, but Carrie wasn't one of them. No matter what had happened, she wanted to honor her commitment to Adam.

She thought about the ring she'd given back. Did she regret that action? No. Although she was in love with Adam, Carrie didn't think they could move forward until they were no longer in danger. She only wished she knew when that might be.

Carrie and Julie had decided to meet at a restaurant in the Galleria, a large shopping center north of Dallas. Julie was already at a table toward the back, and the sight of her friend made Carrie's face light up.

Julie jumped up and met Carrie halfway to the table. The two friends hugged.

"I'm sorry I'm late," Carrie said. "Things were crazy this morning." She took the chair next to Julie and tossed her purse onto the vacant one beside her.

"No problem," Julie said. "Catch your breath, get something to drink, and we can talk." She sipped her iced tea. "Afterward, I have orders from Barry to check out the Nordstrom here. He agreed to pay for our lunch if I brought home something frilly." She raised an eyebrow.

Carrie grinned. In a few minutes the two friends were chatting as though no time had passed since they were last together.

The waitress served salads, and for a moment the two women nibbled, although neither seemed as interested in eating as talking. Finally Julie said, "Now for the reason we're here, I guess. The last time we talked, someone had taken a shot at you, after which you discovered your fiancé wasn't who you thought."

"I've found out even more since then," Carrie said. She leaned forward and laid out all she'd learned from Adam. "The real question isn't whether I love him — despite everything, I still do — but what we're going to do to get out of this mess."

"I don't suppose you've talked with anyone else about the situation," Julie said.

"Who would I tell? My parents pretty much washed their hands of me when I became a Christian my first year in med school. I don't have any siblings — you're the sister I never had." Carrie leaned across the table. "You're my best friend."

"Even though we were both in love with Billy Kiker in the third grade?"

"Even then," Carrie said, and laughed for what seemed the first time in weeks.

Julie took a forkful of salad. "Why didn't Adam tell you all this before he asked you to marry him?"

Carrie put down her fork. "He admits he probably should have, but he thought he'd made a clean start in Jameson and hoped he could get by without revealing his past."

"And you can forgive him for that?"

"When I think about how supportive Adam's been, when I realize how wonderful it's been to have him in my life — yes. He taught me how to smile again, Julie. When he and I first met, I was a wreck, mainly because of what happened to John."

"Stop it! John had a cardiac problem that no one, not even a great diagnostician like you, could have noticed. And even though the odds of a complication like the one he experienced are slim, that doesn't mean it can't happen . . . even with the best possible medical care." She reached to pat Carrie's hand. "You have to accept that."

Carrie inhaled, taking a moment to compose herself. "I know. And I'm making progress there." She took a swallow of tea. "The guilt about John's death isn't as bad as it was, although there are still triggers. But now I'm really frightened for Adam. The shooting, the firebomb, someone trying to kill him — and my life is in danger as well."

"Why doesn't he go to the police?"

"He says there's a possibility someone there might leak his true identity. I don't think it matters anymore, but he won't listen." She drained the tea from her glass, but her throat remained dry. "It's frustrating to feel so helpless. I don't know what's going to happen next."

Julie rattled the ice cubes in her glass, and the waitress appeared with a pitcher for refills. After she left, both women added sweetener to their glasses and drank. Then Julie said, "How would you like this to end?"

Carrie didn't answer at once. When she did, her voice was almost a whisper. "What do I want? I want all the danger to go away — right now, without our having to do anything. Just *poof*." She opened her fist like a magician making a coin disappear.

"Neither possible nor realistic," Julie said. "What is both possible and realistic is that you give Adam your support and help him find out who is after him."

"Even if doing that puts me in danger?"

"Crossing the street puts you in danger. Driving to the grocery puts you in danger. Eating in the hospital cafeteria puts you in danger. And the reward for any of those doesn't approach what you'll get from having Adam in your life. You love him. Period."

Carrie shoved her plate aside. "And that's it? That's all I can do? Julie, I feel so helpless. I need to *do* something."

"Isn't that typical of a doctor? You always

want to be in control." Julie pointed her finger at her friend. "You can't control this. You can brainstorm, you can do what Adam asks, but the main thing you can do is pray . . . for him, for you, for the whole situation."

"I . . ." Carrie's throat tightened. She couldn't get the words out.

"I know, sometimes praying is hard, especially if you haven't done it for a while. But there's no magic formula. Just talk to God. He's been listening all the time. All you have to do is make it a two-way conversation."

Adam could hear the argument in his head as clearly as if there were someone standing beside him making the case. "Leave town." "Don't go to work." "Hide." And to each suggestion, his answer was the same: a resounding, "No." To this point, his response had been to run, but this time he'd stand and fight.

He wasn't going to run, because to do so would mean leaving Carrie behind. Yet, if he stayed, he needed this job — not just for the salary, although that was essential, but because to step away from it would invite the very questions he'd tried to avoid. "Why did Adam do that? Is there something strange about him?" If he simply kept doing what he'd been doing, surely he'd think of a way out of all this.

Was it time to move past his principles and get a gun? No, he wasn't ready to take that step. He'd figure a way out of this without resorting to violence. Of course, if it came to defending Carrie . . . For now he'd stick with the actions he'd already taken to avoid a would-be shooter.

Adam was at his computer, scanning through LexisNexis for a legal opinion to back up some research, when he felt the buzz of his cell phone in his pocket. This was the new one, the one with a number only Carrie knew.

Although Hartley and Evans provided Adam with his own office, they'd been careful to emphasize the firm's open door policy. The attorneys would close their doors only when client privacy required it. Otherwise, everyone's door was to remain open, to promote ease of interaction in the office. It was nice in principle, but Adam needed privacy for this call.

He slid the phone out of his pocket, turned his chair away from the doorway, and whispered, "Carrie?"

"Adam, why are you whispering?"

"I don't want anyone to hear this conversation." He lowered the phone to his lap, effectively hiding it behind the edge of his desk as Janice Evans walked by and gave him a friendly finger wave. He waited until she was past to raise the phone to his ear once more in time to hear Carrie say, "So that's what I've decided."

"I'm sorry. I had to put the phone down. One of the attorneys just walked by. What was that?"

There was no mistaking the exasperation in Carrie's voice. "Maybe we'd better talk another time."

"Carrie, I'm sorry. I can call you in a couple of hours from outside the office."

"By then I'll be up to my eyebrows in patients."

"How about tonight?"

An eternity passed before she replied. "Your motel. Seven o'clock. I'll take the same precautions I did last night. Gotta go now."

"I really —" Adam heard a click. He had no idea what Carrie wanted to say, and he'd have to wait another five hours to find out. But surely she wouldn't agree to a face-to-face meeting again if she wanted him out of her life. Or would she?

"You're sure a popular person."

Adam snapped out of his reverie to see

Brittany standing in the doorway of his office, one hand poised on her hip. She probably didn't realize her pose was provocative. Adam figured she'd been practicing those mannerisms for so long they were automatic by now. Brittany was an attractive young redhead who acknowledged that her life's ambition was to latch onto a handsome lawyer with a great income and a bright future. Since, as far as she knew, Adam didn't fit that description, she'd been pleasant but not seductive to him — thank goodness.

"Why am I popular?" he asked.

"Someone called for you this morning. You were out at the time. They asked if you were usually the one who closed up the office. I told them 'sometimes.' "

Adam's heart raced, wondering if the hit would be in the parking lot this time. He'd have to figure out a way to avoid that. "Did they give a name? Say why they wanted to know?"

"Nope. Just got the information, thanked me, and hung up."

Adam shrugged. "Probably nothing, but thanks."

"Well, I thought you'd like a heads-up."

"Thanks." *I'll be watching for him . . . the same way you'd watch for a snake when you're in the woods.*

Brittany swung away and headed for the coffee machine.

Was this another way to let Adam know the stalker had found him? He'd heard that some killers got a perverse sort of pleasure out of letting their victims know they were about to die. Then again there could be a perfectly innocent explanation for the call. But Adam doubted it.

In Adam's mind there was no question of whether the stalker would strike again. The only unknown was when and where . . . and who would be harmed or killed in the process. Here at the office, he'd have to be constantly on his guard. But outside? What else could he do that might give him a bit of breathing room?

He'd moved to a motel, mainly so he could get a good night's sleep without worrying about another firebomb or bullet. He'd switched to a different vehicle, but he realized that the anonymity that gave him would be short-lived. How long would these advantages last? What was the reflex he studied in college biology? Fight or flight. Some animals did one or the other reflexively. Only man made a choice. But what was his?

He needed wisdom that was beyond his

own power. So he did the thing that had become as natural to him as breathing, the thing that had kept him sane during the last two years. He bowed his head and prayed.

EIGHT

Carrie checked her watch — half past five. If she didn't drag her feet on her hospital rounds, she should be able to get home, relax in a hot bath for a bit, then get ready to see Adam. The more she thought about it, the more she agreed with her best friend's advice. How had Julie put it? There was risk to everything in life, even crossing the street. She had to consider not just the worst possible outcome, but the best.

Carrie didn't want to lose Adam — no matter what. She still loved him — that much was becoming increasingly clear to her — and whatever it took, she was going to help him find out who wanted to kill him, then neutralize them. Together they'd put a stop to it. The reward was worth the risk.

She quickened her pace through the hospital corridors and soon was in the surgical ICU at Mrs. Lambert's bedside. The figure lying there didn't resemble the woman Carrie had seen so many times in her office. There she had been alert, animated, happy to be alive. Now she lay still as a wax mannequin, unmoving and pale. A ventilator controlled her breathing. IV lines and monitor wires were everywhere. But she'd survived the surgery, and that was important.

A quick scan of the chart showed stable vital signs and initial lab values that were no cause for worry. Phil's operative note, although brief, indicated that the procedure went off without a hitch, with the patient tolerating the surgery as well as could be expected for her age and condition. There was no need for Carrie to add either orders or a progress note. Her patient was unresponsive, so conversation was neither necessary nor possible. Moving on to the waiting room to face her family, on the other hand, took a bit of willpower.

If Carrie had any doubt that she'd been replaced in the mind of Mrs. Lambert's family as the primary caregiver, the reception she received in the waiting area removed it. Mrs. Stinson was polite, yet more distant than she'd been earlier. Yes, Dr. Rushton had been by. No, there was nothing Carrie could do, no questions she could answer. Almost as an afterthought, Mrs.

Stinson added, "We've talked it over, and we'd like Dr. Avery to take over Mother's care after she leaves the hospital. Dr. Rushton said that would be okay with you. I hope you don't mind?"

Carrie swallowed the retort that was on her lips. "Of course not. The records are already at the clinic, so it's just a matter of your making future appointments with Dr. Avery." She shook hands with the woman, although it was the last thing she wanted to do, then beat what she hoped was a dignified retreat.

As she stepped out of the elevator, Carrie's first thought, born of habit, was to retrace her steps back to the clinic. But she needed to save time, so she turned in the opposite direction, intending to reach her car by exiting through the Emergency Room. The door there emptied into the common parking area close to where she'd left her car that morning. As she hurried through the ER, her thoughts turned to her meeting with Adam. He would probably —

"Dr. Markham." Doris, the ER charge nurse, bustled up to Carrie and touched her sleeve. "I know you're not on call, but we need your help."

Carrie fought the urge to pull away. She didn't want to get caught, not now. "I'm in sort of a hurry to leave."

"This should only take a minute," Doris said. "The EMTs just brought in an elderly black man who collapsed on the street downtown. Erin thought she'd seen you with him in the ER a few weeks ago."

Carrie looked at her watch. She really needed to go. Then again . . .

"The man's comatose," Doris said. "He has no ID. There's no one with him. We don't even know how to contact his family, so if you recognize him that would really help."

Carrie took a deep breath. "Where is he?"

In a few moments Carrie looked down at a familiar face. She knew Garvin Burnett, knew him well. Mr. Burnett's visits to her office had always turned into prolonged sessions where he talked and she listened. Apparently she was the only person who would sit still long enough to do that for him.

Mr. Burnett was in his early eighties. He had lived at Meadowbrook Acres for some years, clinging fiercely to his independence. He never called it a retirement home, never referred to it as anything but a place where the population all happened to be well up in years.

She'd asked him once about his family, but he shook his head. "No family. But I don't need anyone. I'm fine on my own." When she broached the subject of moving to a section in Meadowbrook where he could get help if he needed it, Burnett bristled. "When I can't take care of myself, that'll be the time to pull the plug on me."

Two EMTs stood beside Mr. Burnett's stretcher. One scribbled on a clipboard, the other adjusted the man's oxygen mask. Carrie turned to Doris, who had taken up station at the foot of the stretcher. "You were right. He is a patient of mine. His name is Garvin Burnett," she said. "How did he end up here?"

The first EMT spoke up. "Got a call that a man had been acting crazy, then collapsed on the sidewalk at Fourth and Mizell. Witnesses told us he had a convulsion right before we got there. Nobody knew him, nobody saw anything else."

Carrie gazed down at the unconscious man. An IV was running, oxygen flowed into a mask over Mr. Burnett's face. The monitor showed his blood pressure to be low, although not at shock levels. Quickly, she ran through the differential diagnosis. Then her memory dredged up the most important fact. The reason she'd seen Burnett in the Emergency Room previously was his diabetes. He had labile, type I diabetes, controlled with some difficulty by daily insulin injections.

Carrie turned to the lead EMT. "He's diabetic. When you picked him up, did you check his blood sugar with your meter?"

"Part of the routine. His blood glucose was so low it was almost off the chart. We gave him glucagon and followed it with 50 percent dextrose, but he never came around."

"Labs back yet?" Carrie asked.

Doris spoke up. "Ordered them stat when he hit the ER, but they aren't back yet. We catheterized him but there was hardly any urine in the bladder."

Carrie nodded. The bladder probably emptied with his convulsion — so much for a urine glucose and ketone. "Okay. My first thought was that his blood sugar plummeted — too much insulin, no food, whatever — and it caused his convulsion and loss of consciousness. But that should respond to the treatment he got from the EMTs. There has to be something else. Let's start looking."

John Sullivan, the ER physician on duty, entered the cubicle. "Carrie, thanks for looking in on him. If you want to give me his medical history, we can take it from here. I imagine you're in a hurry to leave."

Carrie thought about Adam. She should probably take a moment to call him. But before she could act on it, she glanced at the monitor displaying Burnett's vital signs, and warning bells went off in her head. "Thanks, John, but I think I'll stick around for a bit."

Although he was neurologically intact when she examined him initially, Burnett's pupils even then were the least bit sluggish in their response to light. Now his blood pressure was going up and his pulse was dropping. She watched his chest rise and fall, his respirations getting a bit ragged. Cushing's triad. Increased intracranial pressure.

"We need to get him to radiology for a stat MRI of his head," Carrie said to Doris.

Two hours later Mr. Burnett was in surgery, and the answers to the puzzle were clear. The elderly man had wandered away from Meadowbrook Acres, apparently suffered hypoglycemic shock, convulsed, and hit his head on the curb. Although his blood sugar and chemistries had righted themselves with the treatment rendered by the EMTs, the MRI Carrie ordered confirmed her clinical suspicion of a skull fracture with formation of a subdural hematoma — a collection of blood pressing on the brain.

The hospital social worker, working with the staff of Meadowbrook Acres, verified that Mr. Burnett had no family. Carrie and a neurosurgeon certified the operation as an emergency, their signatures on the operative permit substituting for that of Burnett or his next of kin. Tomorrow, if Burnett lived through the surgery, the hunt would begin for a facility to which he could eventually be transferred for long-term care. The sadness already in Carrie's heart because of Burnett's condition mounted as she realized this episode spelled the end to the proud man's independence.

It was fully dark when she finally walked out of the Emergency Room entrance and headed for her car. Her watch showed almost nine o'clock. As she climbed into the driver's seat, Carrie rummaged in her purse and retrieved her cell phone. She scanned the display, dreading what she'd see. Sure enough, there were five missed calls, all from what was shown as "Private Number." No matter what the display showed, she knew what the number represented and who the caller was. It was Adam, on his throwaway phone.

Adam left a message the first two times his call to Carrie's cell rolled over to voice mail.

When each subsequent call did the same thing, he ended them without speaking. For what seemed like the hundredth time, he parted the blinds in his motel room and gazed out. The parking lot was as it had been just moments before when he'd last looked — dark, almost deserted.

He hoped Carrie hadn't gotten cold feet. Adam needed to talk with her. He wanted . . . no, he needed to see her.

Of course, Carrie might have changed her mind. She might be coming to tell him she never wanted to see him again. If that were the case, he'd leave Jameson and find another town, try to start life all over . . . again. But how many times could he do that? Coming to Jameson had turned out to be the best thing he'd done since he began his journey. He didn't want to leave. Adam was determined that the shooter couldn't make him do so — but Carrie might.

He checked the time — eight thirty. There was probably a logical explanation for why Carrie was so late. After all, she was a doctor, he told himself. Doctors got caught on emergencies, and she probably didn't have time to call. No reason to worry . . . yet.

But despite his rationalization, worry was exactly what Adam did. He loved Carrie, and the thought that she might have fallen prey to the gunman who'd been stalking him, once it popped into his head, was almost more than he could stand.

As darkness fell outside, Adam had kept the light off in the room. No real reason, he supposed, but somehow he felt better in the dark — safer, perhaps. He pressed the button on his digital watch to illuminate the numbers. Eight forty-eight.

Should he call again? No, he'd left two messages, and if she looked at her cell phone Carrie would see she'd had multiple missed calls from him. *Just trust her, Adam.*

He tried to still the panic rising in his chest.

It was two hours past the time she'd told Adam she'd come to his motel room. Carrie wondered if he'd still be there. Might he have taken her failure to appear as an indication that she wanted him out of her life? Maybe he was at his apartment right now, packing, loading his car, about to drop out of sight again.

Carrie punched in the number of Adam's new cell phone. On the first ring an electronic voice repeated the phone number and invited her to leave a message. "Adam, it's Carrie. I'm on my way. I'll explain when I get there."

She wanted this to be a face-to-face conversation. Carrie needed to apologize, explain. She'd tell him what she'd told him before, but now it would carry an additional message — she loved him with all her heart, and she was ready to stand with him in his fight to uncover the identity of his attacker and bring him to justice.

Carrie started her car and pulled out of the hospital parking lot. She'd printed the directions to the Rancho Motel before her first visit, but that paper was at home. Check the address on her iPhone? No, that would waste time when she could be driving. She thought she could find it, and after a couple of false turns, she did.

She parked in the back of the units as before, sneaked through the circle of light spilling onto the Coke machine and ice dispenser, and walked along the front row of doors, looking for Adam's room. She thought it was number six, but she wasn't totally certain.

She turned and scanned the parking lot. A few cars were scattered about, but none that she recognized as the black Toyota rental she'd seen Adam driving. Carrie walked back and forth in front of the units, watching for a light in a room, maybe even someone peeking out from between drawn curtains. But the darkness was unbroken.

Carrie pulled her cell phone from her pocket and pressed Redial. Even if Adam didn't answer, she might hear the ring inside one of the rooms. But no sound reached her ears. Again, the call rolled to voice mail on the first ring. Either he was on the phone or had his phone turned off.

She scanned the area one more time. All the windows were dark. The parking slots in front of all the units in the row were empty. She drew the only conclusion she could — Adam was gone.

Where now? How about his apartment? Maybe he'd gone back there for more clothes, something he forgot.

She climbed into her car and started out for The Villas. Adam's apartment was in a complex of four-plexes occupied primarily by young urban professionals. She found it easily enough, but now, with her brain racing a mile a minute, all the numbers seemed to be hiding from her in the dark.

Carrie exited her car and looked around, her confidence boosted only slightly by the container of Mace in her shoulder bag. She unzipped the purse and let her right hand rest gently on the metal cylinder. The lights were on in the apartment, and from behind the door she could hear classical music playing softly. Carrie found the bell and pushed it. Faintly, the first notes of the Westminster chimes sounded inside.

There appeared to be no response at first — no sound of footsteps, no change in the music, no voices. She poised her finger over the bell, ready to push it again, when the peephole darkened. Carrie moved so that her face was directly in the field of view of the person inside. "Adam?" she almost whispered. Then the door opened.

A young man who looked barely out of high school stood in the doorway. He wore faded jeans and a blue T-shirt with DHS written on it. His feet were bare. "Yes?"

Who was this? Adam didn't have a roommate. "I . . . I must have the wrong apartment," Carrie said. "I'm sorry to disturb you."

"Who did you want?" Neither his voice nor his manner displayed any annoyance at having a stranger ring his bell. "I've only been here a few weeks, but I know a lot of the people in the units around me."

"Adam Davidson," Carrie said.

"Oh, you're one unit off." He smiled. "They all look alike in the dark, don't they?" The young man stepped onto the porch and pointed to the next four-plex. "This is 402. He's in 302."

Carrie thanked him and hurried away. She ignored the sidewalk and crossed the lawn directly to the next unit. The front window was dark. She heard no sounds inside. Had Adam already left? Or could he be at her house, waiting for her to finally appear? Carrie took a deep breath, squared her shoulders, and pushed the bell.

When there was no response, Carrie rang again . . . and again. Finally convinced that the unit was empty, she trudged back to her car. Where could he have gone? The next place to look was her house. Maybe he'd gone there, looking for her after she failed to keep their rendezvous.

By now she had the car moving, heading toward her house, driving almost by instinct. If he wasn't at her place, either he'd left town or his stalker had caught up with him. She could picture Adam, lying in some dark place, bleeding from a gunshot wound, his attacker standing over him smirking.

As she neared her house, she slowed and looked around the neighborhood. His car was nowhere to be seen. She parked in the driveway, checked all around the house, including the backyard. No Adam.

Should she stay here and wait for him to call? Logic told her that was wise, but her instincts cried out for her to do something . . . anything. She'd try the motel once more. Carrie shuddered as she drove, praying for safety for Adam . . . and for her. *God, keep him safe until I can find him. And when I do, I won't let him go again.*

NINE

Adam looked at his cell phone, wondering if he should try to call Carrie again. Then he noticed that the display was dark. He'd let his battery run down. He hurried to the parking lot and found the sack with the box his phone had come in. The first charger he dug out was the one for his car. Fair enough. He needed to be doing something anyway. He plugged in his phone and set it on the seat next to him. Then he started his pickup and began to drive toward Carrie's house.

In a few moments a tone from his cell phone got his attention. Someone was sending a text.

He pulled to the side of the road and looked at the phone. "Blocked Number" showed on the caller ID. He scanned the message and his mouth went dry. The words were typical texting, abbreviated but easily understood. He read them quickly at first, then again, more carefully. "DR MRKHM

N ACCIDENT. N SRGRY NOW CENT HOSP. COME QUICK."

He didn't bother wondering who sent the message, what the circumstances were. Carrie had been in an accident and was in surgery at Centennial Hospital. He needed to get there quickly. Adam put the pickup in gear and sped through the night, leaning forward as though he could make the vehicle go faster by doing so.

Adam's phone lay on the seat beside him. A beep made him look at the display. Missed calls. Voice mail. He ignored them. They were probably from the ER, someone with more details about Carrie's condition. He didn't want to take the time to answer. Besides, it might be bad news. And he couldn't stand that right now.

The Rancho Motel was normally fifteen minutes away from Centennial Medical Center. Adam made it in nine. He skidded into the ER parking area and took the first open slot he found, one marked for "Patient Unloading."

He threw the selector into park, turned the key, and paused to whisper, "Please, God. Please let her be all right. I'll do anything —" He slammed the door of his vehicle and sprinted toward the ER's sliding glass doors. Suddenly, to his left, bright lights flared and the engine of a powerful vehicle roared. He glanced in that direction just before a white sedan barreled toward him. Reflexes carried Adam, rolling, to his right and back. He stopped when he was tucked under the front bumper of a car. The vehicle sheltering him rocked and a loud noise assaulted his ears as the pursuing car grazed the front fender just inches away.

Either this was a trap, or someone was taking advantage of Carrie's accident to catch him unaware. Adam rolled out and ran toward his pickup. At the end of the row, the white sedan skidded into a turn, ready to come back for another try at him.

In his pickup, he started the engine and rammed the gearshift into reverse, burning rubber as he backed out of the parking space. Adam turned the wheel, slammed the selector into drive, and stomped hard on the accelerator. He didn't take the time to fasten his seat belt. The sedan was right behind him now.

At the last minute, Adam slammed on the brakes and cut the steering wheel of the pickup sharply to the right. He skidded into one of the parking aisles, barely missing cars right and left. A glance in the rearview mirror showed a flash of white going down the main aisle he'd just vacated.

He had to get out of here. Where was the exit? Adam slowed and began turning randomly right, left, left again, right, until he spotted an arrow and the welcome word "Exit." He screamed out of the parking lot, turned onto the main street that fronted the hospital, and floored the accelerator.

After a number of twists and turns, during which Adam finally took the time to fasten his seat belt, he was in a residential neighborhood. He remembered this one. It was full of streets that dead-ended, interspersed with speed bumps to keep motorists from racing through. Unfortunately, that was what Adam had to do right now. He navigated by dead reckoning, enduring bump after bump, grateful for his vehicle's heavy-duty suspension.

There'd been no headlights behind him for several minutes now. He spotted a house that was dark, with a vacant driveway leading to a closed garage door. He stopped, backed into the drive, killed his lights and engine, and hunched low in his seat. The few streetlights in the subdivision were low-powered, yellowish ones, casting eerie shadows but making Adam almost invisible as he sat there.

He waited — one minute, two, five — and finally decided his attacker had given up the chase. When his pulse had slowed almost to normal, Adam started the engine and drove away, keeping his lights off until he was back on a main street. Two blocks away, he stopped the pickup in the parking lot of a strip mall. He was pretty sure this had been a trap, but what if Carrie had really been in an accident? Adam dialed her cell phone. After three rings, she answered, and relief washed over him.

"Carrie, where are you?"

"I'm in the parking lot of your motel. I've been looking for you everywhere, but I finally came back here. Where have you been? Why weren't you in the room?"

"The battery on my phone went dead, so I missed your call. While the phone was recharging, I got a text telling me you'd been in an accident. At the hospital parking lot, someone tried to run me down. When I managed to get back in the pickup, they tried to ram me from behind. I finally lost them, but the sequence of events started me thinking, and what I've decided isn't pretty."

"What do you mean?"

"First, there's no question that the killer knows you and I have been seeing each other. And that you're important to me — important enough for me to drop everything

131

and rush to the hospital if I thought you were hurt."

"So he's been watching you longer than a few days," Carrie said.

"Right."

"What's next?" Carrie asked.

"We need to meet. Stay right where you are. But keep your car doors locked and the motor running. And if anything looks suspicious, get out of there."

"Adam, this is scary," Carrie said.

And getting scarier every minute. Adam ended the conversation and pulled out into traffic, his eyes flicking every few seconds to the rearview mirror. Suddenly every car behind him carried a potential murderer.

He wondered if he'd ever feel safe again.

Carrie was parked at the end of the row behind the Rancho Motel, not far from a red Dodge, the only other vehicle in sight. When she saw headlights approaching, she pressed the start button of her Prius and put her hand on the gearshift. Her foot hovered over the accelerator. A black pickup pulled in beside her, the door opened and closed, and Adam tapped on her window.

She unlocked the door, and Adam slid inside. His kiss was quick but heartfelt. The next words came out in an urgent hiss.

"Lock the door again."

Carrie swallowed twice. Her heart was hammering. "Adam, you frightened me."

"Sorry, but we have to take precautions."

"Where's your car? I didn't see a black Toyota in the lot."

"I guess I didn't tell you. I changed it for that Ford pickup." He turned until he was facing her across the front seat of her car. "Why didn't you meet me here like we'd arranged?"

"I'm sorry, but I had an emergency I couldn't leave." She explained a bit about what happened.

Adam took almost no time to respond. "I understand." His face was hidden in the dark, but his words conveyed his feelings quite well. "You care about your patients. That's one of the things I love about you."

A car wheeled into the lot, and Adam stopped talking as it pulled into a space at the end of the row and turned off its lights. Carrie hunched her shoulders against an invisible bullet. She wondered if it was true a person never heard the shot that ended their life. She hoped she wasn't about to find out.

Two doors slammed, and a young couple joined hands and walked slowly to one of the unit doors. Beside her, Adam let out a big breath, and Carrie realized she'd been holding hers as well.

"We'd better get inside," Adam said.

Carrie's senses were on high alert as she scurried through the semidarkness beside Adam. She heaved a sigh and dropped into the room's only chair while he closed and locked the door.

Adam perched on the edge of the bed. "Here's the big question," he said. "How did the person who sent the text get the number of this new cell phone? No one knows it except you. I haven't even called my brother to give it to him."

Carrie's answer came without hesitation. "I haven't told anyone."

"I'll accept that," Adam said. "But what if someone had access to your cell phone? Whoever texted me, and I have to assume it was the killer, must have thought, 'This was the last number dialed on her cell phone.' It was a pretty good bet that your last call would have been to me. When would you have made that call? And who had access to your cell phone after that?"

When had she called him last? They'd talked while she was on her way back after lunch with Julie. Where had her phone been since then? "After we talked I put my phone in my pocket. Sometimes I get text messages or calls from the hospital."

"Was it there the rest of the afternoon?"

Carrie started to say yes, but then she stopped. "No. I was seeing that patient in the ER, and while I was bending over his gurney, my phone almost dropped out of my pocket. I gave it to the nurse to stow in a locker in the break room, along with my purse."

"Was it locked up?"

"It's supposed to be." She thought back and felt a chill down her spine. "When I went to pick up the purse, the locker was unlocked."

"So for an hour or two, anyone going through the ER could have had access to it."

"I can't believe someone on the ER staff would do this," Carrie said.

"Not just the ER staff. It could have been someone pretending to be a patient or family member. Almost anyone could have walked through the ER and slipped into that room. It would only take a matter of a minute or two to identify your purse and check the call log on your phone."

"Would they know where to look?" Carrie asked.

"I'll bet I could find the nurses' locker room inside three minutes," Adam said.

"And even if the locker was secured, you can open those things with a bent paper clip." He shook his head. "No, the list of suspects is pretty large."

Carrie couldn't help it. She got up and walked to the window, where she peered through a slit in the blinds. The parking lot was dark and still, but there could be a killer out there somewhere — a killer who had marked Adam for death.

"Let's talk about what I have to do next," Adam said.

Carrie was still at the window with her back to Adam, so he couldn't see her face, but her next words, the very tone, left no doubt of her feelings. "Not just you — we. I'm with you on this. Neither of us is going to be safe until we identify the attacker and see that he's locked up."

"You know this could put you in danger," Adam said.

"I'm already in danger," Carrie said. She turned to face him. "Besides . . . I love you."

Hearing the words made Adam's heart sing. His happiness was fleeting, though, because he knew what he had to do. And it broke his heart.

"I love you too — more than I can say. And that just makes this harder."

"What do you mean?"

"Whoever the shooter is, the driving force behind him has got to be Charlie DeLuca. I could stumble around here for weeks trying to figure out the identity of the person trying to kill me yet never succeed. And the fact that the caller got my number from your phone . . ." He shuddered. "They're involving you in this entirely too much. I'm going to go directly to Charlie."

"I don't understand."

But Adam did. He was through running. He needed to go out and meet the challenge head-on. He needed to confront Charlie DeLuca once and for all — not just for his own safety, but for Carrie's.

Adam walked across the room to the window, where Carrie had turned back to stare into the night. He embraced her from behind. They stood that way for a moment, then she turned and kissed him, a kiss that made his decision even more difficult. "I don't want to go into details," he said. "Even with you. I have to leave town. Let's leave it at that. If people ask, you can simply say, 'He left. I don't know where he's gone or when he'll be back.' That's the safest thing for you."

Carrie's expression melted Adam's heart: a frown, a hurt look, tears. He took her hands in his. "Just trust me," he said. "Give me two weeks. That's all I'm asking."

"Two weeks?"

"Maybe less, certainly no more than that. And I'll call you as often as I can." Adam unlocked the door. "Now, I want you to drive straight home. I'll follow you and make sure you get into your house safely."

The hurt in Carrie's voice was obvious. "If you love me, why can't you share your plans with me? Why won't you tell me?"

"When I went into the Witness Security Program, one of the marshalls took me aside and warned me about telling people my plans . . . even people I trust. 'What they don't know, they can't tell,' was how he put it. You're better off not knowing."

Adam insisted on seeing Carrie safely inside her home. Not until he was sure there was no intruder hiding anywhere did he say, "Lock the doors. Keep the blinds and drapes closed. I'll sit out front until I'm sure you're settled."

Carrie did as he'd asked. When she heard his motor fire up, she moved to the window, pulled back the curtain, and watched Adam's pickup disappear around the corner. She still couldn't understand what had happened. She wanted to help him out of this mess. And now he was gone. She wanted to contribute, but how could she when he was leaving her behind? Carrie had never felt so powerless, so frustrated.

As his taillights faded into the darkness, she turned away from the front window and slumped into a chair in the living room. Carrie reached for the lamp beside her, then drew back her hand. No, she'd sit here in the dark. It was a better setting for her to ponder what might happen next.

Where was Adam going? Would he come back? *God knows.* She marveled at the truth of that offhand thought. She had no idea where Adam was going or what he'd do when he got there. But God did. And all she could do was trust Him.

That was when the tears started — first a few at the corners of her eyes, then a trickle down her cheeks, and finally the floodgates opened, and sobs accompanied it all. Carrie buried her face in her hands and let the tears come. She cried for the loss of her husband. She cried for the danger to Adam. She cried for the relationship with her parents that disappeared when she became a Christian. And she cried for herself, for turning loose of the only Anchor in her life that ever really held her secure.

Her prayer was silent at first, then continued as a whisper, and finally ended with words that echoed through the empty room. "God, I've pushed You away. I've blamed You for things that You didn't cause. I've found fault when You didn't respond to my prayers the way I thought You should. I've tried to be self-sufficient, to do it all without You. And it doesn't work. Please show me what to do. Please help me find the way. And bring Adam back safely. Please. Please. Please."

TEN

Despite knowing that Dave might try to talk him out of his idea, Adam dialed his brother soon after arriving home that evening. The conversation went about as he expected, but in the end Dave agreed to help. "I'll accept that you won't tell me everything you have in mind, but give me a call after you're on the road. I don't want you to do anything foolish."

"Have I ever done anything without thinking it through?" Adam asked.

"Lots of times, but we won't go into that now," Dave said.

Adam spent a restless night, turning over facts and suppositions, looking for puzzle pieces to fit together and failing at every turn, wondering how best to handle things at the end of his journey.

The next morning he rolled out of bed when he smelled coffee brewing, grateful for his habit of setting the automatic coffeemaker each evening. He'd just poured his first cup when the doorbell rang. He looked at his watch. Who could it be at seven thirty in the morning? Surely last night's call hadn't produced results already. And if Carrie needed something, she'd phone. Whatever it was, he might as well meet it head-on.

At the door, he peeked through one of the pair of glass side panels and saw a tall, middle-aged man standing patiently on the tiny porch. His visitor wore a tan, western-cut suit, and his leathered face was topped by a straw Stetson. Adam couldn't see his feet, but he'd be willing to bet they were shod in boots. Whoever this man was, he was certainly a son of the Southwest.

Adam opened the door on the chain and said, "Yes? Can I help you?"

The man reached inside his coat, and Adam tensed. Maybe if he threw himself to the floor, the first shot would miss. He could slam the door shut, lock it, and sprint for the back door.

The stranger pulled out a leather badge wallet, flipped it open, and said, "Keith . . . or should I say, Adam? I'm Sam Westerman, U.S. Marshalls Service out of Fort Worth. Your brother, Dave, said you needed some

142

help. He asked me to drop by and lend a hand."

Still wary, Adam said, "Sam, I hope you won't mind if I seem extra suspicious, but did my brother give you anything to tell me?"

"You mean, like your first car was a Ford, your first dog was a mongrel, and your first girlfriend was named Ann?"

Adam relaxed for the first time in days. He undid the security chain and opened the door. "Come in. The coffee's ready. Let's sit down and talk."

Adam had most of it worked out by the time he walked in the door of Hartley and Evans, LLP, the next morning. He tried to use bits and pieces of the truth as a foundation for his fiction. For instance, it was true that his parents were dead. It was true that he had one sibling, a brother. Even his destination wasn't total fiction. But beyond that, the story was a construction of half-truths and downright lies. Adam thought he could pull it off. And if things didn't play out as he'd planned, he'd simply have to wing it.

Brittany was at her desk, sipping from a steaming cup in her right hand, blowing on the nails of her left. A capped bottle of nail polish was centered on her desk.

"Change your mind about the color of your polish?" Adam asked, his smile leaving no doubt that he was joking.

"Just some repair work," Brittany said, frowning as she inspected her hands. "I was going to get an early start on these papers, but I chipped a nail. And since one of my prime duties is to dress up the place, I figured I should take care of that before things got too busy."

"Are you saying I don't bring class to the office?" Adam asked.

"You're okay, but you really should dress more like Mr. Hartley. One look at him, those custom-tailored suits and designer ties, and our clients know they've got a winner."

Adam took silent exception. All the external trappings in the world couldn't disguise Hartley's true self — he was a poorer-than-average lawyer reacting to a midlife crisis with a series of women. But there was no need to argue the point. "Speaking of the bosses, is either one of them in?"

Brittany put down her coffee and tested the nail. Satisfied that it was dry, she stowed the polish in a desk drawer and pointed down the hall. "Mr. Hartley's in court this morning. Mrs. Evans is in her office. She said she was going to work on a brief, and no one was to disturb her."

"I'll chance it," Adam said, and strode away.

In keeping with the office's policy, Janice Evans's door was open. She was bent over a law book, looking up from time to time to make notes on a yellow legal pad. Adam tapped on the jamb.

Evans didn't look up. "Unless the president or the chief justice wants me, I'm busy."

"Sorry, I'm neither. But I need to speak with you."

Evans frowned, then said, "Come on in. I know you well enough to be certain you wouldn't interrupt me if this weren't important." She leaned back and rested her hands on the open law book in front of her. "What's up?"

Adam adopted a properly somber expression. "I got a call last night from my brother."

"You told us you were an orphan and an only child."

"Yes, my parents are dead. And I told you I didn't have any siblings, because for all practical purposes, I don't. We've been estranged for the better part of ten years. But I got a call last night that my brother's in advanced-stage renal failure. The doctors

145

say only a kidney transplant can save him. And since I'm his only living kin, they want to test me to see if I can be the donor."

"Can the testing be done here? Or in one of the large cities in the area? Dallas maybe?"

"Probably," Adam said, "but if the match is good, they want to do the surgery immediately. It's easier if I go there."

"Where is 'there'?"

Adam took a deep breath. "The surgery would be done at Duke University Medical Center, but right now my brother's at the Federal Medical Center in Butner, North Carolina."

Evans frowned. "Butner. That name's familiar. Why does it ring a bell?"

"Because there's also a Federal Prison in Butner. That's where my brother's serving thirty to life for murder." He waited what he considered a proper interval before adding, "That's why we're estranged."

Carrie exited her car on Wednesday morning, squared her shoulders, and marched across the parking lot toward the clinic entrance. Her task was simple, yet harder than anything she'd ever been asked to do. She knew that every time she told the story of Adam's departure, not only would it cause her real pain, but she'd also have to project an air of shame, as though his leaving represented a failure on her part.

As the glass doors into the clinic slid to the side with a soft *whoosh,* she prepared to face the day. She made it as far as her office without more interaction with clinic staff than perfunctory exchanges of "good morning." Carrie dropped her purse into her desk drawer, shrugged into a fresh white coat, and looked at the top of her desk. As always, her schedule was centered on the blotter — a busy day, but that was good. It might keep her mind off Adam.

Carrie shuffled through the reports, noted the phone messages, and decided there was nothing there that couldn't wait. Technically, she had no patients in the hospital, but even though others had taken over their care, she wanted to drop by and see Mrs. Lambert and Mr. Burnett. Lila met her in the hall, but after a quick, and she hoped normal, greeting, Carrie hurried on.

Phil's note on Mrs. Lambert's chart was, as always, brief and to the point. "POD #1. Doing well." Post-op day one. Had it been less than twenty-four hours since Carrie stood in the ER and watched while Phil took over the care of her patient? She'd thought she was unhappy then. But since that time things had gone increasingly downhill in Carrie's life.

Mrs. Lambert's family wasn't in the waiting room — apparently they'd been sent home to get some rest.

Mr. Burnett was also in the surgical ICU, his condition satisfactory after his craniotomy last night. He hadn't regained consciousness. Carrie knew that when he did, the news of what lay ahead of him would be devastating to the old man. She made a courtesy note on his chart, asking the social worker to page her if she needed assistance from Carrie in getting him into a rehab facility.

It was pretty much a certainty that Mr. Burnett would be unable to go back to independent living. When he fell, the severe head injury changed his life forever. Carrie could identify with that. Her life had changed as well. And she had no idea what would happen as a result.

Some of it had been difficult for Adam, some easier than he'd imagined. Bruce Hartley came in shortly after lunch. Janice Evans quickly buttonholed the senior partner and they disappeared into her office, where they remained, the door firmly closed, for an hour. When they emerged,

Bruce stuck his head through Adam's door and said, "Can I see you in my office?" The tone was pleasant enough, but Adam knew that following Bruce was mandatory, not optional.

Once Adam was seated in Hartley's office, the lawyer leaned back and clasped his hands behind his head. "Janice explained your situation to me, and we're sympathetic. You've been an invaluable asset in the few months since you joined us. We recognize your need to go, but the office has to keep running."

Adam felt his gut tighten. He had to go, whether on good terms or bad, but his employers accepting his story would give credibility to his leaving town. "I —"

Hartley put up his hand to stop Adam. "As it happens, last week I interviewed a woman who recently moved to the area. She's an experienced paralegal, and she's looking for work. I called her, and she's agreed to take over your position on a temporary basis." He pursed his lips. "If you're back and able to resume work in two weeks, we'll give her a good recommendation and help her get a job elsewhere in Jameson. If you're not, then . . ." He let the words trail off and made a palms-up gesture, as though no one could blame him for the action that followed.

Adam shrugged. "I understand," he said. In two weeks, maybe less, he'd have done what he needed to do. Depending on what followed, he'd be back or it wouldn't matter.

After that it was simple. His apartment rent was paid for another three weeks. No need to forward his mail. He never got any. Adam exchanged his rental car for his newly repaired vehicle, tolerating the good-natured kidding about staying away from gunfire in the future. He cashed a check at his bank and told the teller, a notorious gossip, his story about a sick brother who needed one of his kidneys.

The next day his alarm went off at six a.m. A breakfast of buttered toast and coffee was almost more than his stomach could stand. By seven he was ready to go. He loaded two suitcases into the back of his little SUV, took one last look around the apartment, and walked out the back door, locking it after him. It was time for the most important trip of his life.

He plugged the GPS system he'd bought into the cigarette lighter and called up the destination he'd programmed into it the night before. In the cup holder of his Forester were a bottle of cold water and a travel mug of hot coffee. On the seat beside him, his prepaid cell phone lay next to a folded map of the United States. Adam slipped on a pair of sunglasses and pulled away from the curb in front of his apartment. A robotic voice warned him of a "left turn in two hundred feet." He eased the car into the left lane, clicked on his blinker, and tightened his grip on the wheel.

By now, Adam executed avoidance maneuvers like a pro, ignoring repeated demands from the GPS to "when possible, make a legal U-turn." When he was certain he wasn't being followed, he got back on track to his destination. He had no idea what was ahead. He wasn't even certain this was his best course of action. But it was the best he could do. Directions for the drive were coming from the GPS system, but Adam prayed that God would direct his actions.

The first question came at noon.

Carrie was sitting at her desk thumbing through a professional journal and munching on a sandwich Lila brought her from the food court. What was it? Tuna? Ham? It might as well be cardboard. But she had to eat.

She had gone through the same thing after John's death. She had no appetite. Food had no taste. Time dragged by, marked by painful memories of the past and fears of what the future might hold. Would Adam's departure prove to be as hard as John's death? Both almost killed her.

Phil Rushton, a white coat covering his dress shirt and muted tie, tapped on the frame of her open door. "Got a sec?"

Carrie washed down a bite of sandwich — it turned out to be grilled cheese — with a swallow of Diet Coke. She blotted her lips with a paper napkin. "Sure, come on in."

Phil eased into one of the chairs across the desk from Carrie. "You shouldn't gulp your food like that. You'll get an ulcer."

"I've been doing this since my second year of premed. If it hasn't burned a hole in my duodenum by now, I don't think it will." She laid aside the remains of her sandwich. "What's up?"

Phil sat down and crossed his legs, revealing navy over-the-calf socks above black wingtip shoes. "Just checking on how you're doing. I don't want you to burn yourself out. It seems that every time I look up, you're in the office or ER, even when you're not on call. You need some time away."

Carrie decided to say what she was thinking. "Phil, how is that different from what you do? Both of us spend a lot of time practicing our profession, but I guess that's our choice, isn't it?"

Phil nodded. "Touché. And I must admit that you're not burying yourself in your work as much since you began going out with Adam." He looked down at her hand. "I hadn't noticed until now. You're not wearing your ring anymore. Is something going on?"

Carrie was acutely aware of her bare left hand. "I don't want to discuss that." She looked straight at Phil. "Adam's left town. I don't know whether he's coming back or not."

"Why did he leave? Where has he gone?"

"I don't know," Carrie said. She reached up to dab at the corner of her eyes, a gesture that wasn't fake. Just the mention of Adam's departure was enough to bring her to the verge of tears.

Phil rose. "Well, I'm sorry to hear that. You know you're very special to everyone here. If there's anything I can do . . ." He let the words hang for a moment, then turned and left the room.

Carrie leaned back and tried to ignore the urge to cry. She replayed Adam's leaving once more. Was he in danger? Would he be back? Or had she lost the love of her life for yet a second time?

For reasons she couldn't fully explain, Carrie swiveled her chair and reached into the bookcase behind her desk to retrieve a dusty, leather-bound volume. She laid it on top of the journal she'd been reading and opened it to the front page. The ink was fading, but the words were still clear: "To Carrie. Let this be a lamp unto your feet, a light unto your path. Corrine Nichols."

Carrie hadn't thought of that sweet lady in years. But maybe the gift she'd given to a medical student just starting on her Christian pilgrimage was what Carrie needed right now as she struggled to hold on to the spark of faith that flickered within her. She let the book fall open and ran her finger down the pages, looking for direction in a life that was rapidly sinking into despair.

Adam squinted into the sun and reached into his pocket for his sunglasses. His journey took him eastward, and that meant each morning he had to drive into the sun. Couldn't be helped. The quicker he reached his destination, the quicker he could start his search for the puzzle piece he needed. He planned to use every available hour of daylight.

He'd spent last night in a Holiday Inn just west of the Texas-Arkansas border. Their "free buffet breakfast" of juice, Danish, and coffee was about all he could tolerate — not because it was so bad, but because the butterflies that took up residence in his stomach when he started the journey were still fluttering furiously.

Adam intended to call Carrie last night, but by the time he arrived at the motel, he was too tired to do anything but shower and fall into bed. He didn't want to try phoning her during the day — cell coverage was sometimes spotty where he was, and if he did get through, she was hard to reach between patients. Besides, leaving a message for her would be worse than no call at all. No, right now he'd concentrate on his driving. He'd phone her tonight for sure.

The eighteen-wheelers speeding eastward on Interstate 20 made using his cruise control impossible. Instead, Adam guided his little SUV along, speeding up and slowing down, passing and being passed, always careful to stay under the speed limit. The last thing he needed was a traffic stop.

As the driving became automatic, Adam let some of the thoughts he'd suppressed surface. Why had he thought this hare-brained scheme would work anyway? The smart thing would have been to pack up and leave town for good, strike out for a new city and bury himself there. Leaving the relative security of the Witness Security Program had probably been a mistake. On the other hand, it had brought Carrie into his life. And for that, he was eternally grateful.

Would this work? Could he — ? No matter. Adam had to set short-term goals and not look beyond them. First, leave Jameson. Make sure the story got out, one that was believable but left him an option to return. Then make this drive. When he reached his final destination, call Dave and ask for his help in the last stage of the plan. Despite the promise he'd made, Adam hadn't called Dave. Why? Because if he revealed the final step of this scheme too soon, he knew his brother would surely try to talk him out of it.

And if this failed? He didn't want to think about that possibility.

The plan had to work.

Eleven

Carrie was in her kitchen, about to microwave a tv dinner, when her cell phone rang. Once she recognized the caller, all thoughts of food left her. She dropped into a chair and breathed a silent "thank You" to God.

"Adam, is that really you?"

"Yes. It's so good to hear your voice. You'll never know how much I miss you."

"Oh, but I do, because I miss you even more." Carrie had a million questions, but they all fled her brain like dandelion fluff in a strong wind. She asked the one that remained topmost in her thoughts. "Are you all right?"

"Fine. Just tired. But only a few more days to go."

"Where are you?"

"I'm just east of —" Static filled the line, then everything went quiet.

Carrie looked at her phone display. "Call failed." Was it the fault of her phone? No, she had good reception. The problem must be with Adam's phone. Maybe a battery, perhaps poor cell phone reception where he was. She waited a couple of minutes for him to call back. When he didn't, she dialed his number — first his regular cell phone, then the throwaway phone he'd bought — but all she got was a mechanical voice saying, "Your call cannot be completed."

At that moment, what Carried wanted most was to throw something, to vent her frustration with cell phones, cell phone towers, cell phone service providers, and everyone associated with the mass communication industry. Instead, she took a deep breath. It had been good to hear his voice and know he was doing well. That would have to be enough for now.

Before she returned to her food preparation, she murmured a brief prayer. *God, please keep him safe. Bring him back. Please . . .*

"Lila, I'll be ready to start seeing patients in a few minutes." Carrie scanned the list of morning appointments. Nothing unusual there. She decided that she might have time to finish reading the medical journal article that had caught her eye yesterday.

She started digging through the stack on

her desk, but before she could put her hands on the right one, her phone rang — not the primary number, but her back line. She didn't give that number out to a lot of people, but one of them was Adam. Maybe . . .

She lifted the receiver. "Hello?"

"Dr. Markham?"

The voice wasn't Adam's. It wasn't even a man calling. Disappointment replaced hope in Carrie's mind. "Yes. Who's this?"

"This is Doris, in the ER. Your patient, Mrs. Cartwright, is here, complaining of weakness, nausea, sweating. May be the flu — lot of that going around — but I thought I should give you a call. Do you want me to have the ER doctor look at her, or do you want to come over?"

The fact that Shelly Cartwright had come to the ER in the first place worried Carrie. The woman wasn't a complainer. Her husband was in Afghanistan. The couple had a three-year-old son, an unexpected blessing that came while they were in their late thirties, but as far as Carrie could tell, Shelly was doing a good job of handling the stress of being both mother and father during Todd's deployment. This must be something bad if it sent her to the ER.

"Dr. Markham?" Doris's voice carried a

hint of impatience.

"I'll come over to see her. In the meantime, let's get some labs going." She rattled off the tests she needed, including a blood count to look for anemia and a blood sugar to check for low or high values. She added potassium, since a deficiency could contribute to weakness. "I'm on my way."

When Carrie pulled back the curtains around the ER cubicle, she was taken aback by what she saw. The woman on the gurney looked nothing like the vivacious brunette with whom Carrie spoke at church only a few weeks ago.

Doris moved to the other side of the gurney and reached down to pat Shelly's hand. The nurse might have a gruff exterior, but Carrie knew better.

"Shelly, what's wrong?" Carrie asked.

"I feel so silly being here, but I kept getting weaker and weaker."

The history Carrie obtained was of the fairly sudden onset of weakness, sweating, slight nausea. "When did this start?"

"About an hour . . . maybe an hour and a half ago."

"Did you do anything for it?"

"I lay down, drank some Coke, but nothing helped."

"Any pain?"

"No, nothing. I just felt like I was going to pass out . . . still do."

Carrie looked across the gurney and checked the monitor again. Blood pressure had dropped a bit, pulse had gotten a little faster in the past few minutes. Cardiogram complex on the monitor didn't look quite right — maybe hypokalemia?

"Labs back yet?" Carrie asked.

"Not yet," Doris said. "I'll see what's holding them up."

"Just a sec."

Doris turned, a puzzled look on her face.

"Let's hook her up and do a full EKG."

Without question, Doris grabbed the apparatus and began attaching the leads.

In a moment Carrie was looking at the paper strip spewing from the EKG machine. "That explains it."

"What?" Shelly asked.

Carrie held up the wide strip with the full EKG tracing. "You were hooked up to a cardiac monitor that only gives a partial picture of your heart's activity. This is a complete one, and it confirms my suspicion. You're having a heart attack."

"But I don't have chest pain," Shelly said in a "this can't be happening" tone.

"Almost half of women who have heart attacks don't have chest pain," Carrie said.

"But we know what the problem is, and we'll take care of you."

And that's what they did. Oxygen. Aspirin under the tongue. Amiodarone. A beta-blocker. A call to the interventional radiologist, and soon Shelly was on her way to the X-ray suite for a coronary angiogram.

While Carrie waited for the results, she asked Doris if she knew who was caring for Shelly's son. "Sorry, I don't know. Why don't you ask the EMTs who brought her in. Rob and Bill are still here. They're on break in the cafeteria."

Carrie found the two EMTs in a corner, sipping coffee and swapping stories. She didn't make the connection between name and person until the one with his back to her turned, and she saw it was Rob Cole. This might be awkward. Well, she needed the information.

"Dr. Markham, come join us," Rob called.

Bill slapped Rob on the shoulder and grinned. "Yeah, I'm tired of this guy's company."

Carrie pulled up a chair, declined their offer of something to drink, and got right to the reason for her visit. "You guys did the pickup on Shelly Cartwright?"

"Yeah," Bill said. "She was having second thoughts about calling 911 when we started to load her onto the gurney, but she was pale, her blood pressure was a little low, and the neighbor who was with her insisted that she should be seen by a doctor."

"So a neighbor was there," Carrie said. "Do you know if she's taking care of Shelly's son?"

"That's right," Rob said. "The woman's sort of a grandmother type, and I got the impression she does that a lot when the mother has to go somewhere and can't take her son."

Carrie pushed back her chair. "Thanks. I'll have the social worker make contact with her. We need to be certain the little boy's taken care of until his mom is released."

Carrie was a dozen steps away when she heard, "Dr. Markham?"

Carrie turned to find Rob behind her. "Yes?"

"I . . . I wonder if you'd like to have dinner with me while your boyfriend's gone. I've been on my own before, and it's no fun."

"Thanks anyway, Rob, but I'll be fine until Adam gets back."

She turned to walk away, but apparently Rob wasn't through.

"So where did he go? How long is he going to be gone?"

"Rob, I'm sorry. I have to get back to my patient." She turned and hurried away before the young man could say anything else. *Can't he take no for an answer?*

Adam dropped his suitcases and flipped the switch to illuminate the bedside lamp of his motel room. After making sure the door was double locked, he closed the blinds and pulled the heavy drapes together. Then he slumped onto the bed.

He closed his eyes and wondered how Carrie was doing. It frustrated him when his cell service failed earlier today, but at least he'd been able to tell her he was all right. In a bit, he'd call from the landline in his room, and they could talk as long as they wanted.

It had been a disappointment, but not a surprise, when Carrie said she wasn't ready to take back his ring. He wished she were wearing it now. On the other hand, if he did what might be necessary to protect her from Charlie DeLuca, there was a very real possibility Adam wouldn't be able to keep a wedding date anytime soon.

Well, it was too late to turn back. He should reach his destination tomorrow. Now there was another call to make, one that was critical to his mission. He dialed Dave's cell number, but the call, like the one that preceded it earlier in the day, went unanswered. Adam had already left one message. No need to leave another. He'd try again later.

Adam's grumbling stomach reminded him that he hadn't eaten since lunch. No problem — he'd seen signs for several fast food places nearby. One of them would probably be open late. He'd get a burger and malt, then call Carrie. After that, a shower and a good night's sleep.

He started to get up, then fell back onto the pillow. He was exhausted. He'd rest for a few minutes, maybe half an hour. Then he could be up and running.

Adam heeled off his shoes, pulled the spread over him, turned off the bedside lamp, and closed his eyes. After what seemed like only a few minutes, the ring of the phone brought him awake. He grumbled as he sat up and turned on the lamp. Adam snatched his cell phone from the bedside table, but the display was dark. His sleep-clouded mind finally cleared enough for him to realize that the ring came from the room's telephone.

Who could be calling? No one knew he was here. If this was a wrong number . . . He had to clear his throat twice before he could rasp out, "Hello?"

"This is Jeremy at the front desk. We were wondering if you planned to spend another night with us."

Why was this nut calling? Adam had just checked in less than an hour ago. He glanced at his watch and was startled to see it was twelve o'clock. The phone cord barely stretched to allow Adam to pull aside the drapes and peek through the slatted blinds. When he looked out he did a double take. It wasn't midnight-dark. It was noontime-bright. He'd slept for almost fourteen hours!

"I'm sorry. Yes, my plans have changed. I'll be staying one more day."

"Very good, sir. Fortunately we can accommodate you without your having to move. Have a good day."

Adam checked the display on his cell phone. No missed calls, no messages. A growling stomach reminded him that his last meal had been twenty-four hours ago. A cup of coffee brewed in the room's pot, with all the sugar and creamer available, would have to hold him until he could make himself presentable. After twenty minutes, showered, clean-shaven, dressed in clean clothes, he headed for the Denny's near the motel.

An hour later Adam was back in his room,

his hunger satisfied and his mind working at full throttle again. He microwaved the coffee that remained in the carafe and added sugar packets he'd picked up from the restaurant. Coffee in one hand, his cell phone in the other, he sat on the edge of his bed and punched in Dave's number.

What if his brother still didn't answer? What if he was undercover, or somewhere with no cell reception, or . . . After the fifth ring Adam was about to end the call when he heard, "Branson here."

"Dave, it's me."

"Keith?"

"You mean Adam."

"Sorry. I may never get the name right as long as you keep changing it." There was a slight pause. "Where are you? And whose phone are you using? The display on my cell shows private number."

"I'm at an Econolodge in Creedmore, North Carolina," Adam said. "Where are you?"

"I've been undercover down here along the Rio Grande. Had my cell phone off for a couple of days." Adam heard a door close. "That should give me a little privacy. Now, what are you doing in North Carolina? Did you change your mind about running away?"

"Actually, just the opposite." Adam swiveled around to lie back on the bed, propped against the headboard. "I know it sounds crazy, but I need to see Charlie DeLuca."

"You're right. It does sound crazy. But why?"

"I want to talk to Charlie face-to-face and try to convince him to call off his shooter."

"That's not going to work, Adam." Dave used the same tone he'd used years before when he gave sage older-brother advice. "And even if he says he'll do it, what makes you think he'll keep his word?"

"If that doesn't work, then I've got an offer I'm pretty sure he'll take."

"And that is . . . ?"

Adam drained the coffee in his cup, but the lump in his throat didn't move. "I'll make him a deal."

"What can you offer Charlie?"

"His freedom. If he'll call off whoever's been targeting Carrie and me, I'll contact the DA and recant my testimony. Without me, the case falls apart and he walks."

"That's insane," Dave said. "Not only would you be returning a criminal to society, you'd be admitting to perjury. In effect, you're offering to take Charlie's place in prison."

"I know." Adam thought once more about

what was at stake here. "When there was someone trying to kill me, I was willing to take the heat. But Carrie's in it now. And I'll do anything to make her safe again . . . and I can't think of any other way to do it."

"So that's why you're there in . . . whatever the name is."

"Creedmore. Yes. The Butner Correctional Facility, where Charlie DeLuca's serving his sentence, is a fifteen-minute drive from where I am now. I need you to use your contacts in law enforcement to get me access to him. Can you do that?"

Dave's sigh came through loud and clear. "I'm still going to try to talk you out of this, you know. But yeah, give me half an hour to make some phone calls. Give me your number and I'll call you back."

It was actually closer to an hour before Dave called again. Adam spent the time pacing the floor, his mind running in circles, trying to take the rough edges off his scheme. His mind threw up objections, then tried to tear them down. At the end of an hour, there were still some holes he might have to patch on the fly.

"Yes?"

Dave sounded almost sad, but then again, that was to be expected, given the circumstances. "I have the information for you."

"Let me get a pencil."

"You won't need it. I think you can remember this," Dave said. "The good news is that you or anyone else can visit Charlie DeLuca any time. But there's bad news that goes with it."

TWELVE

"A couple of us are going out for lunch today," Lila said from the door of Carrie's office. "Want to go?"

A polite "No, thanks" was on Carrie's lips, but she held it back. Since Adam left, she'd lived her life like a hermit. Breakfast at home with the newspaper, lunch spent at her desk reading medical journals while munching on a sandwich one of the nurses brought from the hospital, a frozen dinner defrosted and eaten in front of the TV each evening. This was how she behaved after John died, except that sometimes she forgot completely about eating. Why not get out? "Sure. And I'll drive."

There were four of them in the group: Lila, two other clinic nurses, and Carrie. For the first few minutes in the car, Carrie's presence inhibited conversation somewhat, but before they reached the restaurant they'd chosen — a barbecue place nearby

— the group was chatting freely.

The food was good, the company even better, and by the time they'd cleaned all the barbecue sauce off their fingertips and gone through the "I had that so I owe this" division of the bill, Carrie felt as though she'd had a respite from her worries.

As she drove back to the clinic, she looked in the rearview mirror and did a double take. There was a dark blue Ford Crown Victoria behind her. Ordinarily, this wouldn't have been a cause for concern, but Carrie recalled seeing it following her car on the way to the restaurant. She struggled to recall the maneuvers to confirm if she was being tailed. She sped up. The Ford stayed with her. She slowed down and changed lanes. The Ford did the same. She made random right and left turns until Lila asked, "Dr. Markham, are you okay? Do you want me to drive? This isn't the way to the clinic."

Carrie looked back and the Ford was nowhere in sight. Maybe it had just been a coincidence. "Sorry. I was thinking about something else." Lila gave her a worried look but said nothing.

When the women exited the car in the clinic parking lot, Carrie felt a familiar tingle between her shoulder blades. She huddled in the center of the group as they moved toward the clinic doors and didn't relax until she was safely inside. Carrie wasn't sure how much longer she could stand it.

Adam, hurry home. We have to bring this to an end.

Adam supposed he could drive to Chicago, but there was no need. Charlie DeLuca was there, but he wasn't going to listen to Adam . . . or anyone else.

Charlie DeLuca was buried in the family plot in one of the nicer suburbs of metropolitan Chicago. He'd experienced a heart attack while in the Butner Federal Correctional Institution, and that was where DeLuca died before he could be moved elsewhere for treatment.

Adam trusted his brother but still felt he had to confirm the information. He dug out his laptop, logged on to the free WiFi the motel offered, and after a few minutes found a tiny obituary from one of the Chicago newspapers. Yes, Charlie DeLuca was dead.

Why hadn't Adam done such a computer search long ago? Why had he just learned the news now? After a moment's thought Adam recognized the reason: from the moment the jury returned a guilty verdict, he'd worked to put Charlie DeLuca out of his mind. The man had been given a sentence that should have guaranteed he'd die in prison, and that was exactly what he'd done.

Adam should have felt relief, but instead the news raised another problem for him to solve. If DeLuca's death occurred several months earlier, why was someone still trying to kill Adam? It made no sense. But the persistent attempts told him one thing — he had to stop the killer another way. And that sent him to a totally different plan, one that left him with mixed emotions at best.

In a few minutes Adam was packed and ready to leave. The desk clerk surprised him by deleting the charge for a second day. "You just missed check-out time by a couple of hours. The maids are still working, and we'll have that room rented by sundown."

He smiled at the unexpected gesture. "Thanks. If I'm back in North Carolina, I'll stay with you again."

As he headed west, back to Jameson, Adam began work on a new plan. This one might not work either, but it was the best he could do. It would require one slight side trip on his journey, but the timing seemed right. And the thought of what he'd do there caused his pulse to quicken. On the one hand, what he was about to do frightened him. On the other, if this worked, both Adam and Carrie might be out from under the shadow of his would-be killer once and for all. Then again, if his plan misfired, he could end up in prison.

Carrie rolled over and squinted at her bedside clock. If she was going to attend church today, she should get up. Of course, that was a big "if." A gentle rain was falling outside, making this a perfect day to pull the covers over her head and sleep in.

She wasn't on call this weekend. The only people who'd look for her at church today were those wanting to ask questions about Adam's absence. Those questions hadn't slowed this week, but she'd finally reached the point where she could answer them almost without conscious thought. *I don't know where he's gone. I don't know why he left. I don't know when he'll be back.* All true and all resulting in a tug at her heart that was almost physically painful.

Adam hadn't called again since their phone conversation was terminated by a tenuous cell phone connection. Carrie had been tempted to try calling him but wasn't sure if he'd have cell reception or if he'd be able to talk. No, she had to trust him. He said he'd stay in touch.

Carrie lay in bed and let the events of the past few weeks unreel in her mind. She felt as though she were on an emotional and spiritual roller coaster. She'd prayed for strength and courage but still felt weak and afraid. Now her lips moved silently. *God, I know You're in control of all things. But I can't help it . . . I'm scared.*

Carrie's prayer was interrupted by the insistent ring of her bedside phone. She'd just been wishing Adam would call back. Could this be him? Even though she knew she shouldn't get her hopes up, she answered the call with more than a little anticipation. "Dr. Markham."

"Carrie, this is Adam."

She flung the covers off, swung her feet over the side of the bed and slid them into slippers. "Adam, I'm so glad to hear from you. Where are you? Is everything all right? When —"

"Easy. I love you. I've missed you, more than I can say."

"I love you too. What —"

"Look, we have lots to talk about when I get back, but I wanted to call and let you know that I'm on my way to Jameson. I should be there late tonight. We can talk tomorrow."

"Are you okay?" Carrie asked.

"I'm fine. But the situation has changed. That's one of the things we need to discuss."

Carrie took in what seemed like half the air in the room, then let it out slowly. "Is . . . is this call safe? I didn't check the caller ID. Are you using —"

"No need for any of that. I realized I've been going about this the wrong way all along. I thought I could protect us both by hiding. I was wrong. And I'm tired of running away."

"What's changed?" she asked.

"I'll tell you when I get back. I had a plan to stop the threats on my life at the source, but now I see they're going to continue no matter what I might do. So I intend to face the would-be killer head on."

"So I don't have to say I don't know where you are?"

"If anyone asks, you can say I called, I've been out of town because of a family emergency, but I'm coming back now."

She ran fingers through her hair. "I don't understand."

Carrie heard the sound of a horn in the background. "Look, I've got to drive, and traffic's heavy on the Interstate," Adam said. "I have to make one stop, then I'm headed home. It will be really late when I get into town."

"I don't care how late it is. I want to see you tonight."

"Okay. I'll phone when I get near your house. I can park a couple of blocks away and go through the alleys, then knock on your back door."

"I thought you were through hiding."

"I am," Adam said. "But I'm not going to lead the person who's after me to your doorstep either. When I face him, I'll choose the place — and it won't be anywhere near you."

After the call ended, Carrie slipped into a robe and headed for the kitchen to have her first cup of coffee and throw together some breakfast.

A few minutes ago she'd been ready to blow off church. No more. Church was exactly where she wanted to be this morning.

As he drove, Adam considered how Charlie DeLuca's death had changed things. He'd hoped he could get Charlie to call off the killer. But Charlie was dead, yet the attacks continued. It seemed to Adam his only remaining option was to identify the potential killer, whoever he was, and neutralize him.

Maybe Carrie had been right. Maybe it was time to go to the police. But what, exactly, could he tell them? *Someone shot at me. Oh, that report I filed about finding the bullet holes in my windshield? I lied about that. Sorry. And somebody threw a Molotov cocktail through a window of the building I was in. How do I know it was meant for me? I just do. But you have to believe me. Somebody even tried to run me over in the hospital parking lot. Did anyone see it? Well, no. But surely you know I'm telling the truth.*

No, this was his best option. It wasn't great, and he didn't really know if he could carry it off, but he didn't see an alternative. So now he needed to buy a gun.

As he rolled through East Texas, he kept an eye on the roadside signs, watching for the right exit. Finally he saw a billboard telling him where to turn for the First Monday Trade Days. Soon he was guiding his car through the streets of Canton, Texas, looking for a place to park. He found a lot where he traded five dollars for a slot into which he jammed his little Forester.

Since moving to Jameson, Adam had heard about First Monday Trade Days in Canton. The activity didn't actually take place on the first Monday of each month, but rather on the weekend before that day.

Since today was the Sunday before the first Monday, Adam was in luck. Although he could undoubtedly find a flea market elsewhere this weekend, one that offered what he needed, he figured Canton would have the best selection.

Adam picked up a map and studied it. Among the stalls where people sold everything from antiques to woodcraft were a number selling guns. But where should he begin? The choices ranged from gun dealers displaying a big inventory in open-air stalls to individuals with a few guns and knives laid out on plain folding tables. While Adam was considering his choices he discovered another option, one the map didn't show.

Adam jumped when a man approached him and said in a low voice, "Looking to buy a handgun?" He shook his head and walked away. After a couple of these encounters, he realized this was the way some individuals operated, choosing to sell a few pistols on a roving basis rather than pay the rental for a fixed space and deal with the paperwork required of a licensed dealer.

Now that he was confronted with so many choices, Adam regretted his lack of preparation. He wanted a dependable handgun, small enough to be carried easily, effective at short range. But did he want a revolver, a semiautomatic, what? He had no idea.

His work in the law office had familiarized him with Texas's "concealed carry" laws. A carry permit would require that he pass a firearms training course. It would also require a more extensive computer background search than he was prepared to undergo. Adam Davidson wasn't a convicted felon, but then again the identity he'd set up for himself when he struck out on his own might not hold up to intense scrutiny. After a few conversations Adam decided his best course of action was to buy a gun from a private dealer, one who didn't fill out the sale form regular dealers used. He could worry about the matter of a carry permit later.

After a number of fruitless stops, he wandered up to a small table tended by an older man wearing a plaid shirt and jeans and lighting one cigarette off the butt of the previous one.

Adam looked through the man's small stock of pistols, but in the end threw up his hands in both disgust and perplexity. "I'm sorry. I just don't know."

"Why don't you tell me what you want, son?"

Why not? Adam gave him the story he'd developed as he went from stall to stall: his wife was being stalked by a former boy-friend, and he wanted a weapon to give her — small enough to carry in a pocket or purse but with adequate stopping power. He didn't mind a used pistol, so long as it was in good condition and reliable.

The man took the cigarette from his mouth long enough to point a nicotine-stained finger toward a small food stand about a hundred feet away. "See that tall, weather-beaten looking man at the table drinking coffee? That's the Colonel. See if he'll sell you that pistol his wife had."

Adam thanked the man and headed toward the food stand. It sounded a bit unusual, but the whole day had been unusual. Might as well give it a try.

The man at the table was leathery and lean. His white hair was the only indication of his age. He wore starched khakis, a white dress shirt open at the neck, and shined engineer's boots. He looked up when Adam approached. "Yes?"

"Sir, my name is Adam Davidson." Adam extended his hand, and the man took it in a grip that was firm without making it a contest of wills.

"Sam Johnson," the man replied. "Most people call me Colonel." He gestured to the other chair at the table. "What can I do for you?"

Adam eased into the chair, then told the same story he'd given the last gun dealer. "He said to ask you if you'd sell me your wife's gun. I wasn't sure what he meant, but I figured it was worth walking a hundred feet to talk with you."

Johnson took a sip of coffee, leaned back, and ran his gaze over Adam's face. Then he tapped the shoebox at his elbow. "I come here every month and bring this. So far I haven't been able to do anything about it. I can't bring myself to be one of those guys who walks the grounds and asks perfect strangers, 'You want to buy a gun?' Guess I've been waiting for the right person. Maybe that's you."

Adam wasn't sure where this was going, but he was curious to know more about the man's story. "I take it there's something special about the gun."

"It was my wife's." Johnson lifted the lid of the box. "Ruger semiautomatic SR9C, mint condition." The man looked into the middle distance and smiled. "Right after we were married, I told her a woman alone — and she was alone a lot of the time when I was deployed — a woman alone needed to protect herself. I bought this. Taught her how to use it."

"You said it *was* your wife's."

"She died six months ago." The man looked away and blinked hard.

"I'm sorry for your loss," Adam said.

"I'm still getting rid of some things," Johnson said. "This is one of them." He shoved the box toward Adam.

The gun showed evidence of care. No scratches marred a black finish that shone with gun oil. The pistol was probably six inches long. Adam lifted it and found that it fit neatly in his hand.

"Weighs about a pound and a half," Johnson said. "It looks like a toy, but one pull of that trigger can leave a man just as dead as if he'd been shot with a .357 Magnum."

The enormity of the step he was taking wasn't lost on Adam. Then he thought of Carrie, and his resolve strengthened. "I guess it's what I need."

"That model can accept either of two magazines. This one's got the smaller one, ten rounds. That enough for you?"

"That will be fine," Adam said. "If ten rounds isn't enough, I might as well throw it at them."

"You're right about that." Johnson leaned back and crossed his legs. "If you don't mind my asking, do you know how to use one of these?"

Actually, Adam didn't, but he thought he could figure it out. "If you mean where's the safety, how do I eject the magazine, stuff like that — no. But I can learn. After that it's a matter of point and pull the trigger, isn't it?"

"Pretty much." Sam took the gun from Adam and spent a few minutes showing him the mechanics of the Ruger. Then he carefully replaced it in the box. "One word of warning. It's something everyone who carries a gun should know. Don't pull it out unless you're prepared to use it. And if you shoot, aim for the torso — the center of the mass. Trying to hit an arm or a leg? That's not going to happen." He paused, apparently considering his words. "I guess what I'm asking you is whether you're prepared to kill someone."

Adam had thought about this for the last hundred miles of his journey. He had his answer ready. "Yes, sir. I am."

"Son, I retired from the army as a bird colonel. Never got the star because I wouldn't play their games. In thirty years I learned to read people pretty well and pretty fast." Johnson uncrossed his legs and recrossed them the other way.

Adam wondered what was coming next. Was Johnson about to back out? There was no way he could have any idea what Adam had in mind, was there?

"I think you're a good man. I doubt that you'll be using this to hold up a convenience store." Johnson took another sip of coffee. "Whatever trouble makes you need this, I hope it helps." He shoved the shoebox toward Adam. "Three hundred cash, including a box of 9 millimeter ammo."

Adam unfolded three hundred dollar bills from his diminishing roll and laid them on the table. He rose and picked up the shoebox. "Thanks."

"As a good citizen, I should remind you that you're supposed to take the class and get a carry permit for that pistol." Johnson unfolded himself from the chair like a carpenter's rule. He stuck out his hand. "Good luck, son."

Adam started back toward his car. He'd need all the luck he could get.

Carrie let the noontime buzz of the café wash over her, providing an auditory backdrop for her deep thoughts. Her Coke sat forgotten, its bubbles rising slowly to the surface. The sight and smell of her Reuben sandwich failed to tempt her. She idly munched on a potato chip and replayed her morning in church.

As she expected, there'd been questions about Adam. After a couple of them she had the new answer down pat: *He had to leave town in a hurry because of a family emergency. That's why no one knew any details. He called me this morning. Things are okay now, and he'll be back tomorrow.*

The sermon? Not the best she'd ever heard, but then again, how much attention had she paid? Her mind had been on Adam. She could hardly wait to see him. She was anxious to hear about his trip. The electronic strains of Beethoven's "Fifth Symphony" cut through the chatter and clatter around her. Carrie picked up her cell and saw that the caller was Lila.

"Dr. Markham, I'm so glad you picked up." Lila's voice was breathless, and Carrie had the impression the woman was on the verge of tears. This was a far cry from the breezy, self-assured nurse with whom she worked every day.

"Lila, what's wrong?"

"It's my mother. She's in the ER, and they've called Dr. Avery to see her. But I really wish you'd come."

Carrie stared at her plate as though the sandwich and chips had just materialized there, surprising her with their presence. She raised a hand and beckoned a passing waitress. Carrie handed over her VISA card, pointed to the plate, and mouthed, "To-go box." There was no way she could fail to respond to Lila's plea. "I'll have them cancel the call to Dr. Avery. What's the problem? I need to tell the ER doctor what I want done while I'm in transit."

The relief in Lila's voice was obvious. "Mom complained of a severe headache this morning. I keep a blood pressure cuff at home to check my own pressure, so I decided to take hers." Her voice broke and the panic returned. "It was two twenty over one fifteen!"

"That's high, but we can get it down. What has the ER doctor done so far?"

Lila's deep breath whistled in Carrie's ear. "They drew some blood, ran an EKG, which I haven't seen, and gave her IV labetalol."

"Beta-blocker. Good choice," Carrie said. The waitress appeared with the check, plus a to-go box and a Styrofoam cup for Carrie's drink. She nodded her thanks. "That's pretty standard. Is her pressure coming down?"

"Yes. Of course, I realize they want it to come down slowly. It's not that. It's what the ER doctor wants to do now."

"Go on." Carrie snugged the cell phone between her ear and shoulder while she added a tip and signed the check.

"He wants to admit her and start a workup for pheochromocytoma."

Pheochromocytoma, a benign tumor of the adrenal gland, was certainly one of the causes to be considered in cases of chronic hypertension, but its incidence was estimated at about one per one thousand cases. And this wasn't chronic. The last time Carrie examined Lila's mother, Mrs. James had mild elevation of her blood pressure — not enough to merit medication, but sufficient to get her a lecture on the need for weight loss. The reported blood pressure now was certainly high, but it was too soon to jump to a workup for pheochromocytoma.

A phrase Carrie had first learned in medical school popped into her mind. She smiled the first time she heard it, but the wisdom behind the words was soon evident to her. Now she frequently repeated the words to medical students when discussing a differential diagnosis: *When you hear hoof beats, think horses, not zebras.* She picked up her food. "You're right. I think that's a bit radical. I'll call the ER right now and be there in fifteen minutes."

Carrie disconnected the call, then pushed the speed-dial button for the ER as she strode out of the café to her car, her lunch in hand. When the nurse answered, she said, "This is Dr. Markham. My nurse, Lila, is there with her mother, Mrs. James. Please call Dr. Avery and tell him not to come out. She's my patient and I'm on my way to take care of the situation. And let the ER doctor know too." She'd give him the horses and zebras talk later — in private.

Carrie pulled away from her parking spot, looked in her rearview mirror, and went cold all over. A dark blue Ford Crown Victoria had dropped into traffic right behind her. Well, she didn't have time to do the deke and dodge thing now. She headed for the hospital. Let them follow her. There should be enough people around to discourage an attack when she arrived, and maybe she could get one of the security guards to walk her to her car when she left. Right now she had to forget about her own safety and focus on Lila's mother.

After she entered the ER, Carrie picked up Mrs. James's chart at the nurse's desk and did a bit of mental arithmetic. Almost an hour had elapsed since Jeff Clanton, the ER doctor, began treating Mrs. James. In that time the woman had received an initial IV dose of a beta-blocker, following which an IV drip delivered more of the drug in a controlled fashion.

The treatment seemed to be working. Carrie headed for the curtained cubicle where Lila's mother lay and saw Jeff Clanton on a course designed to intercept her. Since he was the ER doctor on duty, that might explain some of this. Jeff was a recent graduate of one of the lesser-known medical schools in the south. He'd applied to three family practice residencies but hadn't been accepted at any of them. That wasn't totally uncommon — competition was pretty fierce at some institutions. One told Jeff they'd take him next year, so he was working here both to make a living and get experience until that slot opened up. To this point, Carrie hadn't had any problems with his performance. Jeff seemed anxious to profit from his time in the ER, and this seemed like a chance for her to do a little mentoring.

"Blood pressure's coming down nicely," Carrie said to Jeff as the two doctors stood at Mrs. James's bedside. "What do you think caused the hypertension?"

The ER doctor looked embarrassed. He inclined his head toward the curtains surrounding the ER cubicle. "Uh, think we should step outside?"

"Not at all," Carrie said. "Mrs. James is a retired LVN, and her daughter, Lila, is my clinic nurse. They're used to hearing doctors discuss cases, and I think they need to hear this. Besides, I have a question I want to ask our patient, and I think her answer may surprise you."

"Okay." He cleared his throat. "She says her blood pressure's always been high, but she wasn't on any medication. I took that to mean that this was a sudden spike. To me, that suggested an adrenal tumor, so I asked Dr. Avery —" He paused and gave her an apologetic look. "I would have called you, but he's on call — Anyway, I suggested a pheochromocytoma workup."

Carrie clamped down on her back teeth. *Be cool. He's just out of med school.* "What's the first thing you think of when you encounter a patient with a sudden rise in blood pressure?"

"Several things. Eclampsia, of course — but she's not pregnant. Renal disease, but her BUN and creatinine came back normal. She drinks two cups of coffee a day, no energy drinks, no Cokes. And her only medication is a hormone preparation. That leaves something like an adrenal tumor suddenly becoming active. I know it's unusual, but I think we should rule it out."

Carrie nodded. Jeff was right so far, but there was another possibility, one Carrie herself might not have considered had she not encountered it a year or so before. She turned back to her patient. "Mrs. James, what medicines do you take?"

The woman thought about that for a few seconds. "Just my hormone pill, like he said."

"What other pills — not prescriptions, just pills — what others do you take? What did you take today?"

"Well, you told me I had to lose weight, so I went to the health food store on Friday and got a bottle of weight loss pills."

Carrie glanced at Lila, and she saw her nurse's expression change as the light dawned.

"And did you take one of those today?" Carrie asked.

"Actually, the first one didn't seem to have much effect, so I took two yesterday. This morning I decided to try three. I mean, they're natural, so I don't see how they could be bad for me." She turned to Lila. "I think they're in my purse."

Lila opened the satchel-like purse slung over her shoulder, rummaged for a minute, and extracted a white bottle with a purple and white label that read, "Bitter Orange."

Understanding lit up the younger doctor's face. "I should have asked about nonprescription drugs."

"You don't use the word 'drugs.' You don't say 'medication' or 'prescription.' You ask if they're taking any pills, whether they got them from the doctor or bought them over the counter. You ask what they took today — this day, not regularly."

He nodded. "I —"

"It's okay," Carrie said. "We'll talk about it later. Right now, let's titrate that blood pressure down to a safe level."

Almost two hours later Carrie was ready to leave the hospital. She'd arranged to admit Mrs. James overnight for observation in order to taper the dose of the beta-blocker medication and observe for any heart damage from the episode. Dr. Clanton had learned a valuable lesson about horses and zebras. And Lila couldn't thank Carrie enough for coming to the hospital when she wasn't on call.

"No problem," Carrie reassured her. And it wasn't. Her time in the ER certainly had been more productive and more satisfying than a Sunday afternoon nap.

Carrie almost forgot the blue Ford that followed her to the hospital — almost, but not totally. She found a security guard in the Emergency Room waiting area and approached him. "Would you mind walking me to my car?"

It was a strange request, since it was broad daylight, but the guard either was used to such appeals or was unusually patient. In either case, he rose, giving her neither a puzzled look nor furrowed brow, and accompanied Carrie to her car, one hand on his holstered weapon, his head moving from side to side as though expecting trouble. She wasn't sure if he really believed her or was putting on a show, but in either case she welcomed his presence.

At her car Carrie thanked the guard and prepared to climb in. But just before she slid behind the wheel, she scanned the parking lot and saw a tall man, wearing a Stetson, leaning against the fender of a blue car three rows ahead of her. He was dressed in a suit and tie, and his manner was anything but threatening. He smiled and began walking toward her.

Carrie looked around. The security guard was almost back to his post. She was about to start running toward safety when she heard a soft voice with a definite drawl say, "Dr. Markham?"

The stranger wasn't hurrying, but rather

ambled along as though he had all the time in the world. She found herself rooted to the spot, wondering if a scream would get the guard's attention in time.

The man tipped his hat. "There hasn't been a good time to introduce myself," he said. He reached into his pocket and showed her a leather wallet with a badge inside it. "Sam Westerman, U.S. Marshalls Service. I was asked to keep an eye on you while your . . . er, your friend is out of town."

Carrie wasn't sure how she felt — grateful that Adam was trying, in his own way, to keep her safe or angry that he hadn't bothered to mention it to her. "Thank you. I appreciate it," she said.

After Westerman touched the brim of his hat and ambled away, Carrie climbed into her car. As she pulled into her driveway, Carrie waved to the blue Ford behind her. *Thanks, Mr. Westerman. Thanks, Adam.* She decided she wasn't angry. In a few hours she'd see Adam again. That was enough.

Thirteen

It was almost midnight when carrie heard the tap at her kitchen door. She'd been sitting at the table, a cold cup of coffee in front of her, for almost half an hour. She peeked through the curtains and saw Adam standing on the porch. Carrie opened the door and held out her arms. In a single gesture Adam embraced her and kicked the door shut behind him. Then he kissed her in a way that affirmed his love much more than words could.

"I'm so glad you're back, Carrie said.

"Me too. I've missed you," Adam said. He pointed to the coffee cup. "Is there more of that? I've been subsisting on some of the worst swill imaginable, using it to wash down stale service-station pastries."

In a moment they were settled at the kitchen table with fresh cups before them. Adam reached across to take Carrie's hand. "I have a lot to tell you."

"Such as why you left without telling me more than a bare minimum?" Carrie said. "We're in this together. I never felt so left out and helpless."

"I recognize that," Adam said. "But —"

"Speaking of not knowing, why didn't you tell me about Sam Westerman?"

Adam looked genuinely puzzled. "I didn't? It was on my list to cover in that first phone call." Then the light appeared to dawn. "Oh, that was when our cell phone connection fizzled. After that it must have slipped my mind."

Carrie sighed but squeezed his hand. "Never mind. Tell me about your trip. Where did you go? What did you do?"

"I decided to go to the prison where Charlie DeLuca was held, get in to see him some way or other, and see if I could reason with him. I'd beg him to call off his shooter. And if he wouldn't budge, I'd offer to recant my testimony if he'd promise to leave you alone."

"No!" The word seemed to jump out of Carrie's mouth. Tears threatened to spill from her eyes. "If you did that, you'd go to jail for perjury. I know you were willing to do it for me, but I can't let you."

"Don't worry. It's not going to happen. Charlie DeLuca's dead."

"And you had nothing to do with it?"

Adam shook his head. "No, he had a fatal heart attack about six months ago."

"Wait. If he's been dead for six months, and the last attack came less than two weeks ago, who's trying to kill you?" Carrie said.

"I asked myself the same question," Adam said. "I see two possibilities. Either the order to kill me didn't die with Charlie, or . . ."

"Or what," Carrie said.

"Or the attacks weren't aimed at me. Maybe you were the target."

"I don't —" Carrie stopped. She thought about the patients and families who, for one reason or another, bore a grudge against her. Perhaps Adam was right. "I need to think about that." She looked into his eyes. "Are you willing to go to the police now?"

"And tell them what? No, I'm going to do this myself. I have to make the shooter show himself. What I'd like to do is capture him, but I've got to be ready to defend myself."

"What do you mean?"

He leaned closer to her and lowered his voice. "I have a gun."

Carrie clutched his arm. "I've heard you say before that guns can get turned on their owners. Won't this get you shot?"

"We're already being shot at. I promise I'll only use it to protect myself, or to hold the shooter captive while we call the police."

The discussion went back and forth until eventually she said, "I give up. You're going to do what you want. But please be careful."

"Let's talk about it at dinner," Adam said.

Carrie agreed to meet him at a local steak house the next night. "In the meantime, please be careful."

Adam patted his pocket. "I've been careful for two years. Now I'm prepared."

In his car after breakfast, Adam thought about his next move. He'd called Bruce Hartley last night and related his prepared story, ending with his readiness to return to work.

Hartley seemed a bit taken aback by Adam's call. "Uh, I wasn't expecting to hear from you this soon. I mean, Janice and I need to talk. That is . . . Why don't you come in about ten tomorrow and we'll discuss it?"

Adam had plenty of time to run a couple of errands before meeting with Hartley. First he planned to stop at a store that sold police equipment. He was a civilian, but he figured they'd take his money as quickly as that of a member of the law enforcement community. He needed a holster for his pistol. He could wear one on his belt, concealed by a suit coat or a sports shirt with the tails out. Or he could get an ankle holster to keep the gun out of sight but readily accessible no matter what he wore. That might be an even better choice.

As he drove, Adam considered another problem — getting a concealed carry permit for the gun. It was legal in Texas to carry a handgun but only with a permit. Before the application could be submitted, the gun owner had to complete a mandated course of instruction. That was no problem. Adam was anxious to learn.

But signing up for a course and a carry permit would subject his identity to the scrutiny of a full background check by the Texas Department of Public Safety. With what Sam Johnson had told him, maybe he could just go to a gun range — better still, drive into the country with a box of shells and some empty cans. After all, Adam wasn't planning a lot of long-distance shooting. Simple as one, two, three: get close to the target, point the gun at the main body mass, pull the trigger. He was hoping he wouldn't be doing any shooting, that the threat of the gun would be enough if he came face-to-face with his attacker. But if it came down to it, he was prepared to use the pistol.

As Adam pulled to a stop outside the store, he felt the weight of the gun in his inside coat pocket. The holster would be a step in the right direction. Learning how to use the gun, practicing with it, would be another. After that, it was a matter of unmasking the would-be killer and bringing him to justice . . . whatever it took to do it.

Adam expected to be greeted by a barrage of questions when he walked in the door of Hartley and Evans. Instead, Brittany waved and smiled but continued her conversation with whomever was on the other end of the phone line. Bruce Hartley emerged from the break room with a mug of coffee, beckoned Adam to get his own cup, then disappeared into his office, leaving the door open.

When Adam was settled, Hartley sipped his coffee, leaned back in his chair, and propped one foot on the bottom drawer of his desk. "So you're back quicker than I expected. Did the surgery go okay?"

Adam adopted what he hoped was a properly somber countenance. "I was too late. When I got there, they told me my brother had gone downhill so far that he was no longer a candidate for a kidney transplant. After he saw me he told them to take him off dialysis — said he'd gotten right with God and was ready to go."

"That's tough, man."

"We had a good visit, and he told me good-bye."

"I guess you'll be going back for the funeral."

"No, he didn't want a memorial. He wanted his body cremated and the ashes scattered in some woods not far from the prison. The chaplain said he'd see to it."

Adam could almost see Hartley decide how quickly he could shift gears from sympathy to business. Apparently it didn't take long. "So let's talk about your position."

"You said you were going to hire a temp. How's that working out so far?"

Hartley half turned to stare out the window of his office. "She's worked out very well. Matter of fact, on Friday we offered her a permanent position."

"After a week?"

"She was doing a good job, and we couldn't afford to be short staffed."

Adam clamped his jaws shut to hold back the comments that jumped to mind. He took a deep breath. "So where does that leave me?"

"Janice and I talked before we hired Mary — that's her name, the new paralegal. We decided that if you came back, we'd offer you the same deal we offered Mary."

If I came back? I told them two weeks. "And that is . . ."

"Go to work as a temp, same salary as before. If things go well, and we see there's enough work to keep two people busy, we'll make it permanent. Otherwise we'll give you a good recommendation."

A punch in the gut couldn't have taken Adam's breath away more effectively. True, he'd only worked there less than a year, but in that time he'd come to look on himself as an important part of the practice. Part of his new plan included returning not just to Jameson but to his job, resuming his usual schedule, making himself visible to his assailant. And, of course, he needed the income.

Adam didn't see any choice. "I'll take it. Are my things still in my old office?"

Hartley had the grace to look embarrassed. "Mary moved in there, so we boxed up your stuff and moved it into the storage room next door to her. I'll get a desk and computer in there by tomorrow. You can start then."

Both men rose. Hartley's right hand

moved, but he didn't extend it. Just as well. Adam threw him a curt nod. "I'll be in tomorrow."

In the reception area an attractive brunette turned away from Brittany's desk as Adam walked by. She smiled and held out her hand. "You must be Adam. I'm Mary."

Adam forced a smile and took the proffered hand. "Adam Davidson. Pleasure to meet you."

She held his hand a second or two longer, and he had a vague sense that she was flirting with him. "Likewise," she said.

Adam watched Mary walk away, presumably to her office — his old office, but he'd have to get used to thinking of it in new terms. After Mary was gone Adam looked at Brittany and raised his eyebrows.

Brittany whispered, "There's more to that story than you know."

The woman's voice carried a mixture of amazement and anger. "Dr. Markham, I can't believe you'd charge me for that visit." The middle-aged woman sat primly on the edge of the chair opposite Carrie Markham's desk.

Carrie looked at the door of her office, hoping the office manager or someone who could help her with this argument might appear. She knew she had no chance to change the woman's mind, but was determined to be calm as she tried to explain yet again. "Mrs. Freemont, you came to the clinic, told the receptionist it was an emergency because you were having a heart attack."

"Yes, but it wasn't a heart attack. And it didn't take you long to find that out."

"On the contrary. I left the patient I was seeing to examine you. I took a history. We ran an EKG and some lab tests and found —"

"I know. I'm overweight. I drink too much coffee. I ate some spicy food. It made acid come back up into my esoph . . . whatever that thing is between my throat and stomach. But the pain was really bad. I was afraid I was going to die. I thought it was a heart attack."

Carrie forced a smile. "And I'm glad it wasn't your heart. But, like the grocer and the dry cleaner, we have to charge for services rendered. Of course, if you're indigent . . ."

Mrs. Freemont puffed out her chest like a pouter pigeon. "I'm by no means indigent." She clutched her purse tightly, a purse Carrie recognized as a Dooney & Bourke, well beyond her own price range.

"I'm sure we can work out an arrangement for you to handle the balance of the bill left after your insurance paid."

Mrs. Freemont was shaking her head before Carrie could finish the sentence. "It's not the money. It's the principle."

Carrie had heard this argument before, from Mrs. Freemont and others like her, and she knew that answer was far from the truth. *No, it's the money.* "I'm sorry. If you wish, you can talk with the clinic administrator. But the matter is out of my hands."

As the woman huffed out of her office, Carrie reflected that if looks could kill, she'd be lifeless on her office floor from hateful glares directed at her by Rose Freemont, Calvin McDonald, and a few other patients. And that thought triggered another one . . . one that made her catch her breath. Maybe Adam's alternative theory hadn't been too far off the mark. Maybe she *was* the target.

Carrie peered over her menu at Adam, who seemed engrossed in the dinner choices the restaurant offered. "They didn't hold your job? You were gone a week, and they replaced you?"

"Hartley — he's the senior partner — he made it sound like it was strictly a business decision, and maybe it was. The practice

207

has been getting pretty busy. But what he told me before I left was they were going to arrange for Mary — that's the new paralegal — to work for a couple of weeks while I was gone. He said if she worked out and they saw there was enough work for two, after I got back they'd add her full-time."

"But they didn't wait. And they didn't just add her. They gave her your position and stuck you in some out-of-the-way office."

The waiter came and took their orders. After he padded away, Carrie said, "So that's it? It's a done deal?"

Adam paused with bread in one hand, a knife bearing a pat of butter in the other. "Brittany, the receptionist, told me there was more to the story. So I bought her lunch, and she gave me the real scoop."

Carrie wanted to ask more about Brittany but decided to let that go for now. She began making circles on the tabletop with the condensation from her water glass. "So what's the 'real scoop'?"

"First of all, Mary's a looker. Mid- to late thirties, dark hair, a figure —"

Carrie raised an eyebrow that dared him to go on with his description. "Okay, no need to draw me a picture."

Adam looked over Carrie's shoulder. "No picture, but if you want a real-life snapshot, find an excuse to look behind you. She just came in."

Carrie eased her napkin out of her lap, then bent to pick it up. She gave a quick glance. "Black sheath with a white jacket over it?"

"Mm-hmm."

"Didn't get a good look, but from what I saw, I think you're right."

Adam murmured, "You're about to get a better view. She's coming over." He stood. "Mary, good to see you."

Carrie had always considered herself reasonably attractive: a nice face framed by blond hair and highlighted by green eyes. But at that moment she felt outclassed. Mary had carefully styled, shoulder-length black hair. Her blue eyes sparkled. Her teeth were as white and perfect as the simple pearl choker she wore.

And Mary's voice matched her looks — slightly husky, definitely sultry, every word carrying an implied invitation. "Adam, I thought it was you."

"Mary Delkus, this is Dr. Carrie Markham."

Carrie stayed seated but held out her hand. "Nice to meet you."

"My pleasure," Mary said. She glanced up and frowned. "Well, I see they're serving our dinner, so I'd better get back. Doctor, nice to meet you. Adam, see you tomorrow." She turned and wended her way to a table where an older man rose and pulled out her chair.

"Well, I have to agree. She's a knockout," Carrie said. "Should I know the man she's with? He looks familiar."

"Uh-huh. That's Bruce Hartley. According to our receptionist, Mary lost no time getting close to him. Brittany says the woman must be handling a bunch of confidential files, because she spends a lot of time in Hartley's office . . . with the door closed."

"What did the other partner — what's her name? Evans? What did Mrs. Evans have to say about all this?"

"That's what surprises me. Janice Evans is a very sharp woman. Frankly, I don't know how Hartley got her to agree to the move, but somehow he did."

Their salads arrived, and they spent a few moments eating. After a couple of minutes, Carrie paused with a forkful of lettuce halfway to her mouth. "Seeing Mary with Bruce Hartley, I guess I know now how she got your position."

"Oh, give her the benefit of the doubt. Maybe she really needed the job. And

Hartley says she's good at her work."

Carrie laid her fork carefully on her salad plate. "Men! All a woman has to do is bat her eyes, and you think she's the most innocent flower in creation. Believe me, the female of the species can be much deadlier than the male, as somebody once said."

In a moment the waiter returned and replaced their salad plates with their entrees. After a few bites Carrie said, "Adam, since you told me how long Charlie DeLuca's been dead, I've been rethinking the possibility that the attacks are aimed at me. Maybe you're right."

Adam frowned at Carrie's words. "When I mentioned it, you didn't think much of that theory. What made you change your mind?"

"You mean other than the fact that the first two attacks came when we were together?" Carrie sipped from her water glass. "I realized that it's not so far-fetched that an angry patient might try to hurt me . . . even kill me."

"Did something happen to bring about this change?"

Carrie nodded. "I had a visit from a hateful old woman, a patient of mine. She came to the clinic last month with chest pain and demanded immediate attention because she was having a heart attack. I dropped what I was doing to check her over. We discovered that what she had was chest pain from acid reflux."

They stopped talking as the waiter cleared their plates. They passed on dessert, asked for coffee. When the waiter was gone, Adam leaned forward and took Carrie's hand. "So you'd think the woman would be grateful."

"Nope," Carrie said. "When I gave her the news, I also told her she needed to lose weight, avoid all her favorite foods — caffeine, carbohydrates, carbonation, and chocolate — and take the medicine I prescribed. That didn't sit well with her, so now she's up in arms because she got a bill for my services. I mean, no heart attack, why should I charge her?"

"That's ridiculous."

"Nope, she was really livid when she left. And she's not the only one. For instance, there are the patients like — well, there's this man who brought his wife to the ER with pain in her abdomen. He apparently thought it was indigestion, but it turned out to be a perforated ulcer. By the time she came in, she was in shock. I made the diagnosis and got a surgeon to see her immediately, but she died on the operating table. The man hasn't said as much, but judging from the way he looks at me every time our paths cross, I'm pretty sure he blames me for her death, and he's pretty angry."

"But —"

"Here's our coffee. Let's just drink it and relax," Carrie said. She looked across the restaurant and saw Mary returning her gaze. "We can talk about this later, but not in such a public place."

In a few minutes the waiter came by. "Would you like more coffee?"

Adam exchanged glances with Carrie. He was ready to go, and apparently, so was she. "I think we're ready for the check."

Outside, Adam took Carrie's arm and steered her away from her car. "Get in mine. We need to talk some more."

"No. Let's go in mine. I have somewhere in mind, and it's better if we're in my car."

Carrie led Adam to her silver Prius parked a little distance away from his Subaru. She motioned him toward the driver's side. "Want to drive?"

"No, it's your car. Go ahead and drive."

In a moment the car rolled out of the restaurant parking lot. Carrie took a right at the first intersection. "Let me ask you a question," she said. "Where would you say the safest place is for me to park right now?"

Adam thought about that. "The police station?"

"No," Carrie said. "How long would we be there before someone came out and checked to see if there was a problem? Try again."

"Your house?"

Carrie shook her head. "Not out front. Too dark and relatively isolated. And not in the garage. We'd be essentially trapped in the house."

"So I guess you mean . . ."

"Yep, the hospital."

Adam shivered a bit. "Not exactly a scene of happy memories for me," he said. "Remember, someone tried to run me down there."

"We'll be fine. If anyone sees my car tonight, it belongs to a doctor who's come back to the hospital." Carrie wheeled the Prius into the parking lot nearest the Emergency Room. She chose a dark corner at the front. To their right, grass stretched like a calm black sea. To their left were probably a dozen or more empty spaces before the next car in the row, a huge, silver Hummer. Adam figured it belonged to some doctor who was more concerned with appearances than ecology.

She moved a lever and pushed a button to

turn off the engine. "Now this is simply a doctor's car in the hospital parking lot. And we should have some privacy."

Adam half turned in his seat to face Carrie. "You were going to explain why the attacks could have been aimed at you."

"I've already told you about two of my patients who seem to hate me — truly hate me. I could name a half dozen more. That happens to everyone, even a doctor. And one of these people could be going a little crazy about it."

"I'll accept that the drive-by shooting could have been aimed at you. The same could go for the firebomb at my office. But what about someone setting me up and trying to ram my car right here?"

"I thought about that," Carrie said. "Let me ask you. If I wanted to hurt you, hurt you deeply, what would I do: hurt you or hurt someone you loved?"

"I guess —"

Adam never finished the sentence. Suddenly the driver's side window exploded and Adam heard two sharp cracks separated by a couple of seconds. His first thought was of Carrie. In a single motion, he unlatched his seat belt, lunged across the intervening space, and pulled her toward him, covering her body with his. Before the echoes of the shots had died, Adam called out, "Carrie. Are you okay?" When there was no answer, he said, "Carrie! Speak to me!"

Adam eased up and peered through the remains of the driver's side window. Nothing moved. No one was visible in the dark parking lot. His hand went to his ankle holster, but he left the gun there. First, check on Carrie.

He bent down and touched her shoulder. "You can get up now."

Adam shook Carrie, gently at first, then more vigorously, but there was no response. He touched her head and his fingers came away wet. He held his hand in front of his face, but it was too dark to see. Nevertheless, he was sure — his hand was wet with Carrie's blood.

FOURTEEN

Adam was out his door in a second. He sprinted around the car. If the shooter was still out there, Adam was making himself a target, but he didn't care. All that mattered was Carrie. He opened the driver's side door and unlatched the seat belt that still held her, folded sideways toward the passenger side. He scooped her into his arms and ran for the ER doors that beckoned in the darkness. They seemed a mile away, but he covered the ground as fast as he could. Between ragged breaths, he shouted, "Help! She's been shot. Somebody help!"

At what appeared to be a loading dock for the emergency vehicles, a younger man emerged from between two parked ambulances and jogged toward Adam.

"I thought I heard gunshots. What's going on?" he called as he closed the gap between them.

Adam gulped air. "She's been shot," he

said. "Help me get her inside."

As they approached the double glass doors, light-spill from inside showed Adam what his fingers had already told him: Carrie's face was covered with blood.

As soon as they were inside, the other man called to the woman behind the desk, "We need help. Stat. Dr. Markham's been shot!"

After that, things went almost too quickly for Adam to follow. Two men in hospital scrubs wheeled a gurney into the waiting room, took Carrie from Adam's arms, and gently laid her on the stretcher. A third man, wearing a navy golf shirt and dark slacks, charged through the outer doors, took in the scene, and went into action. Even without a white coat, his demeanor screamed, "I'm a doctor."

The doctor bent over Carrie. "She's breathing." He pried her eyelids apart. "Pupils equal." He put his fingers on her wrist and nodded. "Pulse is steady and firm." He cocked his head toward the doors. "Let's get her inside."

Adam started after them, but the doctor stopped him with a single shake of the head. "Get her signed in. After that the police are going to want to talk to you. If you wait out here, I'll let you know her condition as soon as I can."

The man who had helped him get Carrie inside was still standing by Adam. He touched him lightly on the shoulder. "Are you going to be all right?"

"I'm not sure. I'm more worried about Carrie . . . Dr. Markham."

"The doctor who took her into the ER is Dr. Rushton. He's a cardiac surgeon, not a neurosurgeon, but he's one of the senior staff. Believe me, he'll see that she gets the best of care."

Adam took in a big breath. "Thanks for your help."

"I'm a paramedic." He shrugged. "It's what I do." The man exchanged a few more words with Adam, then slipped out the double doors and was gone.

Carrie's first thought was that she must have overslept. She didn't recall hearing the alarm, and she wasn't sure what day it was, but there was a sense that she needed to get up, get out of bed right away. She'd be late to work.

She opened her eyes, blinked twice to clear the haze that clouded her vision, and discovered she wasn't in her bed. This wasn't even her room. Carrie turned a fraction to the right, but stopped as little men with hammers began a percussion concert inside her head.

"So you're awake."

The voice was familiar, even if the setting wasn't. Carrie cut her eyes to the right while keeping her head still and got a glimpse of Adam leaning over the rail on the side of her bed. In the background she heard phones ring, conversations in hushed tones, the squeak of rubber soles on waxed tile. She sniffed. Yes, there it was, faint in the background — a familiar, antiseptic scent. She was in a hospital.

"Adam —" She tried to clear her throat. "Adam," she croaked once more.

"Here." He ladled a spoonful of ice chips into her mouth. "Suck on these. The doctor says if you tolerate them, I can give you a few sips of water."

Doctor? She sucked on the ice, swallowed, and tried again. "How did I get here? The last thing I recall, we were sitting in my car in the hospital parking lot."

"Maybe I can help you remember."

Another familiar voice, one that seemed less out of place. Carrie managed to turn her head fractionally until she could see Phil Rushton standing beside Adam. "Phil, what's going on?"

This Phil was nothing like the cool, calm cardiac surgeon she knew. His eyes were red-rimmed. Faint stubble marked his face. He looked as though he'd been on an all-night bender. "You've been here a little less than six hours. He —" He nodded to indicate Adam. "He carried you into the ER about nine last night. You'd been shot."

Carrie did a quick mental inventory. Nothing hurt other than her head. She wiggled her hands and feet. "Shot! Where? How?"

Phil frowned, obviously unhappy at the memories of the event. "You were in your car in the parking lot when a gunshot through the driver's side window struck you in the head. The bullet plowed a furrow in your scalp. Of course, the wound bled profusely, as scalp injuries do."

"Did I have surgery?"

"No, you were lucky. The bullet followed the contour of the skull without entering it. It gave you a concussion, but nothing worse. Nothing that should cause lasting damage."

Carrie moved her left hand toward her head but stopped when she felt the tug of an IV line. She inched her right hand upward and felt a bandage on her head. "Did you . . . did you have to — ?"

Phil managed a smile. "No, we didn't shave any of your hair, although the bullet burned a crease up there. I think you can cover it when you style your hair."

"Is her memory loss a problem?" Adam asked.

"No. Retrograde amnesia is common after a concussion. Hers seems to involve a short time span, and that's good. Sometimes the memory comes back, but even if it doesn't, it's probably no major loss. Otherwise, Carrie's neurologically intact."

Carrie turned her head a bit more, ignoring the pain now. She looked at both men — she wanted to see their faces when she got her answer. "Do the police know who did it?"

"No," Adam said. "I told them we were sitting in the parking lot talking when someone took a shot at the car."

Phil spread his hands. "Why would someone do that?"

"I have no idea, Phil," Carrie said. She wasn't about to blow Adam's cover at this point. If the incident strengthened Phil's suspicions that she was involved in something bad, so be it. Meanwhile, she moved to the question that was most important to her right now. "So when can I get out of here? When can I go back to work?"

"We want to watch you for another day to make sure there's no late intracranial bleeding," Phil said. "Then you should take a couple of days off to recover from the shock of all this."

"I don't need a couple of days off," Carrie said. She leaned forward as if she were about to get up. "And I want to leave now. I'm a doctor. I know what to watch for. Can I talk with my neurosurgeon?"

"You don't have one. I took charge of the case myself."

Carrie frowned. "I guess I owe you my thanks — but why you? Why not get Dickerman or Neece to look in on me?"

Phil had the grace to blush. "I was headed for the ER when you were brought in. My first reaction, of course, was to take charge. By the time we knew you were stable, I saw no need to call in a neurosurgeon. I'm not totally incompetent, you know."

"No, Phil. I trust you." Carrie relaxed back onto the pillow as wooziness threatened to overcome her. "And I think I was a bit premature in saying I want to go home. Maybe I'd better rest." She managed a smile. "Thanks, both of you."

Adam said, "You're welcome. And don't forget the guy who helped me get you from the car to the ER. He said he was a paramedic. His name was . . ." He paused, apparently searching his memory. Then his face brightened. "Rob Cole."

■ ■ ■ ■

The rattle of cart wheels and the clatter of dishes roused Adam. He stretched, feeling as though someone had put every bone in his body into a vise before twisting the handle as far as it would go. He opened his eyes, squinted, then looked at his watch. Six a.m.

Carrie had finally dropped off to sleep less than three hours ago. Adam mounted guard from a chair in her room, rousing with every noise. He intended to keep Carrie safe, no matter what it took. He didn't think the potential killer was still in the hospital, but there was no way to know. Unconsciously his hand reached to his ankle, where, through the cloth of his pants, he felt the comforting presence of his pistol.

A light tap at the door preceded the entrance of an older woman. She wore dark blue hospital scrubs, partially covered by a red-and-blue print jacket. "Good morning, Dr. Markham."

Carrie came awake slowly. "I guess I'd forgotten that patients are awakened this early."

The nurse's smile never wavered. "Some of us have been up all night. But I'm glad

224

you got some rest."

The woman, whose nameplate read "Grace," went through a routine Adam had heard Carrie call "vital signs." She helped her patient slide toward the top of the bed, pushed a button that raised her to a sitting position, and said, "Ready for some breakfast? Dr. Rushton said you could have a general diet if you wanted it."

Carrie started to nod, stopped abruptly, and flinched. She said in a soft voice, "Yes, please. Especially coffee."

"Coming right up," Grace said over her shoulder.

Adam looked into Carrie's eyes. They were bloodshot, with dark circles beneath them, and he thought he'd never seen any that were more beautiful. He shuddered as he realized how close she'd come to death last night.

"Have you been here all night?" Carrie asked.

Adam nodded, but didn't speak.

"You don't have to sit here and guard me."

"I'm not about to leave," he said.

"This wasn't your fault," Carrie said.

"I still think —"

"Don't think. Neither of us could have prevented this. The shooter missed, and I'm going to be okay, except for a scar on my scalp."

The conversation paused while a dietary worker served Carrie's breakfast tray. When she'd gone, Carrie said, "I'm not sure how much of this I'm going to eat, but I don't want to feed you leftovers. Why don't you go down to the cafeteria and get a hot breakfast?"

Adam was already shaking his head. "I'd rather stay here."

"Do you think he might make a try for me while I'm here in the hospital?"

Adam didn't have to ask who she meant. "I don't think so," he said, "but I'd rather not take any chances."

"Well, at least go to the nurse's station and let them get you a cup of coffee."

Adam finally agreed, and in five minutes he was back in Carrie's room, Styrofoam cup in hand.

He raised his cup in a toast. "To better days."

She nodded and took a sip from her cup.

"I'm so sorry," he said. "I wish the bullet had hit me instead. I'd give anything to spare you."

"I love you for saying that." She swallowed a bite of toast and washed it down with coffee. "But I'll say it again: this is not your fault. Besides, we don't really know who the bullets were intended for."

"True, they could have been meant for either of us . . . but they almost killed you."

Carrie settled her coffee cup onto the tray and pushed away the wheeled table that held her food. "I don't think I'm hungry anymore."

Adam lowered the head of Carrie's bed to a more comfortable position. "Do you want me to go?"

Carrie hesitated so long Adam thought his heart would stop. Then, in a tiny voice, she said, "Stay. Please."

Adam felt his heart start beating. He could breathe again. "I was hoping you'd say that. And I hope I can bring this thing to a close soon. I want us to begin living our lives again without looking over our shoulders."

Carrie tried to hitch herself upward on the bed. Adam was on his feet in an instant, tenderly helping her. As she leaned back on her pillow, she said, "What did the police say when you talked with them last night?"

"When the policeman taking my state-ment found out my name — and I couldn't think of a way to lie myself out of it — he ran it through his computer. When it spit out the information that I reported shots through my windshield not long ago, followed by having a Molotov cocktail thrown through the window of the building I was in, he got a lot more serious with his questions. I kept insisting that both episodes were probably just malicious mischief. Finally, after he'd pretty well pumped me dry, I followed him around as he checked the shooting scene."

"Did they dig out the bullets like they did from your car?"

Adam shook his head. "Nope. The bullets went all the way through both the driver's side and passenger side windows. They're somewhere out in the field that borders the parking lot, and good luck finding them."

Carrie lapsed into silence. Adam saw her eyes close, and he used the opportunity to slip out of the room and get another cup of coffee. When he came back, she was snoring gently. He eased into his chair, leaned back, and tried to recreate the shooting scene, focusing on where the shooter was.

The Prius was in the farthest corner of the lot, with probably a dozen empty parking spaces to the left, the direction from which the shot was fired. The shooter probably hid behind the nearest vehicle, a Hummer. Call it a hundred feet.

Adam was no expert on handguns, but he figured their effective accurate range was nowhere near a hundred feet. So this was more likely a long gun, a rifle of some kind.

That led him to two conclusions. The first was that it made no difference whether the police compared the bullets fired at him in front of the theater to those fired in the hospital parking lot. Two different weapons were used. In the first attack someone drove slowly by and fired a handgun out an open passenger window. Adam had seen it. The second attack came from farther away, and he was willing to bet the shooter used a rifle.

The second conclusion opened up a whole new train of thought. If the shots came from behind the Hummer, how did the attacker get away? There'd been no squeal of tires, no headlights moving in the parking lot.

Where was the rifle? Surely the police would have found it, but they'd said nothing to that effect. Maybe the shooter stowed the rifle in the trunk of his vehicle, then escaped into the hospital. Or perhaps the person ducked into his car and simply waited until Adam was inside the building before driving away.

Adam's focus had been on Carrie, not suspicious persons in the area. The shooter could have been anyone he'd encountered last night, or someone he hadn't even seen.

Carrie stirred, and Adam eased to her

bedside. She opened her eyes and blinked a few times. "I'm here," he said. "Nothing to worry about. I'm here."

As Adam stepped off the elevator, the smell of food from the cafeteria reminded him that his last meal had been almost eighteen hours ago. The coffee this morning helped, but why not have a quick lunch? No, he didn't want to take the time. The charge nurse promised to keep an eye on Carrie's room while he was gone, but Adam still hated to be away for very long. He had things to do, and he needed to hurry.

Adam checked his watch and decided he'd better call the office first. He stepped outside to use his cell phone. Brittany answered and put him right through to Janice Evans. He explained what had happened and told her that although he planned to stay at the hospital with Carrie today, he'd be at work the next morning. She told him to call if things changed.

While he was outside the hospital, Adam decided to look at the scene of last night's shooting. Carrie's Prius was where he'd left it, surrounded now by other cars. The policeman told Adam last night that he could remove the yellow crime scene tape and move the car this morning. He would have done so except that when he retrieved Carrie's purse, he'd locked the car and dropped the key into it. The purse — and key — were in a closet in her room. So the Prius would stay there for a bit longer.

The driver's side window was partially shattered, and glass fragments dotted the front seat. The passenger side window showed damage as well. The grassy area beyond the car was quiet now. He pictured figures there last night or early this morning, combing the area with metal detectors to look for the expended slugs, occasionally stooping to pick up something, then discarding bottle caps, coins, and other objects that made the instruments whine. Good luck finding that particular needle in this haystack.

He was certain the police had already searched for ejected shell casings as well, but Adam wouldn't be satisfied until he carried out a search of his own. He turned and made his way back toward the ER doors. The Hummer was still there — at least, he thought it was the same one. It was in what seemed to be the right place, and the windshield and back window were covered with dew from overnight. He stood behind the left rear fender of the vehicle, the position from which he figured the shots were fired.

Adam looked around but saw nothing but a few bits of trash. He dropped into a push-up position and peered beneath the Hummer. No, nothing under there except a small puddle of grease near the right front wheel — maybe a bad seal on an axle boot. But that wasn't what Adam was hunting.

He wasn't a hunter. Adam had never fired a rifle in his life. But somewhere in the deep recesses of his mind was a picture, probably from a movie or something, showing a hunter firing a rifle, working the bolt, and shells ejecting to the right side. So he was looking in the wrong place.

He returned to his position behind the left rear fender of the Hummer, faced Carrie's car, and scanned the area to his right. Nothing there. He moved across the aisle, got on his hands and knees, and searched the area under the Hyundai sedan parked there. Still nothing. Finally he reached under the car and felt beneath the rear tires. There his patience was rewarded. His fingertips brushed a small object wedged beneath the edge of the right rear tire of the car. He started to pick it up, then thought better of it. If there were fingerprints, he should preserve them. He used a pen to tease out the shell, then pulled his handkerchief from his hip pocket and picked up the tiny brass casing, then twisted the cloth to make a small bundle that he stowed in his pants pocket.

He might have smeared any fingerprints on the casing when he picked it up. Even if he hadn't, how could he get it checked? Adam still couldn't wrap his head around asking the police for help. There'd be too much explaining to do. Maybe he'd call Dave.

Adam turned and trudged back toward the hospital. At least he was doing something. And, if the opportunity presented itself, he'd do more. He felt the assuring weight of the pistol in its ankle holster strapped to his right leg. He might have been passive for the past two years, but now he was ready to actively defend himself — and Carrie.

FIFTEEN

Carrie sensed, more than heard, movement in the room. She'd been shuttling in and out of sleep, her dreams and semi-waking thoughts a mishmash of men with guns, shadowy figures whose faces melted into new ones before her eyes, and patients tugging at the hem of her white coat to beg for healing.

Now she heard a noise — soft footfalls on the tile floor. She opened her eyes and saw Phil Rushton standing at her bedside.

"Sorry to wake you," he said. "You need your rest."

"No, no. I was through with those dreams — nightmares, actually. I needed to wake up." She lifted her wrist to look at her watch but found it was gone. "What time is it anyway?"

"About noon," Phil said. "Let's have a look at you."

He took a few moments to examine her,

then settled into the chair at her bedside. "You're an extremely lucky woman. An inch lower and that bullet would have cracked your skull, maybe required surgery. Two inches and it would have penetrated into the brain, and you'd be dead or permanently disabled. As it is, you had a concussion. That's all."

Carrie pushed the button to raise the head of her bed. "So am I okay for discharge?"

"You know better than that. I told you yesterday, we need to watch you for a while."

"Phil, I feel fine, except for a headache that would put a mule on its back. I'm a doctor. I know the signs of a problem."

"Knowing the signs is different than being able to recognize them in yourself." Phil shook his head, and his expression told her she wasn't going to win this argument. "I'd like to keep you a few more hours — make sure no late neurologic changes show up. Can we settle on five or six tonight?"

"Not what I'd like, but . . . I never thought I'd say these words. You're the doctor." She shrugged and offered a hint of a smile.

Phil was almost to the door when Carrie called after him. "Phil, how did you happen to be there to take care of me last night?"

He shrugged. "Had to come back to the ER anyway. Heard the commotion, saw you on the gurney. After that it was all reflex."

As Phil went out the door, Adam came in. The two men did a clumsy do-si-do through the doorway before turning to face each other.

"Doctor." Adam reached out his hand. "Thanks for what you've done."

"Glad I could help." He shook the proffered hand, then turned back to Carrie. "I'd wanted to meet this fabled Adam of yours, but not under these circumstances."

"I'll bet you're beat," Adam said. "Are you going to get some rest today?"

"No, but fortunately I only have office hours. No surgery, unless an emergency comes in." He turned to face Carrie. "Let the nurse know if you have any increase in headache, any double vision, any nausea —"

"I know all the signs, Phil. Thanks."

The surgeon grinned and left.

Adam moved to Carrie's bedside. "What did the doctor tell you?"

"I can go home late this afternoon if there's no change." Carrie lowered the head of her bed slightly. "What have you been up to?"

"I stopped in the cafeteria for a quick cup. I'll have to say, the coffee down there is absolutely terrible."

"One of the first things I learned in med

school," Carrie said. "Bad hospital coffee is better than no coffee at all. But I'm glad you ate. Maybe by tonight I'll feel like eating."

Adam reached into his pocket and pulled out a crumpled handkerchief. He unfolded it, careful not to touch what it held. "I found this in the parking lot."

Carrie reached out, but Adam pulled it away. "Don't touch it. I'm going to see if my brother, Dave, can check the fingerprints on it."

"Why not the police?" Carrie asked.

"Because I trust Dave. And I don't have to explain things to him."

Carrie decided not to start that argument again. She stared at the shell casing for a moment. "Twenty-two long rimfire," she murmured.

"What did you say?"

"My dad had a rifle — called it a 'varmint gun.' We lived in Austin, and he used to take me out in the country and let me shoot it. It fired twenty-two caliber long bullets. And I always had to pick up the ejected cartridges, or 'clean up my brass,' as he called it."

"Think this will help me find out who shot at you?" Adam asked.

"Probably the most common rifle in this

part of the country. So don't get your hopes up about using this to trace the shooter."

"Well, we can still check the casing for fingerprints," Adam said.

"You can try . . ."

Adam dropped into the chair. "That's all I can do. I have to keep trying." After a moment he made a "just a second" gesture, rose, and walked out. He returned with a pen and a thin pad of paper. "Got these from the nurse's station. I think it's time to start our list."

Fifteen minutes later Adam dropped the pen and said, "This is ridiculous. The shooter could be anyone who's moved to Jameson within the past six months or so."

"Or someone who was already here, but with a Chicago connection that would let DeLuca's family reach out to them, even after he died."

"Oh, that helps a lot!" Adam said. "Why don't I get the Jameson phone book and stick a pin in a random page?"

"Look at it another way. Let's focus on last night. You didn't see or hear any cars burning rubber out of the parking lot. So either the shooter got away without you seeing them —"

"Which was possible," Adam said. "Remember, I was concentrating on you."

"Or they stayed around. You mentioned that Rob Cole helped carry me in?"

Adam nodded.

"And what was he wearing?"

"A black T-shirt and jeans."

Warning bells were going off in Carrie's mind. "Why would he be there?"

"He told me he was an EMT. I assumed he'd just gotten in off a call."

"No," Carrie said. "If he'd been on duty, he would have had on a medium blue shirt with a logo on the pocket and navy cargo pants."

Adam picked up his pen. "I guess he could have been the shooter. Shot at you from behind the Hummer, dumped the rifle into his vehicle, and emerged to be a Good Samaritan, thinking it would put him above suspicion."

"Or if the target was supposed to be you, when he saw he'd hit me, guilt could have motivated him to help," Carrie said.

"Good point."

"Who else was there when you brought me in?"

"The doctor — Dr. Rushton. He burst through the double glass doors right after I did," Adam said. "He took charge immediately. Seemed like a natural thing."

Carrie frowned. "He told me he had to

see a patient, and I assumed he was already in the ER. But if he came from outside, why couldn't he have fired the shot, dumped the gun, and burst in?"

"Do these guys have something against you?"

"I haven't figured out Rob Cole. He's acted . . . strange. And Phil Rushton? About the time I decide he's trying to ease me out of the clinic, he says or does something nice."

"Like save your life," Adam said.

"I doubt whether his care made that much difference, but, yes."

"And these are just the people we know about. The shooter could have been anyone."

"This is bringing back my headache." Carrie turned her head away and closed her eyes. She was certain of only two things. One, her life was in danger. And two, aside from Adam, she couldn't trust anyone.

"Are you sure you want to leave the hospital already?" Phil Rushton asked.

Adam stood in Carrie's hospital room behind the wheelchair in which she sat. He noticed that she hesitated before answering. He couldn't blame her. In here it was safe, or at least, relatively so. Because there were no metal detectors at the door, Adam had been able to ignore the signs and keep his pistol with him inside the hospital. To get a security guard required a simple phone call. But once she went out the hospital doors, out into the world, Carrie would once more be a potential target for the shooter. And whether he was aiming at Adam or at her, if a bullet struck her the end result would be the same.

"Yes," Carrie finally said. "I'm ready."

Rushton raised a cautionary finger. "Remember to —"

"Yes, Phil," Carrie snapped. "I'm a doctor. I know how to take care of a scalp wound. I know about the complications after a concussion. I know to take it easy for a day or two." She took a deep breath, and when she spoke again, her tone had moderated. "I'm truly grateful for your care. You didn't have to do it. You could have passed me on to the ER doctor or one of the neurosurgeons. Don't think I'm unaware of that. But I'm a grown woman, as well as a physician. I need a measure of independence."

Rushton spread his hands wide. "Okay. But call —"

Adam could tell how much it cost Carrie to keep her voice level. "I'll call you if I need anything. Right now Adam is going to drive me home, where I plan to soak in a warm tub and eat a pint of Blue Bell ice cream. I'll be at work . . . What is today, anyway?"

"Tuesday, late afternoon," Adam chimed in.

"I'll take tomorrow off and be in on Thursday. If you'd let the schedulers and my nurse know, I'd appreciate it."

While an aide wheeled Carrie away, Adam, this time armed with the key, hurried to the parking lot to retrieve her car. The first thing he did was lower what was left of the shattered side windows. It made the car drafty but presented no other problem. Then he swept glass fragments off the front seat. That action brought a sense of déjà vu, as he recalled doing the same thing after the gunshots in front of the theater — gunshots that signaled the start of this nightmare.

Adam pulled the Prius into the circular driveway where discharges were sent on their way. With Carrie belted safely into the passenger seat, he stepped on the brake pedal, pushed the button to start the car, moved the selector lever to Drive, and pulled away from the hospital.

"See, driving a hybrid isn't so difficult, is it?" Carrie asked.

Adam ignored the remark. "Don't you have some flowers to take home?"

"I asked that they be distributed to other patients in the hospital."

"That was generous," Adam said. "When we get to your house, would you like me to stay there with you? At least for —"

"Stop right there!" Carrie turned to face him. "Adam, I love you. I've missed you, but I don't think I'm going to be good company. Once I'm inside, I promise to lock all the doors and windows. If anything suspicious happens, I'll pick up the phone and call 911." She saw the hurt in his eyes. "But you'll be my second call."

Adam nodded. "Would it be okay if I phoned to check on you?"

Carrie looked down at her lap. "Of course. And I'll call you. But I was serious about the long soak and the pint of ice cream."

They were quiet for the rest of the journey. Adam insisted on helping her into the house. He reached down to his right ankle, unsnapped the Velcro fastener securing his pistol, and with the gun in his fist, went through all the rooms. Empty. No evidence that anyone had been there since Carrie left.

Then, with her safely inside the house, Adam pulled Carrie's car into the garage and lowered the door. He found her in the living room, relaxing in an easy chair. He dropped her keys on the front table and pulled out his cell phone. "I'm going to call a taxi to take me back to the restaurant to get my car."

Carrie pushed herself out of the chair. "I'm not sure I've said it, and even if I did, I probably didn't say it enough — thank you."

Adam grasped Carrie's shoulders, kissed her, and pulled her to him. "Believe me, if I could undo all this, I would. But if I did that I wouldn't have you in my life. And right now you're the only thing that gives me hope — you and the knowledge that God's in control. He's got my back in all this."

Carrie looked up at Adam. "Not only yours — mine too. Ours." Tears sparkled in her eyes. "I've kept God at arm's length too long. I'm trying to make Him part of my life now, like you have all along." She buried her head on his shoulder, and Adam felt as though his heart would burst with happiness.

True to her promise, Carrie luxuriated in a warm bath until she felt like a prune. During the soak she consumed the remains of a half-gallon of Blue Bell Rocky Road ice cream she found in her freezer. Now she lay under the covers of her bed, wrapped in her ratty but extremely comfortable robe.

She toyed with the idea of sleep, but it was still too early. Besides, she felt as though she'd done nothing but sleep for the past twenty-four hours. TV? Not really. The critic who called that medium a "vast wasteland" had been right when he'd said it, and it was still true. She picked up the book at her bedside, read a few words, then put it down when she found her mind wandering.

Like good doctors in her specialty, she loved a diagnostic puzzle. She enjoyed the challenge of taking clues, putting them together this way and that, until the mystery began to come clear. Now she was involved in a mystery of her own, one that had life or death implications. And since she had time available, Carrie decided to shuffle the pieces of information she had to see if they formed a pattern.

She retrieved the pad and pen from her bedside table, a necessity for doctors receiving phone messages, and headed the page "Possibles." After a moment's thought, she crumpled and discarded the sheet. As Adam had said before, she might as well pick up the Jameson phone book. On the next sheet she drew a vertical line. To the left of it she wrote "Adam," to the right, "Carrie." Then she drew a line under both names, forming a T-chart. Again, the left-hand column offered almost infinite possibilities. The column under her name was more limited — mainly patients and their family members who could be so displeased with her they might try to harm her . . . or harm Adam as a way to get revenge on her.

There was no doubt in her mind. The top name on the list in the right-hand column was Calvin McDonald. Carrie shivered as she recalled her last encounter, when he passed her in the hall of the clinic and glared wordlessly at her. She remembered thinking, *If looks could kill . . .* Carrie wrote a few more names under his, including Mrs. Freemont, but after a moment she went back to the top and underlined McDonald's name . . . twice.

The ringing of her phone interrupted her thoughts. Maybe Adam was calling to check on her. Or maybe Phil. She was surprised to find that it was neither.

"Carrie, how are you doing?"

"Julie. So good to hear your voice."

"I've been waiting for you to call. Finally my curiosity couldn't stand it any longer. What's going on with you and Adam?"

"Wow, where do I begin?" Carrie hesitated only briefly. Surely it was safe to share her information with her best friend. Besides,

Julie was a couple of hundred miles away. And who would she tell?

Carrie brought Julie up-to-date on all that had happened, including the shooting that came within inches of taking her life. "Now I'm at home, wrestling with the possible identity of the person behind this."

"I presume you and Adam are good?"

"We're more than good." She paused and weighed her words. "I think that, despite everything that's happened, we're closer than ever."

"That's great. I'm glad to see that God's working in your life and Adam's right now."

"I guess He is. While Adam was gone, I started reading my Bible. One particular verse really hit me, one about God giving us a new heart. And I think He's doing that for me."

"Wait a sec," Julie said. "I know the one." There was the sound of turning pages. Finally she said, "Here it is. Ezekiel 36:26. 'Moreover, I will give you a new heart and put a new spirit within you.' "

"Well, that's what He's done," Carrie said. "And I'm grateful."

After leaving Carrie's home that evening, Adam thought about asking the taxi to drop him at the office but soon discarded the idea. Better to start fresh in the morning anyway. He gave the driver the address of the restaurant where he'd left his car. He'd stop by the grocery for provisions before heading home.

He'd been in the Rancho Motel for several nights, then a series of one-night stays on his trip, but now he was ready to go home — his real home. As he steered his car toward his apartment, he ran details through his mind. His complex was primarily filled with young urban professionals, most of them not yet home from work. There were no children playing in the courtyards, no foot traffic to speak of. The possibility of witnesses to an attack was slim. Dusk was approaching. All things considered, Adam decided to redouble his efforts at vigilance.

He drove around the block a couple of times, alert for people sitting in cars or standing in doorways. On the third time, he pulled into the covered parking area provided for tenants but didn't go to his assigned slot. Instead, he chose a vacant spot as close to the back entrance of his apartment as possible. He pulled his pistol from its holster and shoved it into the waistband of his trousers, ready for action. Adam eased out of his car and looked around. Nothing stirred.

He emerged from the car and reached back for two bags of groceries, grabbing one with each hand. Adam decided that if shots were fired, he'd drop the bags, duck for cover, and start shooting. Could he really fire his gun? The picture of Carrie in his arms, blood covering her head, came to his mind. If he needed something to steel his resolve, this was more than enough. He flexed his shoulders to relieve the tension there, then pivoted three hundred sixty degrees. No one was in sight.

From the parking lot, he scurried to his back door, which he suddenly realized he needed to unlock. Adam set the bags on the ground long enough to pull out his keys. He gave another glance around, drew the pistol from his waistband with one hand, opened the door with the other. Holding the pistol at his side to partially conceal it, he picked up one bag and shuttled it inside, repeating the process with the other. He made one last trip outside, locking his door behind him, to move his car to its proper spot. Adam didn't want to start a war with the neighbor whose slot he'd occupied.

The walk to his back door, his arm held along his leg to conceal his gun, seemed to take an hour. Finally he was inside, the doors double locked. When he put the pistol on the kitchen table, he noticed his hand was trembling.

Was this going to be his life from now on? Holding his gun in one hand when he took groceries from his car? Flinching from shadows, jumping at every noise? No! It might be that way until he could get the shooter to reveal himself, but he wasn't going to live like that forever. He recalled a line from his childhood, one he wanted to open the window and shout to the person trying to kill him: "Come out, come out, wherever you are." *And when you do, I'll be ready.*

Sixteen

Wednesday morning sunlight streaming through a small opening toward the top of her bedroom's drawn drapes woke Carrie. She'd kept them and all the other drapes and blinds in the house closed since she came home from the hospital. With all the doors locked, she felt relatively safe.

Since the shooting, her sleep had been troubled. This morning she had vague recollections of dreams that made her sweat and her pulse pound, yet the details escaped her.

When she left the hospital, she'd told Phil Rushton she'd be in on Thursday. That was tomorrow, and as she swung her feet off the bed and shoved them into slippers, Carrie was happy she hadn't followed her first inclination and declared she'd work today. Of course, it was possible that Phil, in his sleep-deprived state, might have forgotten to pass the word along to the schedulers. Oh well. She'd check that in a minute.

She followed the smell of freshly brewed coffee, grateful she remembered to activate the auto-brew feature on her coffee maker last night. A cup in hand, she ambled into the living room and dialed the clinic's back line. Although most of the doctors weren't due in for at least an hour, she was certain Marie would be at her desk, making sure the day's appointment sheets were printed off for distribution to the physicians.

Sure enough, Marie answered on the second ring. "Clinic, this is Marie."

"Marie, this is Dr. Markham."

"Oh, how are you doing? I'm so sorry for your accident."

It wasn't an accident. Someone meant to shoot me. "Thanks. I just wanted to make sure I don't have any patients scheduled for today."

Carrie heard keys clack, then Marie's voice back on the line. "Um, we have you marked out until tomorrow. Was that a mistake?"

"No, it's perfect," Carrie said. "I'll see you Thursday."

She needed today off — not necessarily because of her head wound but because of the stress of the situation. Carrie puttered around in the kitchen, deciding which dish she'd choose for her leisurely breakfast. But in the end she came back to what she had most days — juice, a toasted English muffin, and coffee. She flinched only a bit at the pounding in her head when she bent down to retrieve the newspaper from her porch. A second cup of coffee, a run through the headlines, and Carrie was ready to move on.

She took a long shower, careful to keep her head wound dry, followed by time in front of the mirror styling her blond hair to cover the crease left by the bullet. Makeup supplied the final touch. She slipped on a simple white tee and black slacks, slid her feet into cordovan loafers, and was ready for the day. But what was she going to do? Right now she was the embodiment of the phrase "All dressed up and no place to go."

Carrie brought the remainder of her second cup of coffee to her desk and found the T-chart she'd started last night. She couldn't do much about Adam's side of the list. She had suspicions about a couple of people whose names she knew, but some unknown, unnamed person with a connection to Charlie DeLuca could also be the shooter. But she could whittle hers down pretty quickly. The question was whether she was willing to do it.

Lord, if I do this I'll need more strength and

wisdom than I have. And, truth be told, I'm scared.

She shoved the list aside and picked up her Bible off the end table. Carrie thumbed through it randomly, hoping to find direction, but nothing spoke to her. She reached to replace it on the table, when it slipped from her hands and fell, open, onto the floor. When Mrs. Nichols gave it to her, she mentioned highlighting a few passages. "These may be helpful for you," she'd said.

The open page was in the book of Psalms, and a passage marked in yellow caught Carrie's eye. "The Lord will protect you from all evil; He will keep your soul. The Lord will guard your going out and your coming in, from this time forth and forever."

Carrie nodded, as though in answer to an unasked question. She picked up the phone and punched Redial. "Marie, this is Dr. Markham again. Would you give me the home address for Calvin McDonald?"

Adam's first day back at the law offices of Hartley and Evans was actually easier than he feared. He came in early, as was his custom. A desk, bookcase, chairs, computer, and all the contents of his old office had been moved into the new one. The only clue that it had once been a storeroom was a stray legal journal in one corner, left behind by whoever had done the moving.

When Brittany arrived, the coffee was already made. Adam was in his office digging through the files he'd found waiting for him when she stuck her head through his open door. "The coffee smells wonderful. Thanks. Her Ladyship never comes in early enough to brew coffee, much less offer to do it. Guess she thinks she's too good."

Adam didn't want to get into a gossip-fest with the receptionist, so he made some noncommittal remark and returned to his apparent study of the open law book on his desk. In a moment he heard Brittany's voice back at her desk, answering the phone.

Greetings from Janice Evans came next, then Bruce Hartley. Mary Delkus was the last one in. Apparently good looks granted certain privileges. As soon as Adam felt sure that everyone was busy, he called up an Internet search engine on his computer and typed in a name. It was a name he hadn't thought of since his second year in law school. But it was the name of a person who might help him with one of the most important problems he'd ever faced.

Finally he was able to secure an address, which led him, after more digging, to a phone number. He scribbled it on a yellow

Post-it and shoved it deep into his briefcase. When he was at lunch, he'd make the call. Meanwhile, he had some catching up to do, if he wanted his current "temporary" position to become permanent.

As soon as Carrie got into her car she realized she'd forgotten one detail: the two front windows were missing. Dealing with that was now her first order of business. Fortunately the dealer from whom she'd purchased her car was not only a patient but also a friend. He took her to his service manager and explained Carrie's situation. "I'd appreciate it if you could help the doctor get underway. She's in sort of a hurry."

After completing the paperwork, the service manager pointed to a silver Prius, identical to Carrie's, just pulling into the service drive. "That's your loan car. I'll call you when we get the new windows installed."

"Thanks so much," Carrie said as she drove away. Thank goodness the vast majority of her patients not only liked her, but some were willing to go the extra mile to help her when she needed it.

The house certainly wasn't what Carrie expected. Every time she'd seen Calvin McDonald, the man was dressed in jeans and a

nondescript shirt — sometimes plaid, sometimes denim. The clothes showed evidence
of frequent laundering but were always
clean. Somehow Carrie's mental picture of
McDonald was of a man scratching out a
living on one of the black-dirt farms outside
of Jameson. But the man's home forced her
to revise that image.

The house wasn't outside Jameson's city
limits. As a matter of fact, it was in one of
the nicer sections of town. Rather than the
small white clapboard house with a compo-
sition shingle roof Carrie visualized, Mc-
Donald lived in a two-story red brick home,
set in the middle of a well-maintained yard
surrounded by a recently painted white
picket fence. A black Buick, its surface
unmarred by dirt or dust, sat in the driveway
in front of a two-car garage.

Carrie screwed up her courage and gave
the button beside the front door a tentative
push. She waited, her ears straining to pick
up any sound from inside. As she was about
to ring the doorbell again, the door opened
wide, and she was face-to-face with Calvin
McDonald.

He gave her the same squinty-eyed glare
she'd come to expect, but although the
expression was somewhere between disdain
and dislike, the voice was surprisingly soft.

"Help you?"

"Mr. McDonald. I'm Dr. Carrie Markham. I'm sorry to intrude like this, but I'd like a few minutes of your time."

McDonald's look of surprise lasted only a second. "Come in." He gestured her inside. Carrie wondered if she'd ever pass back out the door again. After all, this man topped her list of people who'd like to kill her. Of course, even if he did, maybe Adam would be out of danger. *Lord, protect me.* She took a tentative step inside, and McDonald closed the door behind her. Then she heard the click of a lock, and a chill ran down her spine.

Carrie was poised to bolt for the door, hoping she could reach it before McDonald intercepted her, when he spoke. "Would you like to have a seat?" He escorted her to what, in an earlier day, would have been called a parlor. Two easy chairs, a sofa, some tables and lamps, and a couple of throw rugs. There was no TV set. Instead, an upright piano sat against one wall. Apparently this was the room for "entertaining company," as her grandmother might have said.

As she eased into a chair, Carrie noticed that although the room was neat, a faint patina of dust covered some of the furniture.

"I apologize for the dust," McDonald said, as though reading her thoughts. "My wife always kept the place spotless, but since . . . since I lost her, I haven't paid as much attention as I should. I have a woman who comes in and cleans, but I've asked her to leave this room alone. It's . . . it's where Bess and I used to sit and talk."

Carrie decided to plunge right in. "Mr. McDonald, I'm sorry for your loss. I tried to tell you that at the time your wife . . . your wife passed away. And I hope you realize I and the rest of the hospital staff did everything we could to save her."

McDonald sat unmoving. No response.

Carrie took a deep breath and went on. "As soon as I saw your wife in the Emergency Room, I made the diagnosis of a perforated ulcer. That's outside my specialty, so I called in a general surgeon. He rushed her to surgery, and I stood by in the operating room in case I could help. Unfortunately, her heart was too weak to tolerate the procedure. The anesthesiologist and I did everything we could to save her, but we were unsuccessful."

Carrie swallowed, remembering the frustration she felt at losing that patient. "I'm not sure anything could have been done differently, but believe me, we gave it our best effort. I'm sorry it happened." She paused, trying to read his expression. It was the same squint-eyed glare she was used to seeing from him. "Now I'm here to make certain you're not carrying a grudge toward me. And if you are, I want to ask your forgiveness."

There, it was out. She held her breath, waiting to see what came next.

"Grudge toward you?" McDonald's glare softened. He wiped a tear from his eye. "The only person I'm angry with is myself. I tried to get Bess to go to the doctor, but she wouldn't budge. I watched her take antacids and sodium bicarbonate, urged her to get her stomach pains checked, but she refused. And when she finally had so much pain she couldn't stand it, I took her to the Emergency Room. I was afraid it might be too late. I prayed it wasn't — but it was." He pulled a handkerchief from his hip pocket and wiped his eyes. "But I don't blame you, Doctor. I blame myself."

Carrie's next words came out without conscious thought. "Then why do you always glare at me when we pass in the halls?"

McDonald reached into his shirt pocket and pulled out a somewhat worn black clamshell glasses case. He withdrew a pair of wire-framed spectacles, hooked them over his ears, and settled them on his nose. "Bess was always after me to wear these, but I hate them. I'd rather squint. Is that better?"

Actually, it was. What Carrie had interpreted as a scowl was gone. McDonald was no longer someone sending a glare of hate her way. Now Carrie realized he was just a lonely old man, sitting day after day in an empty house, missing his late wife.

Carrie started to get up, but something kept her seated. Should she? Maybe it would help him. Maybe it would even help her. "Mr. McDonald, I know something about survivor guilt, and that's what you're feeling. I've been there. If you keep hanging on to it, you'll never move forward. I know from personal experience. Lots of people suffer from it, and they're almost always wrong to do so. Let me tell you a story."

She took his nod for permission. "It's about two doctors. They'd been married since graduating from medical school. It wasn't always easy to make a marriage between doctors work, but they did . . . and they were happy. She found that she couldn't have children, but they decided God had a child out there for them somewhere, so they'd adopt.

"They barely had begun the process when he started noticing fatigue. He was a general surgeon, and he passed it off as working too hard. But the symptoms worsened. She insisted that he see one of her colleagues for a workup. He put it off and put it off, but finally he relented.

"The workup showed an unusual congenital heart problem — it's called Ebstein's anomaly, but the name isn't important. One danger it poses is a potentially deadly rhythm disturbance of the heart. He developed more problems. Medications weren't working. So a specialist proposed a procedure called transvenous radiofrequency ablation."

She saw McDonald's eyebrows rise, so she hurried to explain. "Call it RFA. In it, a doctor inserts a fine plastic tube through a vein in the leg and runs it all the way up to the heart. A wire inside the catheter delivers current to cauterize the abnormal areas responsible for the rhythm problems. It's an accepted procedure, and it's generally safe."

Carrie paused and tried to clear the lump in her throat, but it wouldn't budge. "The risks of something going bad during such a process are small, but they exist. But in this case the wire got into a coronary artery and opened a tiny hole in it. The only chance to save such a patient is immediate heart surgery to repair the damage. In this case, one of the best cardiothoracic surgeons in the state was in that hospital right then. They took the patient immediately to the operating room . . . but he died."

McDonald continued to sit, silent as a statue. Carrie couldn't tell from his expression if he was following the story. She hoped he was. "Naturally, the wife was devastated. She was a doctor. She should have picked up on the clues to her husband's heart problem sooner. She should have insisted that he seek medical attention earlier. She should have been able to prevent the complication — maybe suggested a different doctor, even a different medical center for the procedure. She should have intervened to get her husband to surgery sooner, although she didn't see how she could. She blamed herself every step of the way. She had the biggest case of survivor guilt in the universe."

"It wasn't her fault," McDonald said quietly. "She did her best."

"And so did you," Carrie said. "I should know. I was that woman doctor. The man who died was my husband."

What McDonald said next removed him from Carrie's list of people who might try

to kill her and placed him in a whole different category. "I'm sorry for your loss," he
said. "I'll pray for you . . . for both of us."

Carrie brushed away tears. "So will I, Mr.
McDonald. So will I."

Adam really didn't want to leave the safety
of his office, not even for lunch. But he had
to — not only because he was hungry, but
also to give him the privacy necessary for
an important phone call. Besides, it was
unlikely the shooter would come after him
in broad daylight, and certainly not within
sight of both the municipal courts and the
police station.

The offices of Hartley and Evans were
within walking distance of both those struc-
tures. And where lawyers and policemen
gathered, there were sure to be eating
places, little sandwich shops and cafés
where people could snatch a quick lunch, a
cup of coffee, a late-afternoon snack without
having to go too far. It was to one of these
Adam walked, not hurrying but not daw-
dling either.

Once inside the sandwich shop, he took
comfort from the presence of no fewer than
three uniformed patrolmen and a couple of
plainclothes detectives. The latter didn't
have their badges on display, but they might

as well have carried signs saying, "Police."
Adam ordered a glass of tea and a roast beef
sandwich, then headed for the restroom.
Behind a locked door he dialed the number
he'd unearthed earlier. *Please pick up.
Please be there.*

"This is Cortland."

Adam wasn't sure how three words could
convey a Texas accent so well, but they did
just that. He pictured "Corky" as he typi-
cally saw him in law school: dressed in an
open-necked blue button-down shirt, Levis,
and soiled New Balance running shoes.
Adam hoped Corky had upgraded his attire
since he graduated.

According to Adam's online search,
E. A. Cortland, Esq., had a law practice in
Houston, Texas. Adam was banking on
Cortland's tendency to skip his noon meal,
hoping Corky would answer the phone
himself while his receptionist or secretary or
whoever usually manned the phone at his
office was at lunch. So far, he'd won the tri-
fecta: this was the right Cortland, the phone
number was the one he wanted, and Corky
was the one who picked up the phone.

"Corky, this is Keith Branson." Adam had
to guard his tongue to make it say his
original name.

"Keith, you old dog. How are you?"

"Look, Corky. I have to keep this short, but I'm hoping you can fill in the blanks for yourself. If you do an Internet search, you'll find that my testimony sent my father-in-law, Charlie DeLuca, to jail. Since then I've been on the run. I'm going to give you a number — it's my cell phone. I'm calling in the favor you owe me for getting you through that course on torts. Will you do some digging and call me back?"

Corky acted as though this was the most natural request in the world. "No problem, Keith, although given what you've already told me I'd bet that's not the name you're using these days."

Adam looked at the phone in his hand and discovered he'd pulled his throwaway phone from the brief case. It was just as well. He gave Corky the number. "What I need is more information than I can get from Google or LexisNexis. I need as much as you can give me."

"Sure," Corky said. "But why?"

"Somebody's out to kill me, probably for testifying against Charlie DeLuca. I need whatever you can dig up on DeLuca, especially his associates and family."

"If we both weren't officers of the court, I'd think you wanted me to hack into some sites and circumvent the law."

"Well —"

"Relax. Given enough time and resources, anyone could get this information quite legally. I'm just shortening the process." Adam chewed on that for a minute. Legal? Most likely it was a gray area, but one in which Corky had always enjoyed working. "Okay. So you'll do it?"

Keys clicked in the background. "Sure. Sounds like fun." More clicks. "I'm already into some sites you'd never penetrate. That was D-E-L-U-C-A, C-H-A-R-L-E-S? He'd be in his late fifties?"

"And he'll never be any older. He died a few months ago."

"Give me time to dig. Why don't I call you back this evening?"

"Great. I appreciate it."

"Not a problem." A low whistle overrode the background clatter of keys. "Just to be sure, which family of DeLuca's do you want to know about? Or shall I check into both of them?"

SEVENTEEN

Adam felt the tremor of his cell phone against his thigh. His throwaway cell, the one he'd asked Corky to use, was in his briefcase. This was his regular number. He didn't want to ignore a call, since it might be from Carrie or Dave.

He eased the phone out, held it shielded by his desk, and checked the caller ID. It was Carrie. Adam lifted the phone to his face, pressed the button, and whispered, "Yes?"

"Can we meet tonight? I have some things to tell you."

"Hang on." Adam rose from his desk and moved to the far corner of the little room. He turned his back to the door and pretended to be engrossed in the titles on a shelf of law books. "We need to make this quick. I should have some information tonight too, but it may be late."

"Late's fine. Shall I come by the Rancho

Motel again?"

"No, I checked out before my trip. But I'd rather keep you away from my apartment." He thought a moment. The logistics were possible. "I'll be at your back door about ten this evening."

"Won't you —"

"I'll do what I did Sunday night when I came to your house. The shooter will never know I'm there. Trust me. Just be ready to open the door for me."

"Are you going to call me on your cell when you arrive?" Carrie said.

"I thought I'd just knock."

"Maybe we should have some sort of code so I don't open the door and find myself staring down the barrel of a gun?"

Adam recalled Carrie's special ring for her cell phone. "Sure. How about the opening rhythm of Beethoven's 'Fifth Symphony'? You know. Dah-dah-dah-dah. Four knocks in rapid succession."

They ended the conversation and Adam hurried back to his desk, arriving just as Mary Delkus tapped on the frame of the open door. She looked like a million dollars today in a form-fitting burgundy dress. "Did I hear you talking with someone?"

"You caught me. I was talking to myself. Sometimes I like to present arguments out loud to see how they sound." He gestured to one of the chairs in front of his desk. "Have a seat. What's up?"

Mary smoothed her skirt over the backs of her thighs and sat. "I need to get better acquainted with you," she said.

"Oh?"

"I feel bad." She gave him a look of apology. "I know that I took your job, and . . . well, I'd like to make it up to you by taking you out to dinner."

Adam didn't know what to say.

"How about tonight?" she said, giving him a glimpse of those perfect white teeth.

Adam hadn't known what to expect from Mary's visit, but it certainly wasn't this. He needed to be free to take Corky's call, he had to be at Carrie's late tonight, and he really didn't know enough about this woman to be comfortable going out with her. Maybe the last factor was pure paranoia, but he was taking no chances. "Mary, that's really very kind," he said, "but I have something on the schedule tonight. Maybe another time."

She smiled. "Sure. Think about it and let me know." Adam's eyes followed her as she strode from the office. He had little difficulty understanding how Bruce Hartley was so taken with her. But looks weren't everything. Beauty could be used in so many ways, some of them good, some bad. As for Mary, the jury was still out, but he was getting an idea of which way he'd vote.

When Carrie left Mr. McDonald, she felt somehow freer. For almost a year she'd carried with her a sense that the man hated her, somehow held her responsible for his wife's death. Carrie couldn't bring Bess McDonald back to life, but maybe she'd been able to give some quality to Calvin's life for the years he had left.

Back in her car, after the call to Adam, she wished she'd taken something that morning for her headache. She knew why Phil hadn't prescribed Vicodin or a similar narcotic for the headaches she was sure to have over the next few days. He wanted to avoid masking late symptoms of a complication following her head injury. Carrie's pain tolerance was pretty high, but right now her skull was throbbing.

She decided to stop for a cup of coffee and use it to wash down a couple of extra-strength Tylenol. Maybe the caffeine plus the pills would help stop the waves of pain bouncing around inside her head.

Jameson offered the usual options to those seeking a caffeine fix. The town even boasted a couple of Starbucks. It wasn't Seattle, but still, Carrie had plenty of opportunities to get a cup of coffee and relax.

Her first thought was a small coffee shop near the hospital. After a moment's consideration, she rejected the idea. The place was a frequent hangout for medical staff, and she didn't want to answer a lot of questions about the shooting in the parking lot.

A banner on a building to her right caught her eye: "Now Open: Kolache Heaven." Growing up in central Texas, she'd quickly become a fan of the doughy pastries with centers filled with fruit, cream cheese, or even a sweetened poppy seed mix. The thought of a kolache, together with a steaming cup of coffee, made her salivate. Besides, maybe hunger was contributing to her headache. She wheeled into the parking lot, then waited patiently in line to place her order.

The man in front of her looked familiar, and when he turned she realized why. It was Rob Cole. "Dr. Markham. Glad to see you're able to be out and about. Come to get your kolache fix?"

"Actually, I didn't know I was hungry until I saw the sign. That's when I decided a kolache would be good."

"And you're right. If you've never tried one —"

"I have," Carrie said. She wasn't interested in a long conversation, but she couldn't figure out how to get rid of Rob without being downright rude. The register next to them opened, and Carrie stepped up and placed her order.

Rob reached into his pocket. "Please. Let me buy."

"Thanks, Rob, but no. I'll get my own." She paid for her coffee and a raspberry kolache, dropped her change in the tip jar, and started to move away.

"Looks like there's only one empty table," Rob said. "Could we share it?"

Carrie resigned herself to prolonging the encounter. When they both were seated, she took a bite of her pastry and a sip of coffee. Then she reached into her purse and pulled out a small vial, shook two Tylenol tablets into her palm, and washed them down with more coffee.

Rob watched with interest but didn't comment.

Carrie had an urge to eat her pastry in three or four huge bites, then make her getaway to avoid a conversation with Rob. Instead, she nibbled at the kolache, alternating with sips of coffee while wondering what

273

Rob's conversational opener would be. She didn't have to wait long to find out.

"Dr. Markham, do you have any idea why someone took a shot at you in the ER parking lot?"

She wasn't sure whether he was naïve, rude, or truly interested. In any case, it was none of his business. "Rob, I think that's a matter for the police." She reduced the size of her kolache by one more ladylike bite and decided to turn the tables on him. "By the way — I've not had an opportunity to thank you." She smiled warmly. "You and Adam saved my life. What were you doing there anyway? You weren't on duty."

Rob shrugged, his expression devoid of guile. "I hang around the hospital a lot in my off hours. I don't have a wife or family, and it's not a lot of fun sitting around an empty apartment. I'd just parked and was on my way to get a burger in the cafeteria when I heard the shots and saw Mr. Davidson running across the parking lot carrying you."

Carrie didn't particularly want to make this a long conversation, but her curiosity got the best of her. Besides, there were still a couple of bites of pastry and a little coffee left. "I'm sure it can be lonely, living alone." *I know. I do it too.*

"It is. And I don't plan to be alone forever. I know the type of woman I want in my life. And I intend to go after her."

Carrie looked at Rob and wondered if this was another clumsy attempt on his part to flirt with her. Did Rob actually think she might be interested? Or was there something more behind it?

By the end of the workday, Adam was wrung out from constant tension. He kept trying to work through the pile of material on his desk, but the stack of files seemed to refresh itself every time he whittled it down a bit. Meanwhile, he parried the questions and comments from his coworkers: from Brittany, who thought the behavior of the partners was indefensible; from Bruce Hartley, whose only concern was that briefs were filed on time and paperwork brought up-to-date; from Janice Evans, who sympathized with Adam about the problems that seemed to be hitting him one after another; from Mary Delkus, who repeated her offer to take him to dinner. And in the back of his mind was always the cryptic question of his friend Corky. "Which family of DeLuca's?" Corky had to end the call before he could amplify on that. But by tonight Adam hoped to have some answers.

At about three o'clock, the phone on his desk buzzed. He punched the intercom button. "Yes?"

Brittany's voice was unusually subdued. "There's a man from the U.S. Marshalls Service on line 1. He didn't want to give me his name, but he said it was urgent."

Adam's gut clenched. It could only be Dave, and Dave would only call him at work if he couldn't get through on his cell. Adam eased the instrument out of his pocket and checked the display for missed calls. None.

"It's okay, Brittany," Adam said. "Probably something routine. Thanks."

Adam punched the blinking button. "Adam Davidson."

The voice was vaguely familiar, but it certainly wasn't Dave's. "Adam, this is Sam Westerman. Are you able to talk?"

Adam knew that Sam meant, "Can you talk without being overheard?" His emotions did battle. He wanted to hear what Sam had to say, hear it now, but he had precious little privacy in the office. "Call me back on my cell in five minutes."

"I'll need that number. Dave gave it to me, but I can't find it."

Adam rattled off the number and hung up. He grabbed his coat and briefcase and headed for the door, where he stopped.

"Brittany, I have to get some papers to a marshall so he can serve them. I'll be back in half an hour." He closed the door firmly behind him before the receptionist could respond.

Ten steps away from the building, Adam stopped and looked around. Where could he go? And how did he know this wasn't some sort of a trap? Was it really Sam calling? Could Sam be involved in the shootings? Was Dave — No, that was ridiculous. He had to trust Dave and, by extension, trust Sam.

He'd avoided his assigned spot in the building's parking lot. Instead, his car was in a lot behind the building, which he'd entered via the back door. He headed there now. When he reached the little Subaru, he looked in all directions but saw no one nearby. He beeped the vehicle unlocked, jammed himself behind the wheel, and relocked the doors.

Adam had no time to get settled before his cell phone rang. "This is Adam."

"Sam here. I have some bad news about your brother."

The chill Adam felt would have made his mother say someone was walking over his grave. "What?"

"He was with a group of law officers down

around the Texas-Mexico border. There was a shoot-out, and Dave was wounded. He's okay, but he made me promise to call and let you know."

"Where is he? I need to go there."

"That's the other thing he made me promise. He knew that was what you'd say, so I can't tell you where he is. The wound isn't severe — he'll probably be out of the hospital in two or three days — and he said there was no need to come down."

Adam leaned forward and rested his forehead on the steering wheel. Did he *need* to be with Dave right now? No, he *wanted* to be there, but there was nothing he could do if he went. As always, Dave was right. "Okay, I guess. Can you keep me posted on his condition? Please promise me that."

"I'll call you again tomorrow," Sam said.

"And if he gets worse . . ."

"I'll let you know."

When Adam ended the conversation, he felt more alone than he'd ever felt in his life. His brother had always been there for him. Now Dave was out of the picture, at least for a while. Sam would help — he seemed like a good man — but there was something about the blood bond that made trust automatic.

Now, other than Carrie, was there anyone

Adam could really trust?

Carrie knew she must have eaten something for her evening meal, but for the life of her she couldn't recall what it was, how it tasted, or anything else about it. She fiddled with the TV set, channel surfing without ever locking in on anything. She paced, peered through the blinds every few minutes, looked at her watch, and in general acted like a child waiting for Christmas morning. And all because Adam was coming over.

Even though she'd had one earlier in the day when she returned from her visit with Calvin McDonald, Carrie decided she needed another shower to help her relax. She stood under the hot water for a long time, then dressed in a plain skirt, a simple blouse, and low heels. When she found herself deciding on costume jewelry to complete the look, Carrie decided that was enough. *For goodness' sake, stop acting as though you're waiting for your prom date.*

By nine Carrie decided she needed something to help calm her. How about a drink? She didn't have liquor in the house, and wouldn't use it if she did. Tranquilizer? Same answer. She flopped into an easy chair in her living room and shuffled through the magazines on the coffee table. There was nothing there worth reading. She picked up the Bible that lay beside the magazines. *Maybe this is what I need.*

She was still reading more than an hour later when a sharp *rat tat tat tat* at her back door roused her. She looked at her watch. Quarter past ten. Adam was here.

Carrie hurried to the kitchen. The top half of the back door was glass, divided into six rectangles by a latticework of wood and covered by a half curtain. She pulled the curtain aside far enough to see Adam standing on her back porch, scanning all around, his shoulders hunched as though by doing so he could make himself invisible. He wore dark jeans and a green sweatshirt.

She turned the latch and opened the door. "Come on in."

He hurried inside. "Lock the —"

Carrie was already working on it. She double locked the door and slid a security chain into place.

"How did you get here without someone seeing you?"

"Same way I did Sunday night." Adam wiped sweat from his forehead and finger-combed his hair. "I parked two blocks away, then came down alleys. I kept in shadows most of the way. Your fence was easy enough to climb. I'm sure no one followed me."

"Is this what you're reduced to now? Sneaking around through alleys in the dark? I thought you were through hiding."

"I am," Adam said. "I'm ready to face the shooter, but I want to choose where we meet. And it's not going to be anywhere near you."

For the first time, Carrie saw the pistol in Adam's hand. "Is that . . . ?"

"Yes. It's my gun." He knelt and slid the pistol into a holster buckled above his right ankle. "And I'd feel better if you had one too."

Carrie chose to ignore the remark. She didn't want a weapon, and she wasn't too happy that Adam had one. "Let's go into the living room," she said. "Do you want something to drink? Coffee?"

"I'd jump out of my skin if I had coffee," Adam said. "Maybe a glass of ice water."

In a moment they were settled side by side on the sofa in Carrie's living room. "I think we both have news," she said. "Who goes first?"

She wasn't sure of the reason, maybe it was the cumulative stress of the past few days, but Adam seemed more preoccupied than usual. He snapped out of it long enough to say, "Why don't you?"

Carrie described her visit to Calvin Mc-Donald. "I don't think he could be our shooter. And the more I think about it, the less certain I am that the attacks have been aimed at me." She was ashamed that she felt a degree of relief at reaching this conclusion. "I believe we can strike Mr. McDonald and Mrs. Fremont and all the other patients and families who might have a grudge against me."

"Good," Adam said. "You haven't discussed my real identity with anyone. Right?"

Carrie tried to keep her expression neutral. *Just my best friend. But Julie has no reason to tell anyone.* "No . . . Well, yes. I've talked to Julie Yates." She saw Adam's expression change, and her voice rose a bit. "Adam, she's my best friend. I'd trust her with my life. And I had to talk with someone about this. Can you understand?"

Adam chewed on his lower lip. "I asked you not to tell anyone. Don't you think it's possible that Julie could tell her husband, who might mention it to a colleague, who could be an acquaintance —"

"Stop! Julie promised me she wouldn't even tell her husband. I'm willing to bet my life that she's kept the secret."

"Actually, it's my life we're betting too . . . but, okay. I'll accept that."

"Thank you."

"Let's put that aside. I have a couple of things to share," Adam said. He told her about his brother's shooting. "He's doing okay after surgery, but he'll be out of circulation for several days. He was shot in the shoulder — the right shoulder — so if it comes down to a shoot-out, I won't be able to depend on Dave for a while."

"Was that what you'd planned?" Carrie asked. "Get your brother here, maybe a couple of his buddies, then face down your stalker like the gunfight at the OK Corral?" She knew there was sarcasm in her voice, but maybe it belonged there. Surely Adam wasn't planning something like that.

"No, I don't expect my brother to fight my battles for me. That's not the way we grew up. Besides . . ." He touched his ankle where the pistol rested. "Although I hope it doesn't come down to what you call the gunfight at the OK Corral, if it does I'm ready."

"How else do you think we can resolve this?" Carrie asked.

"I plan to use the pistol to capture the shooter, not shoot him. I never thought I'd even own a gun. But I feel as though I'm backed into a corner, and I'll do anything to defend you . . . to defend us."

She patted his arm. Carrie decided it was time to move on to a topic that wouldn't trigger an argument. "You said you had two things. What's the second?"

Adam paused to think for a moment. "Oh, I called one of my law school classmates. Corky has a brilliant legal mind, but he also can coax all kinds of information out of a computer."

"In other words, he's a hacker."

"He assures me that he could get all this information in a conventional manner. It would just take a lot longer. He describes it as taking a shortcut." He took a deep swallow from his water glass, then set it on the coffee table in front of him. "I asked him to check out Charlie DeLuca for me."

"Why?" Carrie said. "You worked with DeLuca. You were married to his daughter. Don't you know enough about him?"

"I wanted a list of family and close friends, people who might be behind these attacks on me even though Charlie is dead."

"Didn't you meet all those folks at your wedding? Maybe at the rehearsal dinner? The reception?"

Adam grimaced. "Charlie said there was no need for a big fancy wedding. A judge in Chicago, one of Charlie's cronies, married us in his chambers. My brother and the judge's clerk were witnesses."

"What did Bella say? Or Charlie's wife?"

"They did what they'd learned to do — they kept their mouths shut."

Carrie picked up a legal pad and wrote "Charlie DeLuca Family" at the top. "Okay, so what was Charlie's wife's name?"

"Doesn't matter. Corky called me just before I came here. He only had a moment, but he told me Charlie's wife died six months after he went to prison." He picked up his glass, found it empty, and put it down again. "Charlie hadn't been what you'd call a model prisoner. He was in solitary confinement at the time, so he didn't get to go to her funeral."

Carrie shuddered. This was the man responsible for attacks on her life, yet she found herself feeling sorry for him. "So we have 'wife — deceased' and 'daughter.' Do we know anything about Bella's whereabouts?"

Adam described the dead end Corky encountered in that respect. "It's 'like she dropped off the face of the earth' was the way he put it. His best guess was that after the divorce and her father's prison sentence, Bella moved, established a new identity, and we'll never find her."

"But if she showed up here, you'd recognize her."

"Right. I don't think there's a plastic surgeon anywhere who could change her appearance enough that I wouldn't recognize my ex-wife."

Carrie said, "Who else?"

"Charlie apparently had an older brother, but he managed to tiptoe through society without leaving a footprint. No Social Security number, no driver's license — at least, not in his original name. My guess is that he wanted to distance himself from his black sheep brother. Maybe, the same way we suspect Bella did, he wanted to wipe the slate clean. He just did it a lot earlier."

Carrie looked at the almost-blank page in front of her. "What about close friends?"

Adam shook his head. "Nope. Charlie didn't have close friends. He had people who worked for him, people who owed him favors, but any loyalty they had to him probably died when he did, if not before."

Carrie dropped the pad and threw up her hands in surrender. "So I guess that's it. We have no knowledge of anyone connected to Charlie DeLuca who might be trying to get back at you on his behalf."

"I didn't say that," Adam said, raising an eyebrow.

Carrie studied him for a moment. "Okay

. . . ," she finally said. "What?"

"Apparently one family wasn't enough for Charlie DeLuca . . . He had two!"

EIGHTEEN

Adam watched carrie's face as he dropped the bombshell on her, and he wasn't disappointed. Her jaw dropped like a fish gasping on dry land. He couldn't recall ever seeing someone so totally surprised. Then again, he'd been just as surprised when Corky mentioned DeLuca's second family.

"I think you'd better explain," Carrie said.

"Most of this is conjecture, but it makes sense. Charlie's wife — Bella's mother — was something of a shrew. Charlie's law practice and shadier activities often took him to Cicero, which is sort of a suburb of Chicago. That's where he met a woman who was clerking for a judge — maybe a judge Charlie or one of his associates had 'bought,' so to speak. They started seeing each other, and he eventually married her."

"Didn't his wife — either wife, for that matter — didn't they suspect anything?"

"Not at all. Charlie split his time pretty

evenly, and each wife was told his absences were because of business trips."

Carrie picked up her legal pad again. "So what was his name in Cicero?"

Adam grinned. "Charlie DeLuca."

"You're kidding! I can't believe it. He had a second family, a few miles away from the first, both of them under his real name? The man was either incredibly stupid or incredibly confident."

"My personal opinion? He was both."

Adam watched as Carrie wrote "second family" and drew a line under it. Then he told her what Corky had found. Charlie's double life remained undiscovered until after he was about to go on trial. When the second wife learned the truth and realized the second marriage was invalid, she retook her maiden name, found a job at the courthouse, and closed that chapter of her life.

"So she's not going to want revenge," Carrie said.

"Maybe on Charlie, not on me."

"Did they have any children?"

"She had two from a previous marriage — a son and daughter, both grown."

Under "second family", Carrie wrote "son" and "daughter."

"Before you get too carried away with that list, you'd better hear what we know about the children." Adam leaned forward with his clasped hands between his knees. "As best we can tell, the daughter was terribly disturbed by what happened. So disturbed, as a matter of fact, that she entered the novitiate for the Franciscan Sisters. She's currently at Our Lady of Victory Convent in Lemont, not far from Chicago."

Carrie pursed her lips and drew a line through "daughter." "So what about the son."

"He disappeared."

"Don't tell me he followed his sister's example and went into a monastery."

Adam shook his head. "I don't think so. He was working in a hospital in Cicero and going to night school, getting his certification as an Emergency Medical Technician. After he finished his training, he went to work driving an ambulance there. Then, about a week after the bigamy came to light, he simply didn't show up for work. There's no trace of him since then, at least not by his real name."

"So at least we have one possible out of that list," Carrie said. "What was his name?"

"The name he was born with is Robert Kohler. But we have no idea what he goes by now."

Adam expected Carrie to write down the

name. Instead, she gripped the pen so tightly her knuckles turned white. Then she looked up at him and said, "I may know."

Carrie wondered if she was jumping to conclusions. Then again, the pieces seemed to fit together. Adam came to Jameson about eight months ago. Within a few weeks Rob Cole showed up, working as an EMT. About the time it was evident that Adam and Carrie had become an item, Rob started showing more interest in Carrie. She'd thought at first it was infatuation on his part. Now she wondered if it was an attempt to get close to her in order to keep tabs on Adam.

"You're going to think this is crazy," she said.

"No crazier than someone shooting at me — at us. Let's hear it."

Carrie laid out her theory about Rob, watching Adam's face carefully. To his credit, he neither interrupted nor argued. Instead, he listened thoughtfully until he was sure she'd finished.

"Let's look at it objectively." Adam picked up Carrie's pad and pen and wrote "Rob Cole" toward the middle of the page. "There are three things the law looks for in the commission of a crime: motive, means, opportunity. Let's take them in reverse order." Under Rob's name, he scribbled the words *movie, office, hospital 1, hospital 2.* "Let's look at opportunity for each of these episodes."

"I'm with you," Carrie said.

Adam poised his pen over the first line in the list. "So could Rob have shot at us in front of the theater?"

"I don't see why not. Actually, I suppose anyone could."

Adam made a check mark. "Could he have lobbed that Molotov cocktail through the front window of the law offices?"

"Same answer."

Another check mark. "Now we begin to narrow the field. Could he have sent the text that lured me to the hospital parking lot?"

Carrie thought about that for a moment. "Yes. Rob's in and out of the ER all the time. He'd know about the locker where my phone was. And he'd be familiar with the property, including where you'd park if you came to the ER."

A third check mark. "And the shooting in the hospital parking lot?"

"Of course." She waited while Adam made the final check. "You said he was in dark clothes that night, but not in uniform.

We have only his word that he likes to hang around the ER when he's off duty. He could have followed us from the restaurant, shot at me —"

"We've also said that could have been a mistake," Adam said. "Maybe he thought he was shooting at me."

"And when you emerged from the darkness carrying me, he saw what he'd done. So he ran to help you."

Adam ran his finger down the check marks. "All right, we know he had the opportunity. The means presents no real problem here. That leaves motive."

"If he's Charlie DeLuca's stepson from that second marriage . . . We don't know that he is, but if that's true we should be able to connect the dots."

"We need to find out if Rob Cole was originally Rob Kohler," Adam said.

Carrie nodded. She knew two things: that it would be up to her to get that information from Rob, and that she dreaded the encounter.

It was well after midnight before they agreed that their brains were no longer functional. Adam paused by Carrie's kitchen door and wondered if she'd ever forgive him for getting her into this. His doubts were erased by the hug and kiss she delivered, followed by the whispered admonition, "Be careful."

"I will," he assured her.

"And call me when you're safely home."

"I'll make it short. If our friend, the stalker, has some sort of way to track me via my cell phone, that would at least make it less likely he'll know that I'm in my apartment."

Adam slid out the door and ran in a crouch toward the six-foot-high wood fence that separated Carrie's backyard from the alley. The slats were fastened to two horizontal rails. Adam put his toe on the lower of the two boards, grasped the top of the fence, and pulled himself to the top. He rolled over and landed on the narrow strip of grass that separated the fence from the paved alley.

He took a minute to catch his breath, then worked his way slowly through the alleys toward where he'd left his car. The neighborhood was dark. Although there were street lamps in the area, there were none in the alleys. Adam was sure some homes had motion-triggered lights in the backyards, but the fences shielded his movements, so he remained in darkness. The occasional bark of a dog signaled his passing, but he kept moving.

He emerged from the last alley and scanned the area where his vehicle was parked. Other cars sat silent nearby, but all of them were empty — or if there were occupants, they were hidden. Adam gave it a few minutes. He heard no sound, saw no movement. No telltale embers of cigarettes glowed anywhere. The last thought made Adam smile, as he visualized a man clothed in black, lurking in the darkness, smoking a cigarette, occasionally fingering the gun tucked into his belt. *You've seen too many late-night movies on TV.*

He hurried to his car and unlocked it with his key to avoid the beep and flashing lights of the security system. He eased into the driver's seat, glad he'd remembered to remove the bulb from the interior light. He pulled the door closed gently and relocked it. He didn't turn on his headlights until he was half a block away. Then he went through a series of turns to make certain no one was following him. The drivers of the few cars he encountered seemed more interested in getting to their destination than pursuing Adam.

As he pulled into the parking lot behind his apartment, he killed the headlights and scanned the area. He'd made an effort to memorize as many as possible of the cars normally parked there, and he saw nothing out of the ordinary. Rather than taking his numbered slot, he chose a visitor's space toward the end of the row. He recalled his brother's warning about the dangers of predictability. If unpredictability meant being exposed for a longer walk to his back door, so be it.

Before he opened the car door, he pulled up his right pants leg and slid the pistol from its holster. If he was going to need it, now would be the time. Much like a coach giving a pep talk, he reminded himself that although he wasn't a killer, he was the target of one. And if he had to shoot to defend himself, he would.

He eased out of the car and locked it with the key. Adam looked around once more. Nothing moved.

He strode purposefully toward the back door of his apartment and was halfway there when gunfire from behind a Dumpster to his left made him drop to the ground. Two shots in rapid succession were followed by the scream of a car alarm. Adam stood up, pointed his pistol at the area where he'd seen the muzzle flashes, and pulled the trigger twice.

He heard the whine of a car engine revving, the screech of tires on pavement. He got a fleeting glimpse of a bulky vehicle, probably a light-colored SUV, exiting the parking lot. Adam took that as his cue. Already lights were popping on in the apartment building. Witnesses would emerge in a moment, and the police wouldn't be far behind. He sprinted for his apartment, opened the back door, and tumbled inside in one motion. Adam moved toward the center of the apartment, but not before he engaged both the door's lock and deadbolt. Then he duck-walked to an interior wall and eased down against it, trying to catch his breath.

Returning fire had been a reflex, and now Adam wondered at the wisdom of his action. He realized he could have injured, even killed an innocent bystander. Moreover, now the assailant knew Adam was armed. Would that make him even more dangerous?

Should he clear out again, move to another motel? If he stayed, was he endangering his neighbors? He decided that the shooter was unlikely to return that night, so it was probably safe to stay here for the time being. Tomorrow . . . well, he'd decide that after the sun came up.

Adam leaned against the wall, his gun almost forgotten in his hand, and wondered how many more close calls there would be . . . and how many he could survive.

Carrie wished she could call the clinic and tell whoever answered that she wouldn't be in today. Her head was still sore, but more than that, her brain felt like a house after a tornado struck, her thoughts scattered like pieces of furniture, some fragmented, all out of order. And long periods of staring wide-eyed at the ceiling interspersed with occasional troubling dreams had done nothing to refresh her during the night.

But Thursday was Thad Avery's afternoon off, and she didn't want to ask him to cover for her. No, she'd bite the bullet and go to work. She'd done it before, in medical school, in residency training, in practice. If she could care for patients right after the death of her husband, she could certainly power through headache and fatigue.

In the shower, Carrie tried to avoid getting her scalp wound wet but eventually decided she couldn't stand dirty hair one more day. She carefully washed her blond hair, then dried it gently and used a few light brush strokes to style it to hide the scab left by the bullet. She dressed in a white blouse and black slacks and put on a minimum of makeup. It wouldn't hurt if people thought she was pale — maybe they'd take it easy on her.

Her breakfast was a cup of coffee and two extra-strength Tylenol. Carrie wasn't particularly hungry now. If that changed, she'd grab a donut from the break room mid-morning, by which time a pharmaceutical rep would no doubt have left a couple of boxes of them, along with information on the latest drug from his company.

In her car, she pulled her cell phone from her purse, paused with her thumb over a speed-dial button, then changed her mind. She and Adam had agreed to keep communication to a minimum, not so much to avoid electronic eavesdropping as to allow each of them to carry out the tasks they'd set for themselves. Before he left last night — this morning, actually — they agreed to meet again tonight about ten p.m. at her house. She hated the maneuvers he had to go through to get there, but he insisted that was the best way to keep from leading the shooter directly to Carrie.

Either by design or coincidence, the list of patients Lila placed on Carrie's desk was short. She scanned the names and the diagnosis or reason for each visit and felt herself relax a bit. She should be able to handle these, as well any emergencies that cropped up. She also found a note from the receptionist on her desk: "See Dr. Rushton." No explanation. Not a request. A command. She wondered if those had been the exact words Phil had used.

In any case she'd see Phil, but first she wanted to check on her hospitalized patients, review the reports and lab work on her desk.

Hospital rounds were easier than Carrie anticipated. In her absence, Thad Avery, the other internist in the group, had seen both her hospitalized patients, found them to be much improved, and sent them home. Maybe she'd misjudged Thad. Perhaps he really was a nice guy. She'd always figured he had a hand in patients switching from her care to his, but she could be wrong. Maybe it was all Phil's work.

Bolstered by her second and third cups of coffee of the morning, Carrie walked down the hall to Phil Rushton's office. There was never any problem finding Phil. From before sunup to after sundown, Phil was either in his office, in surgery, or making hospital rounds. She hadn't seen him at the hospital and his name wasn't listed on the surgery schedule in the doctor's lounge. Therefore, Carrie figured he'd be in his office.

She looked through the open door. Phil was seated at his desk, paging through a journal, occasionally using a yellow highlighter to mark a passage. She tapped on the door frame. He didn't raise his head, didn't acknowledge her in any way. She tapped again, and in a voice that conveyed neither irritation nor pleasure, Phil muttered, "Come."

Carrie entered and took one of the two chairs on the opposite side of the desk from Phil. He held up one finger in a "give me a minute" gesture. Carrie marveled at the man's ability to focus so completely on the task at hand. She recalled what a colleague had once said about Phil. "His focus is so complete he could burn a hole in a telephone directory with it."

While Phil's head was down, Carrie looked once more at the diplomas and certificates on his office wall. His training had been impressive: Northwestern, Pritzker, Rush. Then, when the puzzle pieces fell together in her mind, her throat tightened and the hairs on the back of her neck prickled.

Doctors as a group might not have a firm grasp of geography, but most of them knew the locations of first-rate medical schools and hospitals. And she knew where all these were: Chicago — the same city that had been home to Charlie DeLuca . . . and his family and friends.

Phil closed the journal and looked up. "Carrie, thank you for coming by. How are you feeling?"

"Fine. Some headaches, some scalp tenderness — nothing that Tylenol doesn't handle."

Phil twirled the highlighter between his fingers. "You know, you seem to be something of a magnet for trouble nowadays. You were in the lawyer's office when the firebomb was thrown. Somebody took a shot at you in the hospital parking lot and barely missed doing grave damage . . . maybe killing you." He looked at Carrie as though he could read the deepest secrets in her eyes. "Is there something going on in your life I should know about?"

Here we go, Carrie thought. *He's building a case to get rid of me on the basis of "improper conduct." Well, I'm not going to let that happen.* "Phil, I'm offended that you'd ask that. My private life isn't the issue here. When I joined this clinic, I signed a contract with all the standard clauses, including the one that lets you terminate me because of improper conduct. But I don't think that gives you permission to delve repeatedly into what I do on my own time." She took a deep breath. "If you're unhappy with my work as a doctor, say so and we can talk about the group buying me out. If not, I'd rather not go into what I do outside the office and hospital."

Phil's response came quickly. "Carrie, I have to ask these questions. If there's something going on that might affect the clinic, I need to know. That's all." He leaned across the desk, radiating sincerity from every pore. "You know I like you — like you a lot. I'm just offering to help."

Carrie marveled at how quickly Phil's manner changed. It was as if he'd flipped a switch, and a caring colleague replaced the all-business administrator. Then again, she didn't totally buy this nice-guy act. "Sorry. I guess my fuse is sort of short these days. Getting shot will do that to you." She shook her head. "Let me assure you that recent events have nothing to do with the clinic or my work here. And on a personal level, I'm fine, and I don't need any help. But thanks for asking."

Phil apparently wasn't through though. "Your ex-fiance — Adam Davidson. You've been seeing a lot of him lately again, haven't you?"

"Yes, but I can't see where that could possibly affect the group."

"I was just wondering. He only turned up here in Jameson a few months ago, right? Do you know much about his past? Is there something there that might be at the root of these attacks?"

Carrie's antenna was tingling. She needed to head this off, and quickly. "I know what I need to about Adam, but I don't see that it's necessary to discuss it with you. Again, that's my private life, and it has no bearing on my professional activities." She looked at her watch, rose, and said, "If that's all, I really need to get started with my morning clinic."

As she walked down the hall, Carrie tried to replay her recent encounters with Phil, now viewing each of them in a whole new light. She felt as though she were trapped in a maze where a new surprise, each one unpleasant, waited around every corner. *They'd need to add Phil's name to the list. How many more suspects? How much longer?*

NINETEEN

Adam had never felt less like rolling out of bed to start a new day. He squinted at the face of his watch and made out "Th." Thursday. The few days he'd been back in town had provided at least a month's worth of excitement. If he could make it through today and tomorrow, maybe he could use the weekend to rest and organize his thoughts. Right now he felt as though he was trying to unravel a tangled ball of yarn, one with multiple loose ends.

The attack last night had left him shaken. He knew he should call Carrie sometime today and give her that news, and he dreaded the conversation. Adam could almost hear her saying, "How much longer?" He'd spent most of the night searching desperately for a way to track down the shooter, but so far he'd come up empty.

After some coffee and a shower, the world

looked marginally better. In his bedroom he repacked his briefcase for the day. He tossed in his cell, then remembered to add the throwaway phone as well, since that was the number he'd given Corky. After that call maybe he could discard this one entirely.

Adam's eye lit on the balled-up handkerchief on the top of his dresser — the cartridge shell he'd picked up in the hospital parking lot. It had seemed like a good idea at the time, but now he wondered if there was any way it would yield usable information. He sealed the brass casing in a plastic sandwich bag from the kitchen and dropped it into his briefcase. Maybe he could check into it later today.

The shell made him think of Dave. He'd planned to ask his brother if he could have it checked for fingerprints, maybe even run the prints through some kind of database. Surely a marshal would have contacts for something like that. But now Dave was out of circulation for a while, in a hospital bed hundreds of miles away.

Adam lifted the semiautomatic from his bedside table, where it had given him a measure of confidence as he tumbled about in fitful sleep. The odor of gunpowder assaulted his nostrils, and he remembered what Colonel Johnson told him during their quick introductory session on the pistol: if you fire it, do two things immediately: clean and oil it, so the barrel isn't pitted by the products of the explosion, and reload it, because you never know how many shots you'll need next time.

Adam ejected the magazine, then racked the slide to clear the bullet that was in the chamber. When he was certain the gun was safe to handle, he set about cleaning it, using the kit sold to him by the clerk at the same store where he bought his holster. He shoved two fresh bullets into the magazine, reassembled the pistol, and set the safety. When he was certain the weapon was ready for action, he strapped it securely into his ankle holster.

Somehow, feeling the weight of the pistol resting against his calf wasn't as comforting to Adam as he thought it would be. In his braver daydreams, the stalker pulled out a gun but Adam's lightning-fast draw allowed him to put a bullet into the assailant's shoulder before the man could fire the first shot. In other, less pleasant fantasies, the gun in Adam's hand was useless while the shooter fired from point-blank range. That vision ended with a black haze descending like a curtain to signal Adam's death.

■ ■ ■ ■

By ten o'clock Carrie was not only caught up, but a few minutes ahead. "I'm going to get some coffee and a donut," she told Lila.

"Out of luck," Lila said. "The Merck rep was supposed to be here today, but he had to cancel." She grinned. "But if you're hungry, I hid a couple of pastries from yesterday in the fridge. They may be a little stale, but I'll share."

"Sounds good," Carrie said.

Lila microwaved the two cherry Danish, and she and Carrie eased into chairs in the corner of the break room, fresh coffee in hand. "Thanks so much," Carrie said.

"Consider it payback for giving up your Sunday afternoon to come to the ER and take care of my mother."

"How's she doing?"

Lila looked at the clock on the wall. "You can see for yourself. She has an appointment with you just before lunch." She took another bite of Danish, chewed, and swallowed. "But I think she's doing fine."

Carrie reflected on the way she'd solved the diagnostic puzzle presented by Mrs. James, Lila's mother, and her hypertension. Diagnostic puzzles and grateful patients would always be an important part of the practice of medicine for her. They were what kept her going, even when it was hard. And the more she thought about it, the more grateful Carrie was that God allowed her to do something that brought her so much pleasure. *Thank You, Lord.*

Adam worked hard to follow his usual routine at work: he came in early, made the coffee, buried his nose in the tasks left for him, and spoke only when spoken to. He hoped if he did that, no one would notice his bloodshot eyes, the frequent yawns, the two tiny pieces of tissue stuck over the cuts he'd inflicted on himself while shaving.

If he were a drinker, the picture could be passed off as the aftereffects of a hard night on the town. But Adam, in sharp contrast with Bruce Hartley, was a teetotaler, and the staff knew it. So if anyone noticed his state this morning, questions were sure to follow.

Other than a brief conversation with Brittany, who was more interested in relating her own experiences of the prior evening than asking Adam about his, he managed to pass the morning with a minimum of interaction with others in the office. That changed at about eleven, when Mary Delkus tapped on the frame of his open office door.

"May I come in?" The question was apparently rhetorical, because before Adam could respond she was settling herself in one of the chairs across from him.

He composed his features into what he hoped passed for a pleasant grin. "What's up, Mary?"

"I'm still wondering if I could take you to lunch. If we're going to be working together, I think it would be nice if we got to know each other better."

Wheels were spinning in Adam's head before Mary finished speaking. Did she want to know about him so she could undermine his chances of getting his permanent job back? Was she setting him up as a fallback if her relationship with Bruce Hartley fizzled? Or — and Adam sort of regretted the cynicism that put this so far down the line of possibilities — was she truly a nice lady who just wanted to get to know a coworker better? Whatever the cause of the invitation, he needed to wriggle out of it. It had always been important for him to maintain the anonymity that prevented anyone from digging too deeply into his cover story. Right now that was more imperative than ever.

Mary raised her eyebrows in a silent

follow-up to her invitation.

Adam tried to deepen his grin. "Believe me, Mary, I'd like nothing better. But I have a luncheon appointment that I can't change, so I'll have to take a rain check."

The raised eyebrows turned into a frown. "Adam, that's twice you've turned down my invitation to lunch. If I didn't know better, I'd swear you were trying to avoid going out with me. It's just a lunch. Nothing more."

Adam spread his hands. "I know, and I wish I could take you up on it. But I've been gone, and I'm trying to catch up." He pulled out his cell phone and opened the calendar function. "How about next week? Maybe Tuesday?"

Mary reached into the coat pocket of her stylish navy suit and pulled out the latest iPhone. She touched the screen a couple of times, then smiled. "I'm putting you down for lunch on Tuesday." The smile stayed on her lips, but her blue eyes conveyed a different message altogether. They said, *No more excuses, mister.*

As Mary left, Adam made a note on his own calendar. This gave him four days before he had to face Mary's questions. And he was sure that there would be questions. The woman might be only a paralegal, but he'd already figured that she'd be great on cross-examination of a witness.

His next step was a phone call. He'd need to be out of the office to make it, which was yet another reason not to accept Mary's invitation. Adam reached into his in-box and pulled out the top sheet. To a casual passerby he'd seem deep in thought. Actually, he was, but not about Jason Whitley's will. He was putting together a cover story to explain his lunch appointment, in case anyone asked. And the way his luck was running, someone would.

Carrie was pleased to find that, as Lila had said, her mother was indeed doing well. Having been sufficiently frightened by the effects of the weight-loss product from the health food store, she'd decided to substitute willpower for herbs and had lost a pound since her last visit. Her blood pressure was behaving. Carrie assured Mrs. James that if she could drop another eight or nine pounds, she should be able to come off her blood pressure medicine entirely.

"You're welcome to join Mom and me for lunch," Lila said as she escorted her mother down the hall.

"Thanks, but I'll just grab a sandwich at the hospital," Carrie said. She left mother and daughter at the checkout desk.

Fifteen minutes later she was flipping a mental coin between the tuna salad and smoked turkey sandwiches. Finally, her choice made, she took her tray to the most remote corner of the food court and slid into a chair at the last open table for two.

When her husband was alive, he and Carrie unashamedly said grace in public, holding hands, taking turns praying. But after his death, she dropped the practice. Although she was back on speaking terms with God, bowing her head to pray in a crowded environment was still beyond her. She decided to compromise. Without bowing her head, she breathed a silent prayer. She knew God wasn't picky about whether the prayer was voiced or simply formed in her mind.

She had a potato chip halfway to her mouth when a familiar voice caused her to stop. "May I share your table?"

Carrie looked up and put aside any idea of a quiet lunch to refresh her mind and calm her soul. The voice belonged to Rob Cole.

"Going to lunch," Adam said to Brittany as he hurried by her desk and out the door.

Although his assailant had never targeted

him in broad daylight, Adam continued the practice of parking in a space other than his assigned one in front of his office building. He hurried to his car, half expecting to hear a shot at any moment, maybe even feel a bullet sink deep into his flesh. Once in the Forester, he let out a breath he hadn't realized he was holding.

He pulled away, one eye on the rearview mirror, and began a series of turns that by now were second nature to him. Eventually he backtracked toward his office and pulled to a stop near one of the small cafés that was a gathering place at noon for lawyers with business in the courthouse nearby. He made casual conversation with a few of the men as he waited to be seated. If anyone at his office asked about his lunch appointment, he was ready to say he met with someone from another law office, exploring the idea of a position there if his return to Hartley and Evans didn't work out. Beyond that he'd be tight-lipped.

Adam settled in at a booth in the back of the café. He ordered a sandwich and waited until it was served. Then he unfolded the newspaper he'd brought with him. Behind it Adam pulled out his cell phone and punched in a number. He hoped his brother was feeling up to answering — wasn't there some rule against cell phones in hospitals? Maybe they'd make an exception for a lawman. Did Dave even have his cell phone with him?

The call rang for the fifth time, and Adam figured it was about to roll over to voice mail. Then there was a click, a pause, followed by a voice, weak but familiar. "Branson."

Adam felt himself grinning. "Dave, it's me. Adam. Can you talk?"

"Let me see. I have the president and the attorney general here in my hospital room, but I guess I can tell them they'll have to wait." This was followed by what started as a chuckle but ended in a barking cough. "Sorry. Still coughing some. They say it's due to the anesthetic."

"Are you okay to talk?"

"Sure. Other than getting tortured by the sadist in physical therapy twice a day, I just lie here and channel surf. I've watched so much daytime TV my brain is starting to rot."

"What do the doctors tell you?"

"They say I got shot in the shoulder."

"You know what I mean."

Dave's voice took on a more somber note. "The initial surgery was done to stop the bleeding and clean up the wound. I'd lost too much blood for them to do more than that right then. I'm getting built back up, but we have to decide soon what to do next if I want my arm to be fully functional again."

Adam couldn't imagine a marshall with an impaired right arm. Did this mean his brother was going to lose his badge? Did they have to pass some sort of proficiency test? Never mind. Those were questions for another time. "Listen, I need to ask you a question."

"Ask away."

"We . . . uh. That is, someone shot at Carrie and me the other night. Grazed her scalp, but we're fine."

Dave wanted all the details, and Adam spent five minutes pouring them out. He finished with, "Now I have a question for you."

"Okay."

"I went back to the parking lot and found an empty shell casing the police must have overlooked. I'm pretty sure it's one the rifle ejected. Do you think it will tell us anything?"

"Sure. Someone who knows a thing or two about guns could tell you the caliber of the weapon."

"Can it be matched with the gun?"

"I've heard they're working on something like that, but at present you can't identify a rifle by the ejected shell casing. You have to compare an actual bullet with one that was test-fired from the gun. Do you have the slug?"

Adam thought about police combing the field with metal detectors. "No, and we're not likely to find one." He decided to ask the other question, although the more he thought about it, the more he realized he already knew the answer. "Do you think the shell might have fingerprints on it?"

"Possibly, but if so, they'd most likely be partials. If that's the case, they might not be enough to provide an identity. Sorry."

Adam felt the wind leave his sails. "So it's not worth running them?"

"Let me talk with a friend. Hang on to the casing, and I'll let you know."

They talked for a few more minutes before ending the conversation with Dave warning his brother to be careful and Adam promising to call again the next day. He folded the newspaper and dropped it on the table for the next customer. Then he rose and walked slowly out of the café, leaving his partially eaten sandwich behind.

Carrie knew what she had to do, but she

crammed a full-fledged argument with herself into the few seconds that followed Rob's request. Part of her longed for a quiet half hour to recharge her emotional and physical batteries before she returned to the clinic for the afternoon. On the other hand, Carrie recognized this encounter as a tailor-made opportunity to embark on the task she'd set for herself last night: find out more about Rob Cole.

She gestured to the empty chair. "Sure, Rob. Have a seat."

Rob unloaded his food and looked around for somewhere to put his empty tray. Finally he shrugged and shoved it under his chair.

What if Rob was the shooter? Would this encounter put her in danger? No, the tables around her were filled with potential witnesses. Oh, if this were a spy story, Rob might try to touch her with the poisoned tip of an umbrella, but it wasn't. This was real life. And the longer she hesitated, the less likely he was to open up to the questions she knew she had to ask.

She was surprised when Rob closed his eyes and bowed his head over his food. His lips moved, although he said nothing. The grace probably lasted less than fifteen seconds, but in that short period of time Carrie found herself rethinking her opinion of Rob Cole.

Carrie took the first bite of her sandwich, chewed, and swallowed while she pondered how to work her way into her questions. Before she could put down her fork, Rob gave her the opening she needed.

"I'm sort of glad this seat was available," he said around a bite of burger. "I've wanted the chance to get better acquainted. But I'm afraid I've put you off, the way I've gone about it."

This was certainly a different Rob from the brash, almost intrusive EMT she'd seen before. "You have to admit, Rob, that all our interactions have seemed more like flirting than getting to know each other."

"I know. Sometimes I come off that way, but I don't mean to. My therapist says it's a defense mechanism."

"Why don't we start fresh?" Carrie said. "Get to know each other."

"I understand you used to be married. What happened?"

Well, he certainly didn't lob her an easy question to start. Carrie felt the hairs on the back of her neck prickle. She'd kept most of this locked up for the better part of two years. Could she share it now? With a man who might be trying to kill her? Her gut tightened when she realized the only way to find out about him was to make the trade.

Carrie closed her eyes for a moment as the memories came flooding back. "John was a general surgeon, in the same group where I practice." She told him of the fatigue, the struggle to get her husband to see a doctor, the eventual diagnosis of Ebstein's anomaly.

Rob raised his eyebrows. "I don't think I've ever heard of that."

It had been hard for Carrie to share the story with Mr. McDonald. It was pure torture to tell it to Rob. "What John had — what was causing his spells of fatigue — were runs of tachycardia. The runs were so brief I never picked up on the rapid heart rate. Then they changed to ventricular tachycardia."

Rob gave a low whistle. "People can die from V tach. What happened?"

Carrie laid out the events in a flat voice: unsuccessful attempts to control the problem with medications, the failure of cardioversion with an electrical current, and eventually the transvenous radiofrequency ablation — the procedure to destroy the focus of heart muscle that threatened John's life.

Finally she bowed her head and squeezed

her eyes shut. She wouldn't cry in front of Rob. She wouldn't. In a moment she looked up and blinked hard before saying, "The catheter punctured one of John's coronary arteries. It's a one-in-a-million thing — but it happened to my husband. They rushed him to surgery to repair it, but it was too late. He died."

"I'm sorry." Rob's simple response seemed sincere.

"Thank you," she said. "I'm trying to move on." She forced a smile. "How about you? Where are you from? What brought you to Jameson?"

Rob took his time swallowing a bite of sandwich and washed it down with water. He sighed. "I grew up in a small suburb of Chicago. Small family — mother, dad, one sister. My dad died the day I was supposed to graduate high school. That turned my world upside down. Instead of college, I started work at a local hospital. Then I found out I could take a night class and become an EMT. It took awhile, but I got through it and even got certified as a paramedic."

"And I'm glad you did," Carrie said. "You're an excellent one."

"Thanks." Rob acknowledged the compliment with a small nod. "My mom remar-

ried, and things were going better. Then —"
He shook his head, emptied his water glass,
looked away. It took him a minute to regain
his composure. "Then my stepdad . . . he
did something awful."

Carrie looked at him expectantly. She
raised her eyebrows but didn't speak. *Let
him get it out. Don't force it.*

Rob pursed his lips and ducked his head.
He was silent for a moment. When he
looked up again, tears glistened in the
corners of his eyes. "He did something so
awful that I changed my name and left
town."

Carrie felt as though she'd just entered a
minefield, where careful steps were necessary, and one misstep would spell disaster.
Rob had given her the opening she needed,
but she had the feeling that if she asked the
wrong question, took him in the wrong
direction, he'd clam up and she might never
get the answers she needed. She needed to
come at it slowly. "How did you end up in
Jameson?"

Rob kept his head down. "There are some
online sites that list EMT jobs. This one
looked good. I always wanted to see Texas.
And Jameson was a long way from where
I'd been living."

She bought time with a swallow of iced

tea, then centered the glass on the napkin beneath it. "Would you like to tell me why you left?"

He shook his head. "This is silly. We started out trying to get to know each other, and now I'm playing true confessions. You don't want to hear this." He shoved back his chair as though ready to spring from it.

Carrie put one hand on his wrist. "Rob, you've said you wanted to get closer to me. Maybe I feel the same way too. But we've never had the time or been in the right situation." For a moment she felt a twinge of guilt for the way she was manipulating him. Then she realized that he might be the same man who'd been trying to kill her and Adam. *Forgive me, John. Forgive me, Adam. You know I don't mean this.* "I've told you about the biggest loss in my life. But what I haven't said is that now I'm trying to go forward, maybe even let someone into my world again. It could be you, but I can't know unless you tell me more about yourself."

Rob's expression was hard to read, and his tone of voice was neutral as well. "What about Adam Davidson?"

She worked to put a frown on her face. "I don't know what kind of trouble Adam's in, but it's almost gotten me killed three times now."

"So there's nothing between you?"

"Let's just say I'm keeping my options open."

Rob eased back into his chair. He placed his hands flat on the tabletop for support as he leaned toward her. "Maybe you're right. It's time to let you know about the real me."

He met Carrie's eyes, but she couldn't read his expression. "What my stepdad did —"

The strident tones of a pager pierced the lunchtime noise of the food court and stopped Rob in mid-sentence. He frowned, pulled the instrument from his belt, and glanced at the display. In one motion he shoved back from the table and stood. "Sorry. Guess lunch is over. Got an emergency call." He grabbed his tray, loaded it with his dirty dishes, and turned to go. Two steps away, he said over his shoulder, "Let's continue this sometime soon. I'll call you."

Carrie's stomach churned, and she struggled not to bring up the few bites of lunch she'd managed to choke down. As she watched him hurry away, Carrie had mixed emotions about her encounter with Rob Cole. She'd been close to finding out what she needed to know about him, but she wasn't sure she wanted to hear it.

TWENTY

At mid-afternoon Adam was at his desk, a cup of coffee at his elbow, poring over the draft of a new will for Elwood Stroud. Stroud was generally held to be the richest man in Jameson, and according to office gossip, his family could hardly wait for the old man to surrender to the ravages of old age. But Stroud was as tough as the trunk of an old elm tree. He'd already outlived many of his friends and most of his enemies, and he apparently intended to do the same with his three children if that was what it took to keep their hands off the money he'd accumulated in his eighty-eight years on the planet.

"Got a minute?" Janice Evans poked her head in the door. Adam had never seen her look anything but "put together," and today was no exception. "Sure. Just working on this draft of Mr. Stroud's will."

Janice covered her mouth, but not before

325

Adam saw the ghost of a smile flicker across her lips. "Let me guess. He wants to change two or three of his million-dollar bequests."

"Uh, yeah. That's about it."

"Mr. Stroud, God love him, has enough money to get by on. He'll never be eating dog food, but he doesn't have anything like the money he describes in his will."

"But I thought —"

"He used to be a multimillionaire. Made it in oil and got out before the bubble burst. But he gave away most of it. Anyone who approached him with a hard-luck story got some money. It's common knowledge that he's paid the college expenses of a couple dozen kids from the poorer part of town. And I know for sure that he's bailed out several men who were about to lose their businesses."

"So why do we keep rewriting his will for him?"

She stepped inside and closed the door. "Because this law firm was one of the businesses he bailed out." Evans lowered her voice. "Bruce told me about it when I joined the practice. He'd piled up some gambling debts — big ones — but couldn't stop. Finally, when the man who held his markers sent someone around to *reason* with him, Bruce knew he had to do something.

He went to Stroud, and they struck a deal. Stroud would pay off Bruce's debts in return for two things: Bruce would never gamble again, and our firm would handle Stroud's legal affairs without charge."

"I'm presuming Bruce kept his end of the bargain." Adam looked at the thick document on his desk. "So this is . . ."

"Yep. And I have to agree with Mr. Stroud that his kids don't deserve a nickel, considering how much of his money they've already blown through. Every one of the wills does two things: makes a nice bequest to his church and arranges for payment of his final expenses. Beyond that, though, despite what the wills say, there's not a lot of money to spread around." She gestured toward a chair. "Do you mind?"

"Of course. This can wait for a while." Adam shoved the paper aside. "What's up?"

"I think you're owed an explanation for what you walked into when you returned from your visit with your brother."

"I'll have to admit I was surprised to find that Mary had my job."

Evans folded her hands in her lap and looked down at them. "I didn't think what Bruce did was right, but . . . well, he is the senior partner, and he sort of insisted." She raised her head and looked him in the eye.

"He was going to let you go, but I did a little foot-stomping of my own. That's why you're still here."

"I appreciate your going to bat for me," Adam said.

"I don't think there's any question that you'll be made permanent in a couple of weeks. But I'm sorry you had to go through this."

She rose and took a step toward the door. "Don't be too harsh on Bruce. I'm sure you're familiar with the legal term 'undue influence.' That's what's at work in his situation right now. You just happen to be the one getting the bad deal as a result of it."

After Evans left, Adam sat staring into space. He hit a key on his computer and the screen saver disappeared. He tapped out a familiar Web address, and in a few seconds the screen lit up with the online site that had largely replaced the familiar bound volume known as Martindale-Hubbell. It was a comprehensive source of information about lawyers in the United States and around the world, and it could answer the question that had formed in Adam's mind.

He clicked on the search box and entered "Bruce Hartley." When the requested page popped up, he scanned it and realized that

328

his list of suspects wasn't narrowing. It was widening.

Adam needed to call Dave and check on his recovery. It was about time to leave anyway, so he'd do it from his car. He slipped into his suit coat and headed out the door, telling Brittany he'd see her in the morning.

Behind dark glasses Adam's eyes were never still as he walked briskly to his vehicle. He'd purchased a Kevlar vest but decided it was impractical for daily wear. Still, he made sure he varied his routine — the times he came to work and left, the place he parked his car, even the restaurants and cafés where he ate. And, above all, he increased his watchfulness.

After the usual aimless driving, he pulled into a strip shopping center, keeping the engine running to allow the car's air conditioner to function. In a moment he was talking with his brother. "How's the recuperation?"

"Kind of at a fork in the road," Dave said. "The surgeon says I'm stable from my blood loss, but it's time to decide what to do about my shoulder. It works well enough, but if I want full function, the best chance is another operation. I didn't understand it all, but apparently the bullet tore things up, sort of like what a baseball pitcher does to his rotator cuff."

"Is that what has to be done?"

"No, I have choices. If I have the surgery, then go through physical therapy, I stand a really good chance of coming out with a normally functioning shoulder in a few months." Dave paused and Adam heard the sound of swallowing. "Sorry. Don't talk much now, and my throat gets dry when I do. Anyway, my other option is to skip the surgery and just do the rehab. Eventually I'd have adequate function in that arm — but I'd probably never be fit for police work again."

"Sounds like you only have one viable choice," Adam said.

Dave sighed. "Yeah, I guess."

"Shall I come down there?"

"No, he's going to discharge me later today," Dave said. "When I asked the doc for a recommendation, he suggested a Dr. Burkhead in Dallas. Supposed to be a cracker-jack surgeon for this kind of stuff. And I'll be a half-hour's drive from you."

"Great. So I can be there for the operation and help you afterward."

"No, I still think it's best for you to keep your distance."

Adam couldn't understand. Dave, as he'd

been able to do all their lives, seemed able to read Adam's mind.

"Your stalker may know who you really are, but he doesn't know about me. Let's keep it that way. I can be your ace in the hole."

Adam figured that a marshall with his right arm in a sling wasn't much of a secret weapon, but he decided not to argue. "After you leave the hospital, would you like to stay here in Jameson with me?"

"Not a good idea. I have a friend in Dallas. I plan to stay with him while I wait to see the surgeon."

Adam wondered what else he'd missed in his brother's life by being on the run these past couple of years. But there was no time for guilty reflection. He was about to ask if Dave had checked on getting fingerprints off the rifle shell when his brother said, "The nurse is here to check my vital signs. Guess I'd better sign off. Be careful . . . Adam."

As he pulled away, Adam wished he could go home to a normal family instead of constantly looking over his shoulder, expecting a bullet to strike him at any moment. Maybe someday. Maybe someday soon.

Carrie's afternoon was busier than her

morning, but she was grateful in a way. Dealing with the patients kept her from thinking about her lunch with Rob Cole. The fragment of his story that he'd shared certainly fit with what Adam told her about Charlie DeLuca's second family and the son who changed his name and disappeared. But if that were the case, would Rob have been willing to open up to her so easily?

Had all his flirting simply been an attempt to get closer to her in order to learn more about Adam? Was Rob toying with her now? Could he have triggered his own pager to end their time together, tired of teasing her, with no intention of revealing his real identity? While they were talking, she'd thought she was close to unlocking the identity of Adam's shooter. But now she wasn't sure about that — or much of anything else about the case.

Carrie was deep in thought as she moved to the next exam room, when she heard, "Whoa. Better look up every once in a while."

She did just that and saw Phil Rushton dead ahead. He waved the papers in his hand and said, "Glad we didn't collide. That hard head of yours might give me a concussion."

Carrie wasn't sure whether Phil was joking or referring to her last meeting with him. "I need to talk with you when you've finished with patients. Call my cell phone." And he was off again.

Carrie tapped on the door of the exam room and stepped inside. She tucked Phil's request into a corner of her mind and concentrated on the patient sitting on the edge of the examination table. From the frown on his face it was fairly obvious that the man didn't want to be there. But the presence of his wife gave Carrie her best clue of the dynamics of the situation.

"Mr. Hoover, what sort of problems are you having?"

"I'm not having a problem," Hoover said, almost before Carrie could finish. "But she . . ." A nod toward his wife, who stood beside him with arms folded. "She's afraid I have heart trouble. Just because of this little pain I get sometimes." As if to demonstrate, Hoover held his clenched fist over his mid-chest.

The check-in sheet Lila had handed her showed Hoover's age as fifty-eight, his height as five feet six inches, his weight two hundred ten pounds. Even without the charted blood pressure of one hundred eighty over one hundred, the man's florid complexion alerted her to the likelihood of hypertension.

Carrie asked a series of questions, which were sometimes answered by Hoover, sometimes by his wife. His favorite exercise seemed to be moving between the dinner table and the TV set. Walking a block or less brought on crushing chest pain that sometimes radiated down his left arm and was relieved slowly by rest.

The rest of the exam, and the EKG that followed, confirmed Carrie's suspicion. Hoover had significant coronary artery disease. His tracing suggested that he'd already had one mild myocardial infarction, a "heart attack" that damaged a small amount of the muscle in that organ. It took the combined efforts of Hoover's wife and Carrie to convince him that the best course was immediate hospitalization. "We'll need to do an angiogram — that's a test where they inject dye into the blood vessels in your heart. That lets us see how much blockage there is. Sometimes a stent can be inserted via the plastic tube that puts the dye into your heart, but sometimes surgery is necessary. We have excellent doctors who do this all the time."

"But my business —"

His wife jumped in at this point. "Arliss, someone else is going to run your business, whether you're in the hospital for a few days or you die and leave it behind. Let's go for the few days' option."

Carrie wrote a note and orders, set up the emergency angiogram, and alerted Phil Rushton's nurse that he might have to do a coronary bypass procedure. She accompanied Hoover to the radiology suite and stood by as he underwent coronary angiography. When she and the interventional radiologist agreed that stent insertion wouldn't be adequate, Carrie pulled out her cell phone to contact Phil Rushton.

Before she could complete the call, Phil walked in. "I was about to call you," Carrie said. "This one is going to require your talents." She summarized the case in a few words. Phil studied the angiogram and nodded.

"I'll talk with them," he said. "Carrie, I presume you have no objection to my taking over at this point?"

Well, at least he's asking. "Just so long as you let me direct his care after you discharge him. He needs weight reduction, control of his blood pressure, a —"

"Sure," Phil said. "I wanted to talk with you, but I guess we can do it tomorrow. Maybe after work, over dinner." And he strode away.

As she watched the surgeon disappear around the corner, Carrie wondered if, despite Phil's assurances, Thad Avery would end up caring for this patient after surgery. She brushed the thought aside. She'd done her best. Mr. Hoover would get good medical care. That was what mattered.

As for the rest of it, she had mixed emotions. She was glad not to have to endure a meeting with Phil, especially if he was going to quiz her about Adam. On the other hand, she was curious to know what he might want. Then she flashed on the information she'd garnered from his certificates — Phil had a connection with Chicago. It wasn't outside the realm of possibility that he had some connection to Charlie DeLuca. Though what kind of connection could it be?

Adam drove carefully, anxious to get home after a trying day but wary that he might be followed. He wasn't sure why he was taking precautions. After all, his stalker knew where he lived — he'd shot at him just the night before — but sometimes logic took a backseat to plain old-fashioned fear. So Adam went through his usual routine: double back, turn without signaling, drive with one eye on the rearview mirror.

He'd spent some time today wondering about whether he should go back to his apartment. Adam had even scanned the yellow pages in search of a motel, but midway through his search he decided that wherever he was made no difference. The stalker would eventually find him. Meanwhile, he could at least enjoy the few comforts left him, including sleeping in his own bed. But his deliberations served to redouble Adam's resolve to unmask the shooter and end this nightmare. He just didn't have the right scheme to do so . . . not yet.

He pulled into the parking lot behind his apartment complex, remembered that he'd parked at the far right end yesterday, so he took a space toward the front and center. He had his hand on his seat belt release when he heard the ring of a cell phone. He pulled his phone from his coat pocket and consulted the display — blank. Then Adam realized what he was hearing wasn't the unique ring he'd purchased for his cell phone, but rather the generic tone of his throwaway phone.

He reached over to the seat beside him, opened his brief case, and pulled out the instrument. The display showed "blocked number." Who was calling? Perhaps it represented a telephone solicitor, robo-

337

dialing numbers. Then again, it might be the stalker, going for a phone call instead of a text this time. *Forget it. Answer it and find out. He can't shoot you through the phone.*

"Hello?"

"Keith? This is Corky."

It took Adam a moment to react to his "old" name. He looked around the deserted parking lot and saw nothing suspicious. Dusk had not fully settled. Maybe he could safely sit here a moment and talk. "Have you found out any more about Charlie De-Luca's family?"

A squeal of tires overrode Corky's voice. ". . . that idiot over there."

"What's happening? Are you driving?"

"Yeah. I'm on the freeway, on my way home, where my wife is waiting impatiently. Usually I-45 in Houston is the world's longest parking lot. Today, for some reason, most of us are going the posted speed, and some are exceeding that. Those are the ones who've turned into Mario Andretti wannabes." A horn honked, and Adam suspected it was Corky's.

"Do you want to call me back?"

"Nah. This is what I do while I'm in the car. It's my version of multitasking." Another horn. Some muttered curses from Corky. "Idiots! All the drivers today are

338

idiots." He heard Corky take a deep breath. "Anyway, there's someone else who might be trying to avenge Charlie DeLuca. And it's someone you wouldn't suspect. It's —"

Adam suspected the sounds he heard next would keep him awake that night and several more: a long blast from two different car horns, a squeal of brakes, followed by a loud crash, then a deadly silence.

"Corky! Corky!" Adam almost screamed into the phone. But there was no answer.

Twenty-One

As Adam exited his car, he hit mute on his cell phone but kept the connection open. Now he sat in his apartment with the door double locked, the security chain in place. The blinds were closed. The drapes were drawn. He hadn't turned on the lights — he still wasn't sure why, but somehow he felt more secure in the gloom. He listened to the sounds issuing from his phone, imagining the carnage at the scene.

At first all he heard were a few muffled thuds. Then voices, all raised, some shouting frantically, added themselves to the mix. Finally sirens provided a wailing counterpoint to the cacophony. He heard the squeal of tortured metal, and someone said, "Let's get him out of there before the gas tank blows." A different voice chimed in, "No, we shouldn't move him. The ambulance is pulling up right now."

Adam closed his eyes and tried to imagine

the scene as the next few moments unfolded. EMTs gently easing his friend from the car. A policeman, or maybe a sheriff's deputy, picking up the phone — maybe removing it from Corky's hand — and consulting the display.

Adam opened his eyes as a deep baritone sounded in his ear. "Is someone still on the line?"

Should he answer? This was his throwaway cell phone. There was no way to identify him through it. And maybe he could add vital information. Was Corky on any medications? Did he have any drug allergies? Then it hit Adam — he didn't know any of those things. He hadn't seen his friend in almost two years. And he'd only called Corky when he needed a favor. Adam cleared his throat. "Yes?"

"Is anyone there?"

"Yes, I'm here."

"Is anyone there?" the voice repeated.

Adam finally realized that he'd muted the phone. He thumbed the button again, and said, "I'm here."

"Who is this?"

"I'm a friend of Corky's — of Mr. Cortland's. I'm in —" Adam hesitated. Caution returned. "I'm not there in Houston. We were talking on the cell phone, and he was complaining about some of the drivers on the freeway. Then I heard a crash. What happened?"

The reply made Adam's blood run cold. "A wrong-way driver hit your friend head-on. A helicopter's on its way to fly him to the nearest trauma center."

Perhaps it was his imagination, perhaps it was real, but Adam thought he heard the *whup-whup* of helicopter blades getting closer. "How is he?"

"That's for the medics to decide, but he looks pretty bad to me."

"Which hospital?"

"Hermann — that's Texas Medical Center. Now who is this? I need to get some information from you."

Adam pushed the button to end the call. There was nothing more he could say to help Corky. He doubted that the police would go so far as to trace the call, but if they did, it would dead end at this cell phone. He'd get rid of it later tonight. He wondered what new information his friend had come up with about DeLuca. Whatever it was, Adam might never know.

Adam's heart cramped as he realized he was thinking of the information Corky had for him as much as about his friend's life. He sank to his knees and spoke in a voice almost too faint to hear, "God, I pray for Corky. I know You can save him. Please do it. Not for me — for him, his family, his loved ones. Please."

Carrie was about to step into the shower, eager for the hot water to ease soreness in muscles tight for too long, when the ring of the phone stopped her. Her first impulse was to ignore it, but that passed quickly. She was a doctor, and she could never ignore the ringing of a phone or the beeping of a pager. She wrapped herself in a robe and answered, "Dr. Markham."

"Carrie, it's me . . . Julie."

Guilt washed over Carrie. She'd let her promise to keep Julie updated slip her mind. The carousel on which she found herself spun faster and faster, and Carrie had been hanging on for dear life. She owed Julie the courtesy of a call, and instead, her friend had to call her.

Carrie moved to her bed and stretched out. "I'm so sorry I didn't call. It's been —"

"No need to explain," Julie said. "But I've been worried about you since we last talked. What's going on? Are you any closer to knowing who the shooter is?"

"The list keeps getting longer," Carrie

said. *And Adam wanted to put you on that list, but I wouldn't let him.* "Someone must've let information slip, but we have no idea who." She told her best friend about what she and Adam had found, ending with Rob Cole's revelation to her just a few hours ago. "So what do I do now?"

"You could direct something at this list of suspects that would make the real shooter declare himself. That is, if you're prepared for a face off."

"That's what Adam wants," Carrie said. "But how do we do that?"

They kicked around ideas. Then Carrie glanced at the clock on her bedside table. "I need to cut this short. Adam's coming by soon, and I really need to clean up."

"No problem," Julie said. "Give me one more minute before you hang up."

"I know," Carrie said. "We need to pray."

"Want me to start?"

"No, I've got this one." Carrie bowed her head, picturing her friend, hundreds of miles away, doing the same.

As she put down the phone and swung her feet off the bed, Carrie flipped on the TV in her bedroom just to have some noise in the house. She looked up as an ad flashed across the screen: "Your kids will love it," the announcer said. Most of the time Carrie ignored such commercials, but this particular one started her thinking. A germ of an idea sprang up, one that might work. Of course, the plan was dangerous. Then again, doing nothing was proving dangerous as well.

Adam stuck to the pre-midnight shadows as he worked his way from his parked car along the alleys to the fence behind Carrie's house. He scanned every driveway, kept his eyes moving, trying to stay concealed while giving the appearance of a man innocently walking to a neighbor's house. The last thing he needed was for someone to call the police.

Since the shooter had already linked Adam with Carrie, maybe these precautions were worthless. Nevertheless, Adam didn't want to lead his would-be assassin directly to her house — not tonight, not any night.

He paused at the fence and looked around to make sure no one was watching, then grabbed the top and pulled himself up. Adam managed to roll over the fence and land in Carrie's backyard without sustaining more injuries than just wounded pride.

He rapped out the code, Carrie opened her kitchen door, and Adam slid through and double locked it.

"This is getting ridiculous," she muttered.

"Not as ridiculous as being killed by a sniper's bullet," Adam said. "And you may recall that almost happened to both of us."

She pointed. "Sit down. I have a fresh pot of coffee brewing."

Once they were at the table sipping from their respective cups, Adam said, "Today I got another call from this law school classmate of mine, Corky."

"The man who was going to hack into sites and get information for you?"

"I told you, he assured me it was just a matter of taking some shortcuts," Adam said. "Anyway, he called me back this afternoon to give me a report." In his mind, he heard again the crash, the sirens, the dire words of the man who'd picked up Corky's cell phone. Adam shook his head as though to dislodge the thoughts. "Unfortunately my friend was in a head-on crash before he could tell me what he'd found."

Carrie frowned and shook her head. "That's terrible," she said. "How is he?"

"I've got to call the hospital later tonight to see. But the man I talked with thought Corky was critical when they air-lifted him to a trauma center."

There was a long silence as each sipped coffee, lost in their own thoughts. Then Carrie said, "So what else happened today?"

"Well . . . Mary, the new paralegal, keeps pushing me to have lunch or dinner with her. I've put her off for another few days, but eventually that's going to happen. I don't know what she's up to, but I don't think her aim is to get better acquainted with a coworker."

"You don't think it's possible she's genuinely interested in you?"

"That's flattering, but no. Besides, she's already got her hooks into Bruce Hartley," Adam said. "I suppose I'm being paranoid, but I get a sense that she's trying to uncover my identity."

"Hmm. I don't know which is worse — her trying to make a play for you or her trying to find out who you really are." Carried studied him for a moment. "I guess we can worry about that when it happens."

"What about your day?" Adam asked.

"Pretty interesting. I had lunch with Rob Cole." She went on to tell Adam Rob's story. "I don't know whether he was about to reveal his real name or if he was just toying with me. But I certainly think he's a prime suspect."

"We seem to keep adding names to that list," Adam said. "Anyone else?"

"Actually, yes, but . . . I don't know . . . ,"

Carrie said.

"What?"

"Well, I was in Phil Rushton's office today and noticed the diplomas on his wall."

Adam's eyebrows went up. "And?"

"All his training was in Chicago."

"That doesn't necessarily tie him to Charlie DeLuca, but it's certainly a potential link," Adam said.

"Not only that, but Phil's been acting sort of funny toward me lately." She paused. "He even asked about you, wanted to know if I knew your background." She shook her head. "I think we have to consider him a suspect."

"I suppose," Adam said. "And I have another name for our list. Janet Evans stopped by my office today — during the course of our conversation she mentioned some gambling debts of Bruce Hartley's that one of our clients paid off. Apparently it saved the firm."

"Really?" Carrie seemed shocked. "What's the significance of that?"

"One of the things Charlie DeLuca was involved in was loan sharking," Adam said. "Anyway, I looked up Bruce in Martindale-Hubbell."

"In what?"

"It's the list of all the attorneys in the

United States. When I saw that he went to law school in Wisconsin, I was about to log off. Then I decided to see where he grew up."

"Chicago?"

"Close. Elmwood Park, which is a suburb of Chicago, with one of the largest Italian populations in the area."

"So he could have had contact with the DeLuca family . . . ?"

"Right," Adam said. "So we have Rob Cole, Phil Rushton, and Bruce Hartley, plus no telling how many others as suspects. Now how do I find out which one is shooting at us? And why."

"Are you really determined to confront the shooter?" Carrie asked.

Adam thought about it for a moment. He clenched his jaw so tight it ached, relaxing it only long enough to say, "If that's what it takes."

Carrie took his hand and squeezed it. "I don't like it, but if there's no better option, I have a plan that might help us identify the person stalking you."

Carrie was at her desk the next morning, sipping on a cup of lukewarm coffee and flipping through her phone messages, when Lila popped her head in the door.

"Can you return Tim Gallagher's call as soon as possible? He phoned early this morning and said it was important that he reach you."

That puzzled Carrie. She had encountered Gallagher a time or two at parties but was pretty sure he wasn't a patient. If he had a medical emergency, he probably would have gone to an ER or urgent care center, not call her office. Maybe this was a personal call. He'd seemed like a nice enough guy — middle-aged, good-looking, if you liked the jock type. But wasn't he married? Besides that, if he was calling to ask her on a date, he wouldn't do it this early in the morning, would he? On the other hand . . . *Oh, stop it. Just phone the man.*

Carrie found the proper slip and dialed the number. Gallagher answered before the first ring was complete. "Coach Gallagher."

Coach? She had a vague memory that he was a teacher, and now that she thought about it, he sort of looked like a coach. "This is Dr. Markham. You said it was urgent that I call you back. Do you have a medical problem?"

"I don't think so, but I'm trying to avoid one." A bell sounded in the background — not a gentle tinkle, but a strident sound followed by a crescendo of voices mixed with the shuffling and slamming of metal doors. "Excuse me. School's starting, and I have an eight o'clock class. Can I call you back at nine?"

Carrie hated setting a time to take a call. She much preferred to do the phoning on her own schedule. Besides, she might not be able to turn loose at nine o'clock. But now Gallagher had piqued her curiosity. "Sure. Tell whoever answers that I'm expecting your call. If I can't get free, we'll have to play phone tag, I guess."

"Thanks. I appreciate it." And he was gone.

Carrie turned to her nurse, who was still in the doorway. "Lila, do you have any idea why Coach Gallagher would need to talk to me?"

"None at all," Lila said. "But when he calls back, don't forget to tell me. I'm dying to know."

It was almost nine fifteen before Lila stuck her head in the exam room door. "Can you take that call you were expecting?"

As it turned out, Carrie had just told her patient she'd order some lab work, then see him back in a few days to evaluate how the new medication was working. Lila was dispatched with the patient to schedule the tests while Carrie went into the office and punched the blinking light on her phone. "This is Dr. Markham."

"Tim Gallagher again. Sorry I had to call back like this. I know you're busy."

"No problem. What can I do for you?"

"Do you like baseball?"

The question came out of the blue and left Carrie wondering what was behind it. Was the coach asking for a date? Did he have some tickets he wanted to give away? "Uh, actually, I do. Why?"

"I'm the varsity baseball coach at Jameson High School. We have a game at four this afternoon, and the doctor who usually attends is sick. We don't anticipate any problems — worst we've ever had was a broken wrist when one of my players disregarded my instructions and slid home headfirst — but I kind of like having a doctor in attendance." He paused, apparently decided she wasn't going to respond, so he continued, "Would you consider coming to the game today? Four o'clock. The field next to the high school. I'd really appreciate it. And I can promise you'll see a good game — we're playing last year's district champs."

The invitation brought welcome memories to Carrie. At her high school, girls hadn't been allowed to play "hardball," but they had a killer softball team. She'd pitched and played shortstop, and they'd challenged for the state championship. If she couldn't be on the diamond, she could at least be near it. Why not?

"Let me check my schedule to see if I can get away early," Carrie said.

"Fine. This number's my cell. Send me a text when you know. And thanks."

Fifteen minutes later Carrie sent Gallagher a message. "See you this afternoon at the game." For the rest of the day she found herself humming "Take Me Out to the Ballgame."

Last night Adam had taken the SIM card from his throwaway phone and destroyed it using Carrie's hedge shears. The phone itself went into a dumpster. Today he spent his lunch hour at Radio Shack, purchasing another prepaid cell phone for the project he had in mind. He paid cash, and when the clerk asked for a name, he said Tony Kubek. If this didn't end soon, he'd run out of names of past Yankee players.

Adam would target the three men he and Carrie decided were the most likely candidates to be the shooter: Rob Cole, Bruce Hartley, and Phil Rushton. It had taken some digging, but now he had the phone numbers he needed to carry out the scheme.

Carrie's idea was an attempt to smoke out the shooter. At first what she proposed seemed unnecessarily complex to Adam. Why not make the phone calls from his own phone, using his own name? She reminded him that even if one of these men was guilty, two were not; what would they think if they received such a message from him? No, this way they hoped only the guilty person would be able to decipher the words. Then, if he responded, Adam would be ready for him.

Of course, the scheme carried risk, but it was a risk Adam was anxious to take. She begged him to call his brother for backup, but he reminded her that Dave's right arm was in a sling, and he was just out of the hospital. No, Adam would do this by himself. He had to.

The first step in his scheme demanded some privacy. Both lawyers left the office a bit early, Bruce accompanied by Mary Delkus, so Adam and Brittany were left to close up. "You go ahead," he told her. "I've got a few odds and ends yet to do. I'll lock up." Brittany usually had a date, and apparently today was no exception. She thanked him, and in a moment he heard the door slam.

Adam eased the new cell phone from its

charging cradle, checked that the battery and signal levels were good, and thought about the message he was about to deliver. He'd found that both Rushton and Hartley were hardly ever home before eight in the evening. Cole, like most of his generation, had no landline, and he often ignored his cell phone while he was on duty, as he was tonight. Adam's plan was to deliver his message to each man's voice mail from an untraceable phone. Then he would see who responded.

He opened his desk drawer and removed a sack that bore the logo of Toys "R" Us. Adam withdrew a black device that looked like one of the respirator masks worn by painters. He held it close to his mouth and spoke into it, feeling quite foolish. As though the words came from Darth Vader, complete with raspy breathing, he heard himself say, "Testing, testing." Adam couldn't resist adding, "Luke, I am your father." Despite the gravity of what he was about to do, that brought a grin to his face.

Well, here goes. He dialed the first number. If, by chance, they answered, he'd just hang up. But after five rings he got the recorded message. At the beep he — or rather, Darth Vader — said, "I'm tired of this. Let's put an end to it. Meet me tonight at midnight, Ridgewood Cemetery, at the stone angel on the McElroy plot." When he pushed the button to end the call, he was sweating. One down, two to go.

After he ended the last call, Adam leaned back in his chair. It was done. There was no turning back. *God, maybe this is crazy. Maybe it's the only way. In either case, I'm going to need Your help. Please.*

TWENTY-TWO

Carrie leaned against the wire fence that separated the playing field from the bleachers and took in the spectacle before her. Dark green grass, so closely mowed it looked like carpet, contrasted with the rusty tan of the infield dirt. Lines chalked with the precision of a stretched string demarcated the playing field. That was where the action took place — "between the lines."

The home team had the first-base dugout, but right now the bench was empty. Jameson players in white uniforms with the word "Eagles" in blue on the front and numbers on the back were in right field, throwing baseballs, stretching, showing the exuberance typical of high school athletes. A middle-aged man whose uniform bore the number *37* stood near the dug-out, hands in his hip pockets.

Carrie called to him. "Coach?"

He turned and flashed a smile. "Dr.

Markham. Thanks so much for coming."

"My pleasure." She gestured to the bleachers behind the dugout. "I'll be up here if you need me."

"Hope we don't, but I appreciate having you around."

The game started, and Carrie let the experience carry her back to her high school days. She'd had a major crush on the baseball team's star, the shortstop. She could still see him in her mind's eye: tall, muscular, with wavy blond hair and sparkling eyes. He'd had his choice of girlfriends, so she thought her heart would jump out of her chest when he asked her out. The evening ended quickly, though, when she discovered his main objective was to score — and not by crossing home plate.

Despite Carrie's love of the game, life — in the form of medical school and all that came afterward — intervened. This was the first baseball game she'd seen in at least ten years. She made a promise to herself that it wouldn't be another decade before she saw another.

Carrie snapped out of her reverie and looked at the scoreboard. It was already the top of the second inning. Carrie did a double take as the visiting Wildcat batter stepped to the plate. High school students certainly seemed larger than they were in her day — at least, this one did. The batter was over six feet tall and probably weighed more than two hundred pounds. He looked more like a football player than a first baseman. She wondered if the Eagle pitcher felt the way David felt when he first saw Goliath.

The first pitch was a slow curve that broke tantalizingly just off the plate. The batter took it for ball one. The second pitch was also outside. Two balls, no strikes. Carrie leaned forward in her seat, her clenched fists resting on her thighs. *Walk him. Don't throw him anything he can hit. Be careful.*

The pitcher peered in to the catcher for the sign, shook off a couple, then wound up and delivered a fastball. Undoubtedly he meant for it to be on the outside corner, but instead it headed, belt-high, for the center of home plate. The batter took a short stride with his front foot and swung so hard Carrie thought she felt the breeze.

A loud *ping* from the aluminum bat resonated throughout the park. The ball might have come out of the pitcher's hand at eighty miles per hour, but the line drive going back at him was probably going a hundred. The ball hit the pitcher squarely in the chest, and he dropped like a felled tree.

The baseball spun to rest in the red clay surrounding the pitcher's mound. The batter, now standing on first base, threw up his hands in dismay. The umpire spread his arms and yelled, "Time." And in the stands a stunned silence gave way to a rising murmur.

Carrie was on her feet in an instant. She sprinted toward the gate to the field while yelling at Coach Gallagher, "Get the AED. Have someone call 911."

His teammates stood in a wide semicircle around the fallen player. The umpire and opposing coaches approached but stayed at a respectful distance. Carrie reached the boy, who lay on his side, his legs drawn under him. She rolled him onto his back, ripped open his jersey, pushed his T-shirt upward, and put her ear to his bare chest. No heart sounds. *Commotio cordis:* a blow to the chest, usually in a younger person, hitting at exactly the right time of the cardiac cycle to stop the heart from beating. She had less than three minutes to get it started if the boy was going to live.

Coach Gallagher knelt by her side, holding what looked like a black backpack. "Ready for this?"

"Open it, then make sure everyone stands back."

Carrie pulled a yellow-and-black plastic case from the pack, happy that all athletic events now were required to have one of these at hand. Every model was different, but the principle remained the same: deliver a jolt of electricity to jumpstart the heart.

She made sure the AED — the automatic external defibrillator — was powered. Then Carrie used the tail of the pitcher's tee shirt to dry sweat from his chest. Quickly, she applied the pads, one on the upper right chest, the other the lower left. Did this one have an *analyze* button? Yes. She pushed it and got the expected result. Cardiac arrest.

"Everyone, stand clear. Don't touch him until I say it's safe." She said a silent prayer and hit the button to deliver a shock. No response. She waited for the machine to recharge, then shocked the boy again. Still no heartbeat.

The clock was ticking. How much time did she have left? Maybe a minute, certainly no more. While the machine recharged again, Carrie debated starting external chest compressions. The books said to wait two minutes between shocks. She couldn't wait. If this one didn't do it, she'd carry out external CPR until the emergency medical technicians arrived. After a few more seconds, she said, "Stand clear. Here we go again."

Another prayer. Another shock. This time there was a heartbeat — faint at first, then growing stronger with every beat. The boy took a shallow breath. Then another. Carrie closed her eyes and breathed a prayer. *Thank You, God.*

She checked the heart rhythm, and it appeared normal. A siren in the background signaled the approach of the medics. In the ambulance she could hook him up to an EKG, start an IV to establish a lifeline for delivery of needed drugs. "I'll ride with him to the ER," she told the coach. "Will you notify his parents?"

"Sure," mumbled Coach Gallagher. He heaved the biggest sigh in the world. "I've never seen that happen. Never even heard of it. But I'm sure glad you were in the stands. Thanks."

Carrie nodded once. "No problem," she said. "I guess God wanted me here."

Adam sat in the office for a few minutes after sending his messages, alternately worrying and praying. Finally he stowed the voice changer in his brief case and eased out the door, locking it behind him. By now it was almost dark and every shadow he passed on the way to his car seemed to be the hiding place for someone waiting to kill him.

When he was finally in his car, he didn't bother doing his usual maneuvering to lose a tail. *If you want me, come and get me.* At home he paced the floor, thinking and rethinking his plan. Could he have improved on it? Maybe. Did it really matter if he'd tweaked it? Probably not.

He dressed in the same clothes he'd worn for his last stealthy trip to Carrie's: green sweatshirt, black jeans, dark athletic shoes. He considered smearing his face with camouflage paint but discarded the idea. He'd feel ridiculous.

Adam thought about calling his brother, but what good would it do? Dave would tell him he was crazy, then offer to drive to Jameson and serve as backup for Adam. And his brother was in no shape to face a gunman. Matter of fact, Adam was probably in no shape, but things had been set in motion, and there was no way to stop them now.

Thoughts of Dave made Adam remember something he needed to do before keeping his rendezvous. He should give Carrie his brother's cell phone number. If tonight's showdown ended badly, Dave would know what to do. Of course, there was no way Adam was going to mention the worst-case scenario to Carrie. He'd just give her the number.

He pulled out his Ruger, ejected the magazine, checked the load. Would he need an extra magazine, more bullets? No, if ten rounds didn't do it, he'd be dead. Adam pushed the thought aside. He slid the pistol into his ankle holster, pulled it out, then repeated the process until he was sure he could draw the gun easily when he needed it.

Adam opened his closet and found the Kevlar vest he'd purchased at the same time he bought the holster. It had resided in his closet to this point, but now was the time to wear it. He'd leave it on the bed until he left though.

Finally he pulled out his cell phone — the regular one — and made one last call. "Carrie, I'm about to leave for the cemetery."

Her voice betrayed her anxiety. "Are you sure you want to do this?"

"I don't *want* to do it. I just don't see any other options."

"Will you call me when it's over? Even if it's late?"

"Sure."

Adam gave her Dave's number. "If any-thing bad happens . . ."

"Don't say things like that," Carrie said.

They talked for a few more minutes before Carrie said, "Adam, I love you."

"And I love you, Carrie. When this is all over, I hope you're ready to talk about our life together."

"We can talk now," she said.

"No, I need to get going. I'll call you when it's over."

"Adam?"

"Yes?"

"Please be careful. I don't want to lose you."

"I don't want to lose you either," he said.

They exchanged more "I love you's" before ending the conversation.

Then Adam donned the vest, checked his gun again, and did a final run-through of his mental checklist. Time to go. It was only ten thirty, but he wanted to be in place early.

Adam chose Ridgewood Cemetery as a meeting site for a number of reasons. It was older and full of tall monuments and a few mausoleums, so he could hide easily. Like most cemeteries there was a fence around it, but the gates were never locked. And it was isolated enough that a gunshot wouldn't attract curious neighbors. Of course that gunshot could be from his gun or that of his stalker, but he was willing to take the chance. Anything to bring this nightmare to a close.

Adam had done some scouting, so he knew where he was going. He'd found an open barn for the storage of equipment and material, and that was where he concealed his Subaru, between a tractor with a bucket for digging on the front end and another that pulled a small mower. It took him ten minutes to work his way through the cemetery to the spot he'd picked for his observation post. He was just settling in when he heard a single, faint noise off to his left. It was more than an hour before the appointed time, but Adam expected the shooter to come early. He eased his pistol from its holster and began a slow belly crawl toward the noise.

A form materialized from the shadow of a mausoleum. Adam stayed in his prone position, raised himself on his elbows, and braced his gun in a firing position with both hands. He flicked off the safety and took up the slack on the trigger. Working to keep his voice steady and authoritative, he said, "That's far enough. Put your hands up. If I see a gun, I'll shoot."

"Adam?"

Adam exhaled deeply, and he felt his heart start beating again. He eased his pressure on the trigger. "Carrie? What are you doing here?"

"I couldn't let you do this by yourself. So I came to help."

Adam dropped his voice to a whisper. "Get over here, and get down. We don't want to alert the shooter."

In a moment they were crouched behind the mausoleum Adam had chosen as his hiding place, peering around the low granite building toward the marble angel marking the McElroy plot. Adam thought about scolding Carrie for coming, but in truth, he was glad to see her. He put his mouth next to her ear and whispered, "Did you bring a weapon?"

She reached into the side pocket of her black cargo pants, pulled out a small canister, and held it up. "Mace," she whispered.

The whine of a transmission alerted them to the approach of a vehicle. Bouncing headlights made the shadows dance as a light-colored SUV pulled up and stopped on the road near the McElroy plot. The driver killed the lights and lowered the window. He sat there for what Adam figured was five minutes, then the window buzzed up, the engine started, headlights flared, and the vehicle drove off.

"Could you see inside the SUV?" Adam asked.

"No," Carrie said. "But I recognized the license plate as it drove away."

"What was it?"

"It was a personalized Texas plate: HRT SRGN. It belongs to Phil Rushton."

Twenty-Three

Carrie figured her adrenaline level was so high she'd be awake the rest of the night. Instead, she was dozing soundly when she felt Adam shaking her shoulder.

"Carrie, it's one a.m.," he whispered. "I don't think anyone else is coming. Let's go home."

She smothered a yawn. "Okay. Can I get a ride with you?"

"Where's your car?"

"I didn't want to leave it here, so I took a taxi."

"A taxi to the cemetery this late at night? Didn't the driver think you were crazy?"

She shrugged, although she knew Adam couldn't see it in the darkness. "I told him this was the anniversary of my husband's death, and I planned to spend the night sitting by his grave."

"Where did you come up with such a story?"

She climbed to her feet, using the edge of the mausoleum for leverage. "Actually, on the first anniversary of John's death, I did just that — spent the night at the foot of his grave." She pointed. "It's right over there." Her voice broke on the last words.

Adam took her arm. "Do you want a moment alone?"

There was a long moment of silence, then Carrie said in a small voice, "I'd like that."

They walked several yards before she stopped and looked around. She took a few steps to the right and let her hand caress the edge of a simple granite marker. "John," she whispered. Then she bowed her head and was silent for a moment. Adam placed a hand on her shoulder, but said nothing.

Carrie's emotions were in turmoil. She was standing at the grave of her first husband, with the man who might become her second at her side. *John, I did the best I could, but we couldn't save you. Now it's time for me to move on. I hope you understand.*

Finally Carrie lifted her head, wiped her eyes, and said, "I'm ready to go now."

When they reached his car, Adam unlocked it and held the door for Carrie before climbing in himself. He eased the vehicle out of its hiding place, flipped on his headlights, and turned onto the main road that ran through the cemetery.

Carrie turned toward him. "What do you think —"

Another set of headlights appeared on the horizon. Carrie saw them and dropped to the floor of the car at the same time Adam whispered, "Get down."

"You can sit up," he said in a moment. "I thought a car was coming right at us, but it was on the road leading here."

"You know, it seems to me that I've spent more time on the floor of your car than a floor mat." Carrie laughed. "I'm sort of tired of that."

Adam turned out of the cemetery and set a course for Carrie's house. "That makes two of us. Do you think we're any closer to finding out who's been shooting at us?"

"Maybe. Why would Phil Rushton take a drive into the cemetery tonight?" she said. "So far as I'm concerned, that makes him our number one suspect."

"You've got a point. Do you think you can find out if he has some kind of excuse for coming?"

For a moment, Carrie said nothing. *Another spy job.* Finally she said, "I'll try."

They rode in silence, until Adam said, "I didn't have a chance to ask about your day."

Despite the late hour, Carrie's voice

brightened. "Really interesting. Have you ever heard of something called *commotio cordis*?"

Carrie was no stranger to doing without sleep, but that didn't mean she enjoyed it. The next morning was Saturday, a day when she tried to sleep a bit later if possible. But not today. Today she had to check on the young ballplayer she'd resuscitated the day before.

If his EKG was still normal and his cardiac enzymes showed no evidence of heart muscle damage, she planned to discharge him. He was understandably anxious to go home, so Carrie promised him she'd be by early this morning. Thus the reason she got up at what one of her medical school class-mates referred to as "chicken thirty."

When the alarm went off, she forced herself out of bed and padded to the kitchen, only to find she hadn't prepared the coffee maker the night before. She fumbled her way through the process until the coffee started brewing. Then she stood over it until there was at least a cup's worth in the carafe. By the time she'd showered, dressed, and chased a piece of buttered toast with two more cups of coffee, Carrie thought she might make it through the day.

At the hospital, she was moving down the hall toward the ballplayer's room when a familiar voice stopped her. "Carrie, hold up a second." Phil, a cardboard cup of coffee in one hand, a stack of papers in the other, was coming toward her full tilt.

Carrie turned and waited. Phil stopped so close to her that she smelled the fumes issuing from the Starbucks cup. She would have killed for some of that coffee but didn't think Phil would share. Come to think of it, he wasn't the kind to share anything. She put what she hoped was a neutral expression on her face and waited for him to speak.

"Your patient, Mr. . . . The man you referred, the one with the heart attack . . ."

"Mr. Hoover. A. J. Hoover," she said. "What about him?"

"He came through the surgery very well. He's in the SICU if you want to drop by. I'll let you know when I'm ready to discharge him, but feel free to write any orders you think he might need."

"Thanks," Carrie said. "I'll go by the surgical ICU and see him before I leave." What was going on? It wasn't like Phil to be this considerate. She expected that by now he'd have Thad Avery standing by to take over Hoover's post-op care. She frowned, wondering when the other shoe would drop. Surely Phil wanted something.

"We never had a chance to talk about dinner. How about tonight?"

There it was — the shift from rigid taskmaster and senior partner to caring colleague who wanted to get closer to her. She still wasn't comfortable going out with Phil, but she really wanted to follow up on his appearance in the cemetery last night.

"Phil, I think I'd better get some rest tonight. I was up really late." She covered a yawn, a real one, although it did add plausibility to her story.

"Probably just as well to put off our dinner." He yawned as well. "After I finished Mr. Hoover's surgery, I had to take care of a patient with a gunshot wound to the chest. It was almost midnight by the time I left the hospital."

Carrie waited. *Go on. I've given you an opening.* She raised her eyebrows in an invitation to tell her more.

"After the case I called home to check my messages. I usually don't have any — the answering service calls me on my cell — but there was a strange one on my landline last night. It was from someone inviting me to a meeting at the cemetery at midnight. Well, curiosity got the best of me, so I swung by on the way home — stopped at the appointed place, but there was no one there." He shrugged, then took a deep draught of coffee. "They must have called my phone by mistake."

"That's curious." Carrie did her best to keep her expression neutral. "Do you have any idea who could've called?"

"Not really," he said. But there was something behind his eyes Carrie couldn't read. Was he lying? She couldn't tell.

Carrie shrugged. "Well, that's certainly weird. Anything else?"

Phil looked around. They were standing near the nurse's station, and people were coming and going in a steady stream. "No, it can wait. Maybe I'll see you later. If not, why don't you drop by my office first thing Monday morning? We can talk about scheduling that dinner too. Right now I'm going home to take a nap." He finished the coffee, tossed the empty cup into a wastebasket, and plodded off down the hall.

Carrie ended her rounds with a stop in the cafeteria. After inhaling the fumes from Phil's coffee, she considered getting an espresso from the food court but decided to make the trade-off for plain coffee from a container that wasn't cardboard, consumed at a real table in a relatively quiet setting.

After a quick trip through the cafeteria line, she was at a table, holding a mug of coffee in both hands, smelling the aroma and feeling the caffeine energize her tired body. She closed her eyes, leaned back in her chair, and tried to analyze what she and Adam knew.

As she recalled, Phil Rushton once said he grew up in a poor part of Chicago. Like most medical students she was sure he either borrowed money or someone financed his medical education and specialty training. Could it have been DeLuca? Was Phil now repaying the debt by trying to kill Adam?

And Bruce Hartley, the senior lawyer in the partnership where Adam worked, had been in trouble for gambling. Could De-Luca have been the one to whom Hartley owed the debt? It seemed unlikely that he'd torch his own office, though what better way to direct suspicion away from himself? Adam said that if Hartley wanted someone shot, he'd hire it done. Still, so far as Carrie was concerned, he was a suspect.

To complicate things further, Charlie De-Luca had another family — a bigamous relationship with a woman living in a Chicago suburb. When the truth about Charlie came out, the wife had the marriage declared void and her daughter became a cloistered nun. The stepson, trained as an EMT, disappeared. Could he have surfaced in Jameson as Rob Cole? Was Rob Cole really Robert Kohler?

Carrie was halfway through her coffee when she realized someone was easing into the chair next to hers.

Rob Cole, looking like someone who had just finished pulling an all-nighter, smiled across the table and raised his cup in a salute. "Mind if I join you?"

"Tough night?" Carrie asked.

"Yes and no. I ended up working a double shift. One of the other paramedics was sick. But it turned out to be a good night. Took a mother in labor to the hospital just in time for the baby to be born somewhere besides the back of an MICU. And probably saved the life of a guy who got shot in the chest."

"Dr. Rushton said he did surgery on a patient like that," Carrie said. "So I guess your night wasn't a total waste."

Rob looked at the ceiling as though trying to decide. "No, it was okay. I had some other plans, fairly important ones, but I guess there'll be another time."

He started to push back his chair, but Carrie stopped him with a hand on his arm. "Rob, you got called away while we were still talking yesterday. Why don't we finish that conversation?"

Rob eased back into his chair. "Honestly, I can't remember what we were talking about."

Carrie paused to gather her thoughts. She had to approach this carefully. "You were telling me about the reason you changed your name and moved away."

"Oh yeah." He rubbed the back of his neck. "I guess it was the total disappointment after I found out my stepfather really wasn't my stepfather. I'd really taken to him. My sister and I were so happy to have a dad again. When we found out he had another family, that the whole marriage to my mom was a sham, my sister just cracked up. She decided she had to get away, so she cut all ties with us. She . . ." He shook his head. "I can't talk about it."

Carrie plastered a shocked look on her face. "That's tough, Rob." She took a deep breath. "I understand your need to get away for a fresh start, but why did you have to change your name?"

"Sis and I were proud of our new family. Mom's husband said he wanted to be more than a stepfather. He wanted to be our father. Then we found out these terrible things about him. I . . . I ran away. I changed my name because it reminded me of what we had, what he made us lose."

Carrie took a big swallow of coffee. Here it comes. "And what was your stepfather's name?"

Rob hesitated so long she thought he was going to evade the question. Finally he spoke. "Du . . . Lu . . . It was Luciano."

Carrie looked into Rob Cole's eyes, hoping to find a clue there. Had he started to say "DeLuca," then changed his mind? Or was the subject painful enough that he stuttered over his stepfather's name. Was he toying with her? Was this simply a part of the game for him, a game that would end with a bullet for Adam . . . or her . . . or both?

Carrie decided to take a chance and attack the problem head-on. "Rob, I don't think your stepfather was named Luciano. I think his name was DeLuca. Charlie De-Luca."

Rob reached out for his coffee cup, but instead of grasping the handle, he encircled the thick mug with his hand. He didn't lift it — just squeezed. Carrie watched his hands tremble and his knuckles turn white. She was afraid the mug would shatter, and she shoved her chair back a few inches to avoid the splatter of hot liquid. When she looked up from the cup into Rob's eyes, they were burning into hers. For a moment she thought he might hit her, or throw the cup at her, or lunge across the table and grab her by the throat.

Carrie was on the verge of calling out for help, when, like a balloon deflating, Rob relaxed back into his chair. He leaned forward so that their faces were just inches apart. "I don't think I want to talk about this anymore. And I've changed my mind. I don't want to get to know you better after all."

TWENTY-FOUR

Adam had the office to himself on Saturday morning. After he set the coffee brewing, he used his computer to get the phone number for Hermann Hospital in Houston. It turned out that the facility's official name was Memorial Hermann-Texas Medical Center, but he finally found what he needed. He picked up the phone on his desk, then replaced it and dialed the number on his cell phone. The firm would probably have no problem with a long-distance call, but he didn't want to leave any record. He couldn't give a reason for his caution, but he'd learned to trust his instincts. And his instincts always told him to leave as few footprints as possible.

He started with patient information, then was transferred to the ICU, where he was put on hold for what seemed an interminable length of time as the ward clerk found a nurse who'd talk with him.

"Who's this?" she asked in a voice that was a study in neutrality.

"This is Ad— Sorry. This is Keith Branson. I'm a friend of Mr. Cortland's. I was talking with him yesterday when the wreck happened."

"Which Mr. Cortland would that be?"

"All I've ever called him was Corky. Give me a sec." He searched his memory. What was Corky's listing in Martindale-Hubbel? That was it. Edgar A. He relayed this information to the nurse.

"Are you a colleague?" she said. "A lawyer?"

"Yes. Corky and I were in law school together."

"Then you're familiar with HIPAA."

It was a statement, not a question, and Adam knew what was coming next. He had come up against a wall — a wall called "patient privacy." Although he knew that the intent of the Health Insurance Portability and Accountability Act of 1996, known as HIPAA, was good, he longed for the old days when a friend could find out someone's condition without the patient having to include his name on a list of those cleared to receive that information.

The argument didn't last long, mainly because Adam knew the nurse was acting properly. He thanked her and hung up. But he still wanted to find out about Corky. This meant more work with the computer, and using Switchboard.com he soon determined that E. A. Cortland lived in a rather nice suburb of Houston and had a listed number for his residence.

Before he dialed, Adam tried to recall something. He was pretty sure Corky hadn't been married when they were in law school. Had Corky mentioned his wife's name on the phone? No, he had not. So Adam was calling blind. But he'd done that before.

The phone was answered on the fourth ring by a man's soft voice. "Cortland residence."

"This is a law school classmate of Corky's. I understand he was in a bad accident yesterday, and —"

"Let me stop you. This is his father-in-law, and I guess you're calling to get the details. Well, the service is day after tomorrow at the —"

It was like a punch in the gut. The man was still talking as Adam disconnected the call. He laid his phone on the desk and put his head in his hands. He felt sorrow about the loss of a friend as well as guilt at having let that friendship lie dormant for so long. But along with all that, Adam felt despair as he watched his hope of learning the hidden secret about Charlie DeLuca's family disappear into the coffin with Corky.

"Is someone in here?"

A familiar voice interrupted Adam's thoughts. The office door was locked, so he'd assumed he'd be alone this morning. But it was Mary's voice that had startled him, and Mary had a key.

He was trapped. There was no way to avoid an encounter with her. "Back here," he called.

"Be right there."

In a moment Mary appeared in the doorway, holding two cups. "The coffee pot was still full, so I figured you hadn't had yours yet. I poured an extra cup for you. Black okay?"

"Sure. Thanks." Adam took a sip and put the cup on his desk.

"What are you doing?" she asked.

Apparently Mary had no hesitancy in asking questions. He drank a bit more coffee, hoping the caffeine would keep his brain sharp. "Just finishing a little extra work. What brings you in today?"

"Actually I was driving by and saw your car here, so I thought I'd stop and see if you were free for lunch."

"Uh, that would be nice, but I've got to

get home to meet a repairman. The cable's acting funny, and with the weekend coming up, I want to watch the games. I think the Rangers are playing the Yankees on Sunday." Adam thought he was right. He wasn't really much of a sports fan, but he was hoping Mary wasn't either.

She frowned, almost as though the rebuff was expected, and took in half her coffee with a couple of gulps. "Well, I'd hoped we could do it earlier, but I still have you down for lunch on Tuesday. Right?"

Adam was tired of putting off what seemed inevitable. "Sure. Let's set the details when we see each other Monday morning."

He addressed himself to the computer, attacking the keys furiously as though writing a document that had to be completed by sundown or the world would end. In actuality he'd opened a blank Word document and was typing gibberish, but she couldn't see the screen from her vantage point across the desk.

The ruse must have worked, because Mary took the hint. She put her cup down on a side table near Adam's door. "I won't keep you from your work. Have a good weekend."

Adam heard the door open, then Mary called, "See you Monday." The door closed, and in a moment he heard a car drive off. He waited another couple of minutes, then sneaked to the front of the office and peered out the window. The parking lot was empty. Once more he'd avoided giving Mary a chance to probe too deeply into his background. And maybe the identity he'd created would hold up under her questioning anyway, so he had nothing to worry about.

He hoped so. He had enough worries on his plate as it was. There was no need for another.

Carrie was halfway through her front door, her arms laden with groceries, when her cell phone rang. She hurried into the kitchen to deposit the sacks on the kitchen table, then pulled her phone from the pocket of her slacks and checked the display. Adam. She could feel the smile spread across her face.

"What's up?" she asked.

"Have you caught up on your sleep after our late night?"

"Not really. I had to see some patients this morning. But I ran into Rob Cole at the hospital. Adam, I think he's really Charlie DeLuca's stepson."

"Why do you say that?"

After she finished describing her encounter, Carrie said, "I don't think there's any doubt that he's the son of Charlie DeLuca's second wife. And he's very angry right now — I don't know if it's at you, or at his stepfather, or at me for confronting him with it. And I have to wonder why he showed up in Jameson. I mean, coincidences happen, but this is a big one."

"Well, I've been busy too," Adam said. "I think we need to get together to share information and plan our next move."

Carrie dropped into a kitchen chair and brushed a strand of hair from her forehead. "Do you want to come by again tonight?"

"No!" The force behind Adam's retort startled her. "I'm tired of sneaking around in the dark. This is no way to live. I want to bring this thing to a close, and in the meantime, I want us to be able to be out in the daylight. I'm beginning to feel like a vampire."

Carrie grinned at the image. "What do you suggest?"

"It's Saturday, and I think we should celebrate the weekend. Let's have a picnic. It's a beautiful spring day, too pretty to be inside."

"Where? How?"

Adam was picking up steam now. "I know a place. I'll pick up the supplies, then swing by your house to get you." There was a pause, apparently for him to check the time. "It's eleven now. I'll see you at twelve. Okay?"

It was closer to twelve thirty when Adam pulled up in front of her house, but Carrie had filled the time with her own preparations. When she saw Adam's car, she hurried out the front door, locking it behind her, and climbed into his little SUV.

"What's in the bag?" he asked.

Carrie held up a shoulder bag, about the size of a briefcase. "Stuff we may need. Now let's see where you're going to take me."

The drive took about half an hour, but it was through lesser highways lined with the spring wildflowers of Texas — bluebonnets, paintbrush, a few early Gaillardias — and they both enjoyed the scenery. Adam kept an eye on the mailboxes along the road, and at one he turned onto a one-lane gravel road lined on both sides by fields of corn. He followed the curved roadway to a small farmhouse, pulled into the yard, and shut off the motor.

"Here we are. There's a table on the front porch with a couple of chairs. We can set up our picnic there and enjoy the isolation."

Carrie stepped up onto the porch and looked back. The cornfield was better than a privacy fence. There wasn't a sound around them — no cars, no humans, not even any farm animals. It was the perfect spot for a getaway. "What is this place? Doesn't someone own it?"

"A farmer lived here alone after his wife died. Then he passed away. His only child, a son, lives in Kansas City. Our law firm is handling the estate. We're supposed to sell the property, furnishings and all, and send him the money. Meanwhile, it sits here idle." He reached into his pocket and pulled out two keys on a metal wire loop. "Water comes from a well. Electricity is still on. There's no phone, but that's a plus."

Carrie gave a happy sigh. "Let's stay here forever," she said.

"Or at least until we get tired of it." Adam uncovered the top of a wicker basket he'd carried from the car and spread the cloth on the porch table. "But let's eat first. I'm starved."

Adam unloaded bread, deli meats, cheese, and a couple of soft drinks, the bottles still wet with condensation. From her bag, Carrie added two apples, chips, and napkins. Adam pulled utensils and more napkins from the basket.

In a moment they sat down to a perfect picnic meal. They looked at each other, and without a word, they joined hands across the table and bowed their heads. "Shall I?" Adam said.

Carrie surprised herself by saying, "No, let me." She took his silence for assent, and said, "Dear God, I've shut You out of my life too long. All I can say is, I'm sorry. But You already know that. I'm grateful You've brought Adam into my life. However this situation ends, we know that You're in control. We leave it in Your hands, and thank You for bringing us this far. We pray that You will bless the food and our time together. Amen."

They ate in silence for a moment, both lost in thought. Finally Adam said, "What about our other suspect? Did you find out why Phil Rushton was at the cemetery last night?"

"He gave a reasonable explanation for his presence there, and it's sort of a stretch to find a motive for him, even if he does have Chicago connections."

Adam rubbed his chin. "And I don't think Bruce Hartley's the guy. He's got Chicago roots too, but frankly I don't think Bruce has the guts to do something like this."

Carrie leaned back in her chair and pushed her plate away. "So how do we approach Rob? Do you have enough to go to the police? Can your brother help us?"

Adam shook his head. "Not really. I guess my next move is to confront Rob. Maybe if I make him mad enough, he'll show me he's the shooter. And if that happens, I'm ready." He reached down and patted the gun in its ankle holster.

"You're not going to shoot him in cold blood, are you? We're not even sure he's the one who's been trying to kill you. All we have is suspicion."

Adam shook his head. "I'm not a murderer, even if I'm backed into a corner. But I'm certainly prepared to protect myself if it comes to that. And if he pulls a weapon . . ."

Adam didn't complete the sentence, but Carrie knew what was coming next. He had a gun. She shivered, despite the sunny day.

Adam didn't want the day to end. Maybe he could buy the farm and they could live here in peaceful serenity. *Get real.* Yeah, that wasn't going to happen. It wasn't even practical to consider it. But they'd had a great afternoon together, a needed respite, offering them both a chance to recharge their batteries. Now it was time to get back to the real world.

It was late afternoon when he pulled up to Carrie's door. "Give me your keys," he said. "Let me check inside first."

He could see her hesitate, her sense of independence doing battle with the reality that danger could lurk around any corner.

"Pull into the driveway," she said. "We'll go in together, and you can look around inside to make sure everything's okay. After that I promise I won't open the door for anyone . . . except you, of course." She punctuated the last sentence with a peck on the cheek. "Thanks for a wonderful day."

"What about church tomorrow? Can I pick you up?"

She seemed to consider it. "Call me later tonight. We'll talk about it then."

He made a thorough inspection of the house, even checking under beds and looking behind clothes in all the closets. When he put his pistol back into its holster, he said, "All clear."

"Thanks. And thanks again for a wonderful afternoon." The kiss she gave him wasn't on the cheek, and it lasted quite awhile.

Adam stepped back. "Tell me there'll be more of those."

Carrie smiled. "As many as you want."

"Does that mean . . . ?"

"Not yet," Carrie said. "Let's get everything settled first."

As Adam drove to his apartment, he realized the potential danger he'd faced today. If his stalker had followed him, he could have wiped out both Adam and Carrie in the isolation of the farm. Maybe there had been a sudden decision on the part of the stalker to stop trying to take Adam's life. Maybe shooters took the weekend off — or not. Maybe Adam had just been lucky.

As he neared home, he watched the rear-view mirror carefully. He went through the usual maneuvers to check for a tail. And in the parking lot, he chose a different space to leave his car. Once inside he double locked his door. The first thing he did after that was to remove the Ruger from its holster and put it on the kitchen table.

He'd no sooner put his feet up and turned on a baseball game — the Rangers were indeed playing the Yankees and the score was tied — when his cell phone rang. Caller ID was no help, labeling the call "private." He shrugged. Might as well answer.

"Hello?"

"Adam? Adam Davidson?" It sounded like Bruce Hartley, but the voice was somehow different.

"Yes."

"It's Bruce."

Why was Bruce Hartley calling on Saturday afternoon? Was he about to fire Adam, doing it by phone? Did he want to talk about something at the office? Adam wracked his brain and came up empty. "What's up?"

"Sorry to bother you on a weekend. Our firm is the executor for the Caraway estate, and we finally have a buyer for the house. I'm meeting him and the Realtor there in half an hour." Bruce paused, and Adam heard him take a couple of deep breaths. "Aren't you a notary?"

"Yes. You insisted I become one when I went to work for the firm."

"Well, I need you to meet us and notarize some documents." The words seemed to gush out, as though Bruce couldn't wait to say them. "I know it's Saturday afternoon, but this is the only time the buyer can do this, and we need to get it wrapped up."

Adam searched his memory and came up blank. "I don't think I know where the Caraway place is."

Hartley gave him directions to a house on the outskirts of town. "Can you make it in half an hour? If we don't get this done, I'm afraid the buyer will change his mind."

"I'll have to go by the office to get my notary stamp first," Adam said.

"Just hurry."

This was unusual, but if the Caraway

property had been vacant for some time, he could understand why Bruce might want to get the buyer's signature before he changed his mind. It seemed to explain why he was in such a hurry.

As Adam drove to the office, he thought about calling Carrie but decided not to disturb her. She'd had a late night, and most likely was taking a nap — which was what he'd like to be doing. He yawned at the thought. Oh well. One of the downsides of the legal profession was getting calls at night or on weekends, although he thought he'd left that behind when he shifted into his new identity as a paralegal. This would be a good story to share with Carrie when he talked with her later that night.

Carrie browsed in her refrigerator and finally assembled what might pass for an evening meal. She'd much rather be eating with Adam, but they'd settled on a phone call tonight. Besides, she'd be with him at church tomorrow — she'd already decided they would go there together, despite the risk.

She settled into a comfortable chair in front of the TV, her food on a tray in front of her, and flipped through the channels until she came to an old movie, one she'd seen years ago but wouldn't mind seeing again.

When the phone rang, she turned off the TV, expecting it to be Adam. He was a bit early, but that was okay with her. She missed him already.

"Hello?"

"Dr. Markham?" It was a man's voice, unfamiliar to Carrie. And it carried a tone of stress that she couldn't categorize.

"Yes, who is this?"

"Never mind. If you want to see Adam Davidson alive again, come to the old Caraway place right now. Come alone. Don't make any calls — no police. We mean business." The words were unaccented, almost mechanical, as though the speaker were reading them.

"What's going on? Who is this?"

"Here are the directions you'll need. Write them down. If you're not here in forty-five minutes, Davidson dies."

Carrie grabbed a pen and paper and scribbled the directions. "Wait —"

A click in her ear signaled the end of the call.

TWENTY-FIVE

Carrie wondered if maybe this was all a gigantic hoax, someone wanting money. She'd get to the rendezvous, only to find a note sending her somewhere else, and eventually she'd be told to leave some huge amount in unmarked bills at a desolate location. Maybe someone had learned of the attempts on Adam's life and decided to use the situation to get some money from her, while Adam dozed at home in front of his TV set.

She had to be sure. Carrie phoned both Adam's cell phone and landline, but there was no answer. She tried again, and once more her call rolled over to voice mail. She thought about going by his apartment, but that might make her miss the deadline the anonymous voice gave her.

She made what preparations she could, then jumped into her car and headed out. The roads were blessedly empty, and she edged her speed up to about ten miles an hour over the speed limit. What would she do if a policeman stopped her? Would she ask him to hurry and give her a ticket? Would she tell him everything and beg for help? Her instructions had been "no police," and she didn't want to risk violating that admonition.

Forty-two minutes after she hung up from the threatening call, Carrie wheeled her Prius to a stop outside a house on the outskirts of Jameson. Adam's car was parked beside a white SUV. Light was visible from behind curtains in the front window. Aside from her and whoever was in the house, there didn't appear to be another soul anywhere around.

She breathed a silent prayer. *Help me deal with whatever's in there.* Carrie unzipped her shoulder bag and let her fingers roam among the contents until she found the canister of Mace. It wasn't much, but it was the only weapon she had. She wished she'd followed Adam's lead and armed herself with a pistol. Now it was too late.

She exited the car and hurried up the steps onto the porch. Should she knock or just go in? The front door was locked, which answered her question. It had two inserts of leaded glass, allowing her to see movement on the other side but no details. She rapped sharply on the door and saw a figure in black walking toward her. Carrie took an involuntary step backward as the door swung inward and she found herself facing Mary Delkus.

"Right on time," Mary said. Her shoulder-length black hair framed a beautiful face, one that Carrie had only seen once before, but which was hard to forget. Mary wore a loose-fitting black sweater, tight black jeans, and dark running shoes. The color of the clothes matched the boxy-looking pistol she held. "Come on in."

Once Carrie was inside, Mary reached back with her foot and kicked the door closed. An incandescent bulb with a frosted shade hung from the room's ceiling. With one exception, there was no furniture. That exception immediately caught Carrie's eye. In the corner, a middle-aged man with a receding hairline and a frightened expression was secured to a straight chair by multiple layers of duct tape that encircled his body like a silvery cocoon. Another strip of tape covered his mouth.

"That's Bruce Hartley, senior partner in the law firm where Adam — or should I say, Keith — works," Mary explained. "He made the phone call to you, and it only took the slightest bit of prodding."

Carrie noticed for the first time that Hartley's feet were bare, and there was blood on them as well as the hardwood floor beneath. She couldn't be certain, but it appeared that the nails were gone from some of his toes.

Mary gestured with her gun. "I believe the person you came to see is in here." She herded Carrie through a door into the kitchen.

Adam sat in a straight chair in the middle of the room. He was bound with duct tape, his hands secured behind him, his legs taped to the chair legs. Adam's mouth was sealed with another strip of tape. When he saw Carrie, his eyes widened, then a look of apology swept over his features.

Mary glared at Adam. "I know. You want to talk with her. Maybe I'll untape your mouth just before you die, so you can say your last good-byes."

Carrie's mind was swimming, but she thought she'd put things together. She turned full-face to the woman, trying to ignore the gun in her hand, and said, "You're the shooter."

The woman looked directly at Adam, and Carrie detected a gleam of madness in her eyes. "Bright girl you have here, Adam. I think I'm going to continue to call you Adam. That's the name under which I located you. And that's the name that will be on your tombstone."

"Why?" Carrie said. "Why are you doing this?"

Mary shrugged. "Simple. After a little persuading, Adam told me how he dug into the family tree of Charlie DeLuca. Unfortunately he didn't look hard enough to find out more about Charlie's brother, who was a silent partner in almost everything. When it became obvious that the DA was after Uncle Charlie, my dad rolled up everything he could — gambling, prostitution, protection — and moved it to Kansas City. He changed his name to Delkus, greased a few palms to have Gino DeLuca and his family disappear from public records, and started over again."

"So you're Charlie DeLuca's niece," Carrie said. "Did Charlie ask you to avenge him? Is that why you're doing this?"

Mary grinned. "Did he ask? No. He didn't have to. We're Italian. The code of *vendetta* originated centuries ago in Sicily, and we still believe in revenge. My Uncle Charlie didn't die in prison — he died the day his freedom was taken from him." She glared at Adam. "Now the man responsible for that is going to die. And you're going to do it."

"But —"

"Enough!" She turned her gaze and the gun back on Carrie. "I intended to kill him, but then I decided it would be even better if you did it." She pointed to a black backpack on the kitchen table next to Adam. "I was in the stands when you used one of these to restart that boy's heart. It seems to me that an electrical shock should be able to stop a heart as well as start it. So that's what you're going to do."

Carrie's response was a loud "No!"

Mary's eyes hardened even more. "If you don't, then I'll simply shoot you and take care of him myself. But my way will be slower . . . and a lot more painful."

The germ of an idea tickled at the back of Carrie's mind. It was risky, but it might work. Besides, it could buy some time, and every second was precious. She delayed her answer as long as possible. Just as she saw Mary's lips start to move, Carrie said, "You win."

She moved to the table and pulled the defibrillator from its pack. This one was different from the unit she'd used at the ball field. "I need to figure this out," she said. "Why don't I just make him hurt a little first?"

The gun in Mary's hand was still pointed at Carrie. "So long as you finish him off."

"First, I have to put on the electrodes. One goes on the chest." She unbuttoned Adam's shirt and pulled it open to expose his chest. "And one goes on the leg." She reached down to push up his right pants leg. Her hand touched an empty holster.

"Looking for this?" Mary reached beneath her sweater and pulled Adam's pistol from the waistband of her jeans. "Good try. By the way, I was watching you at the ballpark. I know how this works. Both electrodes go on the chest. Do it right." She emphasized her words with a gesture from her gun.

Carrie searched desperately for words to calm this woman. "I don't . . . I mean —"

"If you don't stop stalling," Mary said, "I'll work on Adam the way I worked on poor Bruce. I understand that having toe-nails pulled out isn't pleasant." She tucked the Ruger back in her waistband, but kept her own pistol trained on Carrie.

"No, please." Carrie blinked to clear her eyes of tears. She needed to delay, but she was almost out of options. She fumbled as much as she dared, but in a moment the electrodes were in place on Adam's chest, held there by the adhesive on the pads.

"Now set the machine and push the button," Mary said.

"I have to figure this one out." Carrie had to keep Mary talking. "How did you find Adam?"

"His trail wasn't hard to follow. And once I found him, it was a delicious coincidence that he was working in a law office. My training is as a paralegal, so I decided to get a job in the same office."

"Just like that? How could you be so confident you'd get the job?"

Mary laughed, but it was full of evil, not mirth. "Once I met Bruce Hartley, I knew I could have the job, Bruce's car, or anything else I wanted. I wasn't sure where Adam had gone, but I figured he'd be back, and I was right."

"So all your efforts to get to know him —"

"That's enough! Stop delaying. Find out which button to push to stop his heart. If I have to do it with a bullet, I will, but first I'll make him suffer."

Carrie's fingers roamed across the keyboard, then hovered over a button. She looked at Adam. "I'm so sorry." She pushed. The display showed "normal rhythm."

Mary peered at the unit. "You pushed the diagnostic button. You're not going to do this, are you? Well, I'll have to do it the old-fashioned way. Maybe I should shoot you first though." She raised her gun until it was pointed directly at Carrie.

"That's enough. Drop the gun, turn around, and freeze!"

The voice was one that Carrie had heard only once before. She'd heard it on the phone when she called before leaving for this meeting. Dave Branson was taller than his brother, slightly stockier, and the facial resemblance was striking. He was dressed in jeans, boots, and a flannel shirt. There was a badge of some kind affixed to his belt on the left side. His right arm, from elbow to fingertips, was contained in a navy blue sling.

Mary didn't turn. Instead, she kept the gun trained on Carrie. "I don't think so. And who might you be?"

Dave's voice betrayed no trace of tension. "U.S. Marshall David Branson. And you're under arrest for kidnapping, attempted murder, and probably several other charges that I'll leave to the authorities. Now I'm warning you. Drop the gun and turn around with your hands up."

An evil smirk lightened Mary's face. "Another family member. Good. The history of *vendetta* includes a number of instances of wiping out the entire family of the murderer. I was going to be satisfied with her." She nodded toward Carrie. "But you're just a bonus."

"Last warning. Drop the gun."

"Not on your life," Mary said. Suddenly she whirled to level her pistol at Dave.

Carrie was watching Mary's gun hand, and almost missed the tiny puff of smoke that issued from the end of Dave's sling. The report wasn't as loud as she expected a gunshot to be. But there apparently was enough firepower behind it to do the job. Mary took a step backward and collapsed onto the floor. Her gun skidded into a corner. Blood gushed from her chest, and frothy pink bubbles formed at the corner of her mouth.

Dave rushed over to Carrie. "Are you okay?"

"Yes. Cut Adam loose, will you? I'll see about Mary."

Carrie knelt beside the woman and put one finger on her neck to feel for a carotid pulse. It was feeble and irregular. Blood continued to gush from a wound high in Mary's chest. With every labored breath Carrie could hear the sucking sound of air rushing into the chest cavity, robbing Mary's lungs of the ability to take in precious oxygen.

Sucking chest wound. Got to seal it. Carrie grabbed the roll of duct tape from the kitchen table. In one quick motion she pulled Mary's sweater up to expose the gunshot wound. The bleeding was slowing already. Not good. She tore off several pieces of the waterproof tape and applied them over the bullet hole. The sucking sound diminished in intensity, but Mary's breathing was shallower, slower, more labored.

"Mary, open your eyes. Look at me."

The woman looked up, blinked rapidly, then moved her gaze from Carrie's face to the ceiling, as though she could see something written there. She took one deep, ragged breath and let it out slowly through pursed lips.

"Dave, call 911!" Carrie shouted.

"Already did it. How can I help here?"

The blood pulsating from the wound was darker now and had slowed to a trickle. As Carrie watched, the flow stopped. The bullet must have caught a major blood vessel, maybe the aortic arch. Carrie placed two fingers on Mary's neck. The feeble carotid pulse beat she'd felt earlier was now gone. Full cardiac arrest.

Carrie's first reflex was to pump Mary's chest, but if there was no blood to circulate, cardiac compressions wouldn't help. She looked helplessly at the defibrillator on the kitchen table, the leads hanging loose where Dave had ripped them from Adam's chest.

"Can I do something?" Dave asked again.

"There's nothing you can do — nothing anyone can do now."

Carrie had the knowledge. She had some of the equipment. But she couldn't save the patient. The woman who'd tried multiple times to murder her and Adam lay dead before her. And strangely enough, she felt no triumph — only frustration. Maybe that was what being a physician was about. Carrie tried to save them all, even her enemies. Some she could. Some she couldn't.

The verse ran through Carrie's head again: "I will give you a new heart." The words weren't meant to describe a beating, pumping organ, although certainly Mary could use one of those now. Instead they referred to a spiritual awakening. Surely this scenario would have played out differently if Mary had claimed that promise. But now it was too late.

TWENTY-SIX

Mary's body lay where she fell while investigators took their pictures and memorialized the scene. Adam didn't need any of that though. He'd remember every detail for the rest of his life.

Bruce Hartley sat in the chair from which he'd been cut free, trying to drink from the glass Adam handed him. His hands shook, and most of the water dribbled down his chin, but he didn't seem to notice. He took a few sips before looking up with eyes as sad as a spaniel's. "Adam, I swear, I had no idea what she was trying to do."

"I know, Bruce. She took advantage of you." No need to berate the man. Anything Adam wanted to tell Bruce, the lawyer was probably already telling himself. And if he hadn't yet, he would. "I know she forced you to make that phone call to Carrie. And it's apparent that you held out as long as you could."

A tear rolled down Hartley's cheek. "She . . . she took pliers and pulled out my toenails. I couldn't stand it any longer."

An EMT put his hand on Hartley's shoulder. "Sir, we're ready to take you to the Emergency Room. Do you want to walk to the ambulance?" Then he saw the lawyer's bloody feet. "Never mind. I'll get the gurney."

A sheriff's deputy approached Adam, with Dave and Carrie right behind him. "Mr. Davidson, let's hear your story one more time."

Adam began slowly at first, not eager to relive the harrowing moments, yet knowing he must. "When I walked in, Mary was here with a gun. Hartley was already secured to a chair. After she restrained me, she held a script in front of him and forced him to read it to Carrie."

"And how did she force him to do that?"

Adam pointed to a bloody pair of pliers still under the chair where Hartley had been. "Eventually he made the call. Then Mary silenced him with tape over his mouth and sat down to wait for Carrie."

The deputy scribbled a few notes. "Why did she do all this?"

It took Adam the better part of an hour to give the deputy what he needed, with Carrie and Dave adding information where it was needed.

Dave surrendered his off-duty gun, the one he'd concealed in his sling. Ballistic tests would confirm that a bullet from his Taurus .38 Special killed Mary, but he'd given her every chance to surrender. Instead, she chose to turn and aim her gun at him. Her last words — "Not on your life" — had been prophetic.

The deputy was putting his notebook in his pocket when a stocky, older man with a badge pinned to his golf shirt approached the group. Dave stuck out his hand. "Len, sorry to get you out tonight."

The man smiled. "Sorry you had a spot of trouble, Dave." He turned to the deputy. "Got what you need?"

"Yes, sir," the deputy said.

By now Adam had figured that this was the county sheriff. The man said, "You folks can go. I need you to stop by my office on Monday so we can get formal statements." He shook hands all around, and when he came to Carrie, he said, "Ma'am, I think it was pretty gutsy, the way you tried to save the life of a woman who'd been trying to murder you."

Carrie shook her head. "I did what any physician would do. I only wish I could have done more."

Even as she spoke, Carrie wondered at the truth of her words. What would she have done if the wound hadn't been mortal, beyond her ability to treat in the circumstances? What if, for some reason, use of the defibrillator could have saved Mary's life? Would Carrie have applied it, or would she have stood back and watched her enemy die? Although she hoped she would have done the right thing, Carrie was glad the decision had been made for her.

Carrie fought to keep her eyes open as she drove back to town. Adam was right behind her in his car. When she'd told him she had one more stop to make before going home, he insisted on being with her.

She wheeled into the Emergency Room parking lot and felt reassured when she saw Adam bring his car to a stop beside hers. They exited and walked together toward the ER entrance.

"I guess there's no need to feel like I'm in someone's crosshairs anymore," he said.

"It's going to take some time for it to soak in," Carrie said, "but I think you're right."

"Are you sure you want to do this?"

"Yes. This is the last piece of the puzzle, and I can't rest until I deal with it."

They moved through the sliding glass doors, and Carrie made her way to the desk where the clerk and triage nurse sat. "Is Rob Cole driving tonight?"

The clerk nodded through the double doors leading into the Emergency Room. "He and his partner just brought in a patient." She looked at the clock on the wall. "They're probably taking a break before their next call. Do you need to see him?"

"I'll find him," Carrie said. "Thanks."

She indicated that Adam should follow her. In the ER she navigated a maze of gurneys, patients, families, staff, equipment, and miscellaneous roadblocks, her eyes moving constantly until she spotted Rob heading for the break room. "There he is. Come on."

They caught Rob at the coffee urn, drawing a cup.

"Rob, we need a moment of your time."

Rob's initial reaction was that of a trapped animal. His eyes shifted back and forth and his body language warned of impending flight, but in a moment his features dissolved into another emotion — shame. "Dr. Markham, I'm sorry I acted that way. It's . . . I can't talk about it."

"I think I can help you," Carrie said.

"Let's sit down."

A sofa and two overstuffed chairs, long past their prime, were arranged along two walls of the break room. Rob, Carrie, and Adam found seats and sat for a moment in uncomfortable silence.

Carrie decided to get right to it. "This is about Charlie DeLuca." She noticed the tensing of Rob's muscles at the name, but she plunged on. "You see, someone has been shooting at Adam and at me. We thought it might be you, trying to avenge Charlie's imprisonment."

"But —"

"No, we've discovered it wasn't you. It was Charlie's niece." Carrie shook her head. "She's no longer a threat."

"What happened?"

Carrie took a moment to explain. "But the reason we're here now is that we want to help you. And to do that, we need to know why you blew up at me when I mentioned DeLuca."

"I told you. I don't want to talk about it."

"Rob, we'd like to get you some help."

Rob moved his cup from hand to hand but made no attempt to drink. He looked at the ceiling. He looked at the floor. Finally he looked into Carrie's eyes. "I've been seeing a therapist, but I still . . . struggle. I guess that's why I've acted sort of funny toward you. He says I don't know how to relate to women, at least not appropriately."

Carrie opened her mouth but caught Adam's quick shake of the head, so she waited for Rob to continue.

"When Charlie DeLuca was indicted, there was something else we found out, something that was even worse than bigamy, worse than the crimes that sent him to jail." He tossed his half-full paper cup into the trash. "It was what he'd been doing to my sister. It was so terrible . . . Well, she couldn't forget it. So she left us to become a cloistered nun. Now her name is Sister Rafael. We haven't seen her — can't see her — since this happened. She withdrew from the world because she found out how terrible the world can be."

Carrie leaned forward in her seat and noticed that Adam did the same.

"The night before she left home, my sister told me this, but made me swear not to let our mother know. She was glad Charlie De-Luca wasn't really our stepfather. She was glad he was going to prison. Her words were, 'I hope he rots in hell.' Then she told me about how he'd come into her room every night when he was at our house and . . ." He put his head in his hands and started sobbing.

Carrie let out a breath she'd held for what seemed like an eternity. She could guess the rest. And her heart broke — for Rob, for his sister, for Adam, and for all the others who'd been affected by the sins of one man.

On Monday morning Adam dressed for work, but this time he didn't strap on the ankle holster. His gun was in the sheriff's property room, and that was fine with him. If they chose to check it for fingerprints, they would find his, along with those of Mary Delkus, but he doubted that would ever happen. The case was closed.

Adam parked in his marked spot at the law office and carried his briefcase through the front door without a single glance over his shoulder. He walked by Mary's office, the one that used to be his. He wasn't sure what would happen next, but whatever it was, he'd handle it. As he and Carrie had said to each other again and again yesterday, God was in control. That was enough.

Brittany poked her head in his door. "I've already made coffee. Would you like some?"

"That would be nice. Thanks."

She was back in a moment, holding two cups. She put one on his desk and said, "I've heard what happened over the weekend. I'm sorry for what you've been through."

Adam started to respond when he heard the phone ringing at Brittany's desk. She held up a finger. "Sorry, I've got to get that," she said, then turned and hurried away.

No sooner was Brittany gone than Janice Evans came in. She looked at the chair opposite his desk with raised eyebrows, and Adam said, "Please. Sit down. What's up?"

"I talked with Bruce last night. He told me some of the story. Then I called a friend in the sheriff's department and got the rest of it. You had a busy day."

"How's Bruce doing?"

Janice sipped her coffee and seemed to choose her words carefully. "Bruce was hurting from having his toenails pulled out, but he was also hurting because he'd been so stupid. We all thought he hired Mary and let her lead him around because she was so good-looking. That may have been part of it, but the other part was that Mary's father, Charlie DeLuca's brother, held Bruce's gambling debts years ago."

"Was that when Elwood Stroud bailed him out?"

"Yes. Although Bruce's debts were settled long ago, Mary said if he didn't do what she wanted, she'd see to it that word got around about Bruce's gambling history. Apparently there were some stories from back then that might get him in trouble even now with the ethics committee of the bar association."

"Is he still worried that might happen, now that Mary's dead?"

"He doesn't care. Bruce is ready to get out of the rat race. He told me he wants to sell his share of the partnership to me."

Adam drank some of his coffee, cringing at the bitter taste. He'd better get there early the next day to brew it. Brittany had lots of good qualities, but making coffee wasn't one of them. "Well, sounds like things are ending okay."

Janice leaned toward him. "Bruce heard you tell the police your backstory, and he passed that information on to me when we talked. I'd always thought you were too good as a paralegal, and that explains it." She removed her glasses, and Adam saw only sincerity in her gray eyes. "With Bruce leaving, I'm going to need another lawyer here. Is your license still current?"

"It is in Illinois. Does that state have reciprocity with Texas?"

"I looked it up last night. As it happens, it does. I hate to lose a good paralegal, but

418

good lawyers are scarce too. And I have an idea you're a very good lawyer. Would you consider joining the practice?"

Adam knew he should say, "Let me think about it." He probably should even say, "Let me pray about it." Instead, he said, "I'd be thrilled to."

"Great. We'll start drawing up an agreement later today." She rose, but stopped to ask him, "I suppose your law license is in your real name. Do you want to go back to being Keith Branson?"

Adam had to think about that for a moment. "You know, I've had several names since this all started. It wasn't so bad getting used to them, but I've always regretted giving up my family name." He blinked a couple of times. "My parents are dead, and my brother and I are the last surviving Bransons. David saved my life, and I'm proud to share his last name. I think I'd like to go back to being Keith Branson . . . Dave's brother."

Carrie planned to start her Monday by quietly telling a few people what had happened over the weekend, but apparently the grapevine worked well, even when the staff wasn't together at the clinic. It seemed everyone already had the news.

Lila met her at the door. "How are you doing?"

"I'm fine," Carrie responded. Actually, she was better than she'd been in weeks — better than at anytime since Adam's windshield shattered and gunshots propelled her into the nightmare that just ended. "Is my patient list ready?"

"On your desk," Lila said. "But Dr. Rushton wants to see you first thing. Would you like some coffee?"

"In a few minutes," Carrie said. "I don't think this will take long." She had successfully resisted Phil's repeated requests for the two of them to get together. Now it was time to face the music. She searched her memory for something she might have done that would bring down the wrath of the clinic's managing partner, but nothing came to mind. Oh well. She'd see soon enough.

Carrie tapped at the open door of Phil's office. He rose and walked to her, enfolded her in a hug, and led her to one of the chairs in front of his desk. He took the one beside it and turned it to face Carrie. So far this was a totally different Phil Rushton than the one she'd come to know, respect, and sometimes dislike.

"Are you okay?" he asked. "Would you like some coffee?"

"Nothing, thanks. And I'm fine — thanks for asking." She leaned forward in the chair. Might as well get this out of the way. "Phil, you need to know that strange message you got came from Adam." She went on to explain about the three suspects in the shootings and why Phil was on the list. "Obviously you were innocent, and I want to apologize for suspecting you and for the way it might have influenced our relationship."

Phil shrugged it off. "No problem. I can see why you might think that, with my Chicago connection." He shifted in his chair. "And that brings me to the reason I've been wanting to meet with you."

Carrie frowned. "O-o-okay."

"You already know that I'm from Chicago, did all my training there. I've always wanted to go back, and now I have the chance. I've received an offer to head the division of cardiothoracic surgery at Loyola in Chicago. I'm going to take the job."

Carrie had trouble processing that for a moment. Phil was leaving? Then again, this was a great honor, and he'd be foolish not to grab the opportunity. He deserved it.

"Wonderful. Congratulations."

"That means we'll need another cardiothoracic surgeon here." Phil reached back to his desk and lifted three thin manila folders from it. "Here are three men we need to interview."

Carrie wasn't sure what to say. "What can I do?"

"You'll head the search committee, along with two other clinic members of your choice."

"Why me?"

"Because I'm suggesting that you replace me as managing partner. You've been here as long as any of the other doctors. You're levelheaded. You've demonstrated that you can be cool in stressful situations, and this job has a lot of them."

"I'll need to —"

Phil held up his hand. "I know. I've sprung this on you without warning. Why don't you and Adam talk about it over dinner tonight? I've made a seven o'clock reservation at The Grotto for you to have dinner on me. It's all taken care of."

Back in her office Carrie had the phone in her hand, ready to dial Adam, when it struck her. This was great news, but it was the kind to share face-to-face.

When Adam answered, his first words were, "I was about to call you. I have something I need to tell you."

"Me too. But I'd like to see the look on

your face when I share my news."

"Can you spare some time at noon?" he asked.

"Sure," Carrie said. "Come by my office and we'll have lunch together." *And will I have a surprise for you.*

Keith — he'd have to get used to that name again — could hardly contain his excitement. He checked his watch every fifteen minutes, and finally at eleven twenty he couldn't wait any longer. He grabbed his coat and told Brittany, "I have a luncheon meeting. See you in a couple of hours."

Keith had trouble holding his car under the speed limit, he was so anxious to see Carrie, to share his news and hear hers. When he was halfway to her office, he reached a decision that sent him on a detour. Despite the delay, he was waiting in Carrie's office when she walked in at noon.

She kissed him and started to shed her white coat. "Where should we have lunch?" she asked.

"We'll get to that in a minute. But before we do, let's talk about our news."

"Okay, you first," Carrie said.

He told her about the offer from Janice Evans, his opportunity to resume his law practice and take back his real name.

"Wonderful."

"You're sure the name change won't be a problem for you?" he asked.

Carrie didn't hesitate. "This isn't just a chance to reclaim your name. It's the opportunity to reclaim your life." She grinned. "I may call you Adam a couple of times, but I promise that from now on you'll be Keith Branson to me," Carrie said. "And I'll love you, whatever you're called."

Adam beamed. "Now what's your news?" he asked.

Carrie shared what Phil Rushton told her. "All this time I was worried that he wanted me out, but instead I have a chance to become the managing partner of the clinic."

"Sounds like good news all around."

"It amazes me," Carrie said. "There were times when I couldn't see any way out of the predicament we were in. But God brought us through it . . . and brought me back to Him in the bargain."

"So what did you tell Phil?" Keith asked.

"Nothing, yet. He thought you and I could talk it over at dinner tonight," Carrie said. "He made seven o'clock reservations at The Grotto, his treat. Want to pick me up at a quarter to seven?"

"Sure." Keith pointed to the picnic basket on the floor. "And as for lunch, I figured you'd be pressed for time, so I thought we'd eat here. I have deli sandwiches, chips, and soft drinks."

Carrie smiled. "As I recall you put together a mean picnic lunch." She pulled a pile of medical journals off the small table in the corner of her office and dropped them on the floor. "Want to spread it out there?"

"I wish we could go back to that farmhouse and have a real picnic."

"So do I."

Keith arranged the food on the table. Then he brought over one of the chairs from in front of Carrie's desk and gestured to her. "Have a seat."

She did so. "Now join me."

"Just a second. There's one more thing in the basket." Keith reached in and pulled out a paper napkin twisted into a small bundle. "I guess this is sort of corny, but after all we've been through, I wanted to do it right this time." He dropped to one knee in front of Carrie. "There are no secrets anymore. And it's never been a secret that I love you." He unfolded the napkin and held out the engagement ring. "I hope you're ready to accept this now. Dr. Carrie Markham, will you be Mrs. Keith Branson?"

At first, Carrie's eyes glistened. Then tears

ran down her face, but the smile that accompanied them told Keith they were tears of happiness.

There was a catch in Carrie's voice when she said, "Yes." Then her kiss told Keith that everything was right with the world once more.

READING GROUP GUIDE

1. What was Carrie's relationship to the Lord at the beginning of the book? Do you think the chasm was justified? Can you put your finger on the factor(s) that brought her back?
2. Contrast where Carrie and Adam were in their Christian walks at the beginning of the book. What do you think was the cause of the difference? Do you think you might have felt the same in their situations?
3. Was there any justification for Adam hiding his past from Carrie? Is there ever a valid reason for a lie or partial truth? Why or why not?
4. What is your mental image of Adam's older brother? What was their relationship? Why?
5. Phil Rushton is a complex character. What was your overall opinion of him? If you didn't know about Phil's marital and family status, what would you guess it

was? Why?

6. For a long time, Adam resisted getting a gun. What pushed him over the edge? Do you think he would have used it?

7. What was your takeaway message after finishing the book?

ACKNOWLEDGMENTS

Readers may have the idea that novels spring, freshly formed and complete, from the fertile minds of writers. Far be it from me to disillusion you, but it doesn't happen that way. For instance, here's what it took to put this novel in your hands.

I'm privileged to have a wife who is my first reader, my biggest fan, and my most discerning critic. Kay helped me shape this story from its inception to the final step along the way. Thank you, dear. I truly couldn't do it without you.

My fantastic agent, Rachelle Gardner, has believed in me when others didn't. She presented this concept, and the novel that followed, to my editor, Amanda Bostic, who applied her editorial talent to point me in the right direction. Then Traci DePree exercised her special touch to help me improve the story even further. I appreciate all of these ladies so much. They deserve chocolate . . . or at least a round of applause.

While I was writing, Kristen Vasgaard was designing a dynamite book cover. After the edits were completed, Becky Monds and the rest of the Thomas Nelson crew shepherded the novel through production. Meanwhile, Katie Bond and Laura Dickerson got the word out so readers would know about the book. My sincere thanks go to every one of these good folks.

My writing journey has been long and, at times, difficult. Along the way I've received encouragement, instruction, and mentoring from lots of people, including (but not limited to): Karen Ball, James Scott Bell, Colleen Coble, Brandilyn Collins, Alton Gansky, Jeff Gerke, Dennis Hensley, Randy Ingermanson, DiAnn Mills, Michael Palmer, Gayle Roper, Barbara Scott, Terry Whalin, and too many more to mention.

And, of course, I've been blessed with the support of my family and friends through it all.

Finally, I'm grateful for my loyal readers and the opportunity to share these words with you. Thanks for coming along for the ride. I hope you enjoyed it.

ABOUT THE AUTHOR

Dr. Richard Mabry is a retired physician. This is his sixth published novel of medical suspense. His previous works have been finalists for the Carol Award and Romantic Times Reader's Choice Award and have won the Selah Award. He is a past vice president of American Christian Fiction Writers and a member of the International Thriller Writers. He and his wife live in North Texas.

The employees of Thorndike Press hope you have enjoyed this Large Print book. All our Thorndike, Wheeler, and Kennebec Large Print titles are designed for easy reading, and all our books are made to last. Other Thorndike Press Large Print books are available at your library, through selected bookstores, or directly from us.

For information about titles, please call:
(800) 223-1244

or visit our Web site at:
http://gale.cengage.com/thorndike

To share your comments, please write:
Publisher
Thorndike Press
10 Water St., Suite 310
Waterville, ME 04901